THE MEN OF ELITE METAL: PLATINUM, ZINC, & FRANCIUM

REBECCA ROYCE

The Men of Elite Metal: Platinum, Zinc & Francium

First Published in the Elite Metal Anthologies published by Never Settle Publishing.

New Publication: The Men of Elite Metal: Platinum, Zinc, & Francium

Copyright @ 2019 by Rebecca Royce

Ebook ISBN: 978-1-951349-26-4

Print ISBN: 978-1-951349-27-1

Cover art by German Creative

Final Proof Editing: Meghan Leigh Daigle

Formatting: Ripley Proserpina

Published by Rebecca Royce

www.rebeccaroyce.com

❀ Created with Vellum

FOREWORD

Dearest Reader,

Once upon a time in author land, a bunch of authors who loved each other's work got together and put out three volumes of connected stories. The idea was both simple and complicated. The guys (and a few girls) would be Alpha, dominant, into various elements of BDSM, and all fighting back against an organization that tried to have them killed. It became a three-volume endeavor.

Well...all good things must come to an end. Recently, the rights came back to us individually, and now I am putting out my three stories on their own. They are Platinum. Zinc. And Francium.

For information on the other characters mentioned or the other authors who wrote these stories, please check out the works of Jenn Kacey, Anna Alexander, Heather Long, Virginia Nelson, Roxie Rivera, Sabrina York, and Saranna DeWylde.

Thanks for reading!
Rebecca

PLATINUM

PLATINUM

Platinum stared at the man across the table and tried to think of all the reasons why killing him was a bad idea. *One*—they were in public. He actually liked coming to Bone Daddy's. Getting kicked out for attempted murder would greatly affect the bars he could go locally to have fun. Bone Daddy's was pretty much it.

Oh, who was he kidding? If he took the son of a bitch down, the charge wouldn't be *attempted* murder. If Plat wanted to kill Tony De'Fallipi, he'd succeed even without his sniper rifle.

A man's neck could be broken multiple ways. Snap. Crunch.

He took a pull from his beer.

Two—and it really was imperative he make a quick internal list to hold off his murderous rage—his teammates wouldn't appreciate having to clean the mess. They'd assist without a doubt. Only Copper alone would never let him live it down. She'd want him to talk about why he'd committed murder in the middle of the day. In a bar.

The sheer amount of time spent managing the fallout would cut into his reading hours.

And finally—*three*—much as he hated to admit the sad truth, it really wasn't Tony's fault he was such a complete and total incompetent jackass. A certain portion of the population had to be born naturally stupid. Platinum could only blame himself for hiring him.

"Are you going to say something?" Tony fidgeted with the coaster on the table. Platinum specialized in noticing details. At the moment, he zeroed in on the tear in the corner of the cardboard drink holder. The picture on top—a pirate holding a beer—seemed ragged, half-destroyed.

Why was the bar using broken coasters? Were they running short on funds? He'd invest in the place, secretly if need be. Losing Bone Daddy's wasn't an option.

"Say something." Tony threw the coaster down on the table and it bounced once before settling on its side. Plat watched the movement for an extra second before he turned his gaze on De'Fallipi.

Tony needed to lose weight, in a big way. Maybe take off two hundred pounds. He hadn't been as obese the last time Plat met with him. He smoked, everything he had on reeked of it, and if the yellow stain on the side of his mouth indicated anything, probably chewed tobacco.

At five-foot-five inches, the gray haired mess in front of him was a foot shorter than Plat. He really hoped said mess wasn't about to have a heart attack. The last thing he wanted to do was to have to resuscitate Tony on the floor of the bar.

"When was the last time you went for a physical? Had your sugars checked?"

Plat really shouldn't care. He'd left medical school behind when he'd been kidnapped and brought into the Elite Metal fold. When he agreed to rejoin his brothers and sister in arms to make right a major cluster fuck, he'd given up healing and fully embraced the sniper within him once again.

Still, old habits died hard. Old personas too, it seemed.

Tony coughed violently before he answered. "Are you kidding? I told you the weird kid I've been watching for you for a year is missing, and you want to ask about my last physical? Are you on something? Meeting you here in a nowhere bar, never getting any answers. It's a good thing your checks cash each month."

His temper surged again. Outside of his team, there wasn't a soul alive who would notice a change in him. Control and patience were his best friends.

The knocking on death's door private investigator in front of him pushed all of his buttons. "I heard what you said."

"I mean, why have I been watching a seven-year-old? Do you have some sick perverted thing about him?"

Platinum stood up. "Thank you for your help. The checks will be stopping. Permanently. I'll take it from here. He's eight, by the way."

"The kid is missing. If I can't find him, he's gone." Tony shrugged "You won't make it further than I did."

"Doubtful. Seriously." Plat leaned forward. "And if you ever call the kid weird again, even in the back of your mind, I'll put a bullet in your head. You'll never see it coming."

Since he'd spoken more in the last ten minutes than he talked usually in a week, he turned on his heel and left the bar. His son was missing. It might be nothing, or it could mean Platinum's demons finally figured out how to hit him where it hurt. He'd spent his whole life trying not to make any connections. One drunken assignation with a woman he barely remembered and boom, the universe gifted him with a kid he'd known nothing about for six years—a permanent soft underbelly. Even if Kent never learned his father existed.

One of the two people he cared about in the world was unaccounted for...

Rose was okay, she had to be.

The kid who never knew him, and the woman who probably hated the ground he walked on.

～

Two years earlier

He'd spent the morning watching The Boy. It was easier to think of him in the abstract than by the name The Boy's mother bestowed upon him, Kent. Besides, *Elijah* knew how flexible names were. He'd owned so many in his life, he wasn't certain what his real designation was anymore.

The government called him Elijah Jones. The name worked as well as any other. He was Elijah—a fake name for a brand new life. His previous self, according to public records, died overseas—killed in action. Since the new life was what he had, he needed to find a way to make it work.

New York City was loud, busy, and anonymous. The city worked perfectly for his current situation. Outside of class, he never talked to anyone. His son, The Boy—Kent, he tried to remind himself—seemed social enough.

He hadn't inherited the introverted nature the men in *Elijah's* family seemed cursed with. Must come from his mother—a woman he barely remembered except for some heated, drunken images. A little more than six years earlier he'd made a baby—a fact he'd not known for the last six years.

Eli might never meet his son. He'd accepted the facts of the situation. He could, however, funnel money from his hidden trust fund to the child, allowing him to attend private school—a necessity, it seemed, in all except a few neighborhoods in New York City.

Occasionally, he could watch him from afar while he ate his lunch.

Elijah hadn't finished his sandwich. Glancing down, he stared at his half-consumed Subway concoction. The Boy didn't need him to spy on him all the time, but he felt compelled to do it, nonetheless. As it turned out, The Boy had faced struggles in his young life. His mother died in a car accident when he was two. Her mother, Jessica, cared for him.

Leaving him to Eli hadn't been an option, since he hadn't known the kid existed. Uncle Sam apparently kept his mail from him and who knew what else. He'd gotten the *I'm pregnant, you have a son, where the fuck are you, deadbeat* letters all at once. Since his previous persona, the man he'd been born as, Tim O'Connell, 'died' it wasn't likely he'd ever speak to The Boy at all.

It sucked.

At least The O'Connell money—hidden away where the IRS couldn't touch it—would give his son a hell of an education. Anonymous donations. Scholarships. The Boy would want for nothing, ever.

Except a father and a mother. The same way as Eli. Like father, like son. Only in his case, Thomas O'Connell hadn't been dead, fake or otherwise. He'd been busy with his fourth wife and fifteenth mistress. Most of the time, the old man hadn't remembered he fathered any offspring.

Eli jumped in his seat when the woman plopped down next to him. He hadn't seen her coming or felt her approach in his gut. *Jeezus—how out of practice have I gotten?* Years as a Marine sniper trained him better. People never snuck up on him, ever. New York and medical school were making him soft.

"You don't mind if I sit here, do you?" The woman smiled cheerfully. She possessed red hair and blue eyes, as well as a string of freckles over her nose and cheeks that gave the appearance of youth. Probably looked younger than she was. Eli pegged her between twenty and twenty-five.

Maybe it was the *Star Wars* t-shirt she donned throwing him off. The women in New York were always so put together. Did anyone older than a college student strut around Manhattan in *Luke Skywalker is my Hero* clothing?

And what did it say about him that his cock hardened so instantly when her perfume—*was it vanilla?*—hit his nostrils?

"You don't, do you?"

Oh, she wanted an answer, and he supposed he should get used to giving them. He was going to need a bedside manner, and he might as well figure out how to communicate with strangers sooner than later.

"The bench doesn't belong to me."

If he'd met this woman in a bar, he would know what to do. A few drinks, some giggles—hers not his—and back to his place, where he would either introduce her to or continue her education to some serious rope play. On a park bench? He had no earthly idea what he should say.

"Are you studying on your lunch break?" She pointed to his *Atlas of Human Anatomy* and smiled so brightly, he thought she might actually start to glow. "Because if you're studying, I'll control myself from yapping. I swear, I can. I do have a habit of chatting up strangers. A born extrovert, I guess. I've never met a person who couldn't be a friend. I tell my kids to believe in friendship, anyway. Well, camaraderie and stranger danger."

Eli's mouth fell open. The woman could really talk. And it was so fucking delightful. Maybe he could ask her to continue. She could yammer on and on. He'd sit and...listen.

First, he'd have to say something, too. Or she might stop. "I'm not studying."

"Oh, good. So then you won't mind if I bother you. Unless you do?" She looked at him with wide eyes, and despite the fact he didn't know a damn thing about her, he would have promised to climb Mount Everest in a tutu if she wanted.

"I don't. Please...talk."

She grinned from ear to ear, showing a dimple in her left cheek. "Oh, wow, a dangerous request. I have a hard time shutting up. Although, I can listen too."

"I guess both abilities are important since you have to talk to your kids and wait for their responses?" His remark seemed a good, benign question. She'd already brought them up, so they must be safe to discuss. "How many do you have?"

"Twenty-two."

He'd taken a sip of his water, and he almost spit it out. "Are you kidding?"

"No." She paused. "Why? Did I sound as if I was?"

"Twenty-two is a lot of kids. Are you, what, twenty?" How did she function? No, he had to have misunderstood. No way could she have twenty-two children.

Throwing her head back, she laughed. He immediately shut up. Elijah didn't talk in long spurts very often, and when he did, it was to give instructions to other snipers or members of his team. These days, he spoke only when he needed to in school or study groups.

No one laughed at him. Ever.

"I'm sorry, you misunderstood me." She giggled once more. "They're not *mine*. Although, I appreciate you thinking I'm twenty. I'm actually twenty-six. When I talk about my kids, I mean the ones I teach." She pointed at the Coleto school across the street, where The Boy went. "I'm a Kindergarten teacher. I have twenty-two kids I work with five days a week. Except for two hours on Mondays, which it is right this very second now. I go to a seminar at the West Side Park center to learn some techniques on using manipulatives for the exceptional child." She shifted in her seat. "Anyway, I'm going back there, only they're in recess. I give myself ten minutes here. I can see them, and the classroom aid, across the street. I sit and watch. It's kind of Zen."

"And you talk to strangers."

She shrugged, and her red hair moved up and down on her shoulders. "I guess talking to grownups is Zen to me too."

It dawned on him she might be The Boy's teacher. He'd read the woman's name when he'd paid the tuition bill. All the information had been laid out in the welcome letter.

Easy way to find out. He extended his hand. "I'm Elijah Jones. Eli."

He'd given himself the nickname on principle. If the government named him, he'd make it his own somehow.

"Oh, hi." She took his hand and shook. "I'm Rose Smith. Look at us, Smith and Jones. It's British Television. Oh, *Doctor Who*."

Rose looked at him expectantly, as if she wanted him to understand the reference. As it was, he'd gotten really into nighttime television, since he didn't sleep more than two hours a night. It was always on in the background while he learned how to heal the human body. It had taken him much less time to figure out how to end a life than to keep someone alive, which was probably, perversely, why he did it.

In the sunlight of the park, however, there was Rose to consider. Particularly because she was The Boy's teacher. His very, very adorable borderline hot kindergarten teacher who sat out on these benches every Monday.

Falling into character was an old habit. "Were you a *Doctor Who* fan before the reboot, or did you start to watch with the Ninth Doctor and his Rose?"

She patted him on the knee. "You understood what I'm talking about. You referenced science fiction and don't think I'm crazy."

"I guess I do know my television." He wouldn't promise to always understand every reference.

She looked at her watch. "Well, I guess it's time for me to make my way back to my day job. This was fun." She twirled a piece of her hair on her finger. "Any chance you make a habit out of being here? I might see you on a park bench again?"

He picked up his book. Class needed his attention. "I think there is more than a small chance I'll be out here." Especially considering he developed his new habit to quasi stalk The Boy on Mondays during recess.

If he could have figured out how to take his binoculars and sonar to watch him in the building without anyone on the street noticing or having to break into someone's apartment building, he would do so. Class scheduling made it impossible for him to follow the child home.

"Great." She stood up. "It's nice to make a friend so randomly."

"I don't think we'll be friends. Not exactly."

Her face pinkened when he spoke, which was exactly the response he'd hoped for. Eli didn't want many things for himself out of life. He'd met most of his goals. He did, however, want Rose Smith tied up in his bed while he gave her what she needed. Even if she didn't understand she required it yet.

"Oh."

He stood up and took her hand in his, giving it a squeeze. "Better return to your kids."

"Right." She smiled and fled toward the crosswalk.

If she also happened to be able to tell him a few small details about The Boy, the child he'd never meet personally, well then, so be it. Why couldn't he achieve two things he wanted at once? The government required him to live a completely benign, hidden life. It was beyond time to find some fun in it.

Rose talked. He'd be happy to listen. Except in the bedroom. There, she'd be tied up and want to obey.

Now

Platinum stalked toward the car. What could have happened to Kent? Young children with grandmothers who wouldn't let them eat anything with red dye number five in it—he knew because it was a fact Tony presented him with at the last meeting—didn't simply disappear in such a way where professional private eyes couldn't find them. His danger radar went off in a big way.

"Stop it." Copper grabbed his arm. "Whatever happened in there, whatever you need to get done, you can't run off and not tell Chrome or Steele where you're going. Fuck it, Platinum, you've been trained better."

"It's personal."

She shook her head. Copper was the strongest, toughest woman he'd ever known. Why she decided to make friends with him, when most everyone else left him to his own devices, never ceased to puzzle him. Copper and Mercury were thicker than thieves, only whatever relationship those two shared—or didn't—he wouldn't pretend to understand. Copper had gone and fallen in love with someone other than Merc, and everyone seemed okay with it.

"Yes. And?" She wasn't going to let it go.

"I have a kid." He could hardly mutter the words. A year of impossibly long days passed since he'd thought about The Boy, let alone told anyone—even the people he trusted with his life—about Kent's existence.

"I think you'd better go see Poppy. Whatever it is, you can't hide it from the uppity-ups. Whatever happened, it's only going to make things harder."

Damn it. He hated when she was right.

Plat wasn't going to find Kent if Tony hadn't been able to, not without resources his team could provide. They usually worked in groups of four, each member reporting to Chrome or Steele, depending on who was heading that particular mission. He couldn't ask anyone else to be involved. Any danger he took on would be his own.

None of those facts meant he couldn't ask permission to go, so he didn't end up with his teammates chasing him down assuming he'd gone off the reservation.

Steele would talk to Poppy and Poppy would manage Warbucks.

"I'll call Steele."

Copper patted him on the back. "Good."

"Could you do something for me?"

She raised an eyebrow. "Maybe."

"Good answer." Never make a promise until you knew what it entailed. Not unless it was in the field. Then he knew she'd do what he asked as he would. Team relationships were the only friendships Plat ever understood.

"What is it?"

"There's an asshat in the bar named Tony. I think he's about to drop dead. I don't want him to do it here, too many questions." He really didn't want to have caused problems for Bone Daddy's. Tony Di'Fallipi dying at the table minutes after Plat walked away seemed a headache he didn't need. Plus, needless death irked him. Why let someone die when you could save them?

Some deaths had to happen, others didn't.

"I'll take him out, and maybe I'll drop him at an ER."

"Thanks." He unlocked the car. First Steele then Kent.

"Platinum," Copper called his attention. "Sometime you're going to have to tell me how you ended up with a kid."

"Copper, if you don't understand how it works, then Gabriel is doing something really wrong."

His teammate hooked up with her guy months ago, and as much as Plat didn't understand how any of their group could manage to have a real social life, Copper seemed happy, which meant she needed to be ragged about it every chance he got.

"Fuck you, Platinum."

"I'm pretty fucked. Trust me."

～

THE SNIPER WAITED FOR HIM. She held the gun in her hand

and sat with her back to the tree. Waiting. Waiting for him. The woman surprised her. She hadn't expected there to be a fourth person involved in the little game. It should have been two snipers and the child. The woman didn't belong in the mix, and yet, here she was.

Dragging the child away from home before he could be gotten to. Taking him to the remote cabin with the shades drawn. The woman was changing the plan, and The Sniper hadn't expected it.

Plans changed, and she changed with them. Just as her husband taught her, before he was murdered. An unprovoked bullet through the head fired by the man who called himself Platinum.

All she needed to do was wait. Patience was the sniper's greatest tool. Platinum would die. Soon.

And his kid would watch.

2

___

Rose paced the room for maybe the hundredth time. In the way only children could do, Kent Matthews slept fitfully on the coach. He was safe. For now. Only, he almost hadn't been. Her head spun. Why did today happen? What if she hadn't run into Kent on the street? Would he have died, too?

She took a steadying breath and knelt on the floor. Instinct made her keep the shades closed, and although she'd never been tested the same way before, she trusted her gut when it told her not to phone the police. At least not yet.

Kent's grandmother was dead. Murdered in her bed, and if Kent's story was true, then whoever did it wore a uniform —a cop's uniform—and had pursued him.

Rose hadn't believed him at first, and she still wasn't certain he'd gotten the cop part right. Until someone took a shot at Rose. While talking to Kent, a bullet whizzed right by her head. The sound of it—a violent humming—before the devastating thwack as it cut into the man passing her. Heads made a sound when they exploded—and pink mist.

So much pink mist. It sprayed everywhere. It splattered her shirt. The world narrowed and grew darker in those seconds. She'd grabbed Kent and run to her parents' cabin in upstate New York. Located on the outskirts of New Paltz on a dirt road never used, the cabin offered them a sanctuary. A place she could keep him safe, at least for the present.

Her folks left her the place and she'd been holding off selling it for the sentimental value. Once a week, she checked on Kent, her favorite student from her class two years earlier. She'd never admit to playing favorites and doubted the kids in her class noticed it, but Kent touched her heart.

No mother or father left in the world to care for him. They shared their orphan status. A scholarship child who attended Coleto on grants, he had only his elderly grandmother to love him, and she did the best she could. It could have been Rose's story, only her trip through guardians and semi poverty hadn't started until a week after her fifteenth birthday.

The truth was, Rose was always drawn toward teaching and helping the difficult children, the ones the other teachers clenched their jaws to talk about. As if no one who went to a swanky private school in New York should ever have any behavior problems.

She'd never seen the testing results from his IEP. It hadn't been done until first grade, but she'd lay money on the fact he possessed a gifted IQ to go with his attention problem. His grandmother trusted Rose, and though the administration might have frowned on it if they'd known, she'd continued to see Kent outside of school at least once a week for tutoring.

Thank the stars she did.

"Kent's not a liar," she spoke aloud to the quiet room. "If

he says it's the police who killed his Maw Maw, then it's the police. End of story. And apparently, the police are shooting at me."

She rarely focused on how alone she was or how precarious the isolation left her. She had an aunt in Arizona who hated her. Oh, the other woman would never use the actual word 'hate' to describe their relationship, except when it came down to it, Aunt Pressley thought Rose too strange to deal with. Apparently, attending comic book conventions made her beyond crazy in her straight-laced auntie's book.

Other than the disappearing aunt, her family was gone. Her grandmother passed away on Rose's twentieth birthday, finally letting go after years of horrific pain from cancer. Tears slipped out at the memory. Damn it. She needed to stop being so maudlin.

The shooting happened. She needed to face facts. None of her friends would be able to help, nor would she really want them to. God forbid someone got hurt. Kent needed her, and she was going to keep him safe.

All of the police force couldn't be involved. She'd driven hours from New York City. The New Paltz police must be trustworthy. Rose walked to the phone. Her cell phone barely seemed to have a single bar. Not enough to actually complete a call. However, her parents' cabin still held a landline. She paid the eight-dollar monthly bill to keep it for emergencies. Teaching paid her very little, and she would have liked those eight dollars for extra small niceties.

With their current predicament, she was glad she'd bothered. Hand shaking, she picked up the receiver from the table next to the couch where Kent slept. It took her a full second to realize she didn't hear a dial tone.

"Oh, what the hell?" she whispered, and then checked to see if she'd bothered Kent. He didn't stir, his head pressed on the small pillow, his mouth hung open slightly in sleep. One piece of his white blond hair fell over his forehead, and she smoothed it away.

The color was so unique. It always reminded her of...

No. She cut off the direction her thoughts took. She would not, could not allow herself to think of *him*. Elijah Jones had blown into her life, then detonated it when he vanished a year later.

Her ex couldn't be in her mind during her current situation. She needed help, and he wouldn't have been any.

Of course, he might have been a shoulder to cry on, and his big strong arms would have held her close. Assuming he'd actually shown. She was musing about the guy who vanished. She'd arrived to see him, only to find he'd moved out of his apartment, all of his stuff gone, and any trace of him having existed, disappeared.

She'd thought he was a medical student. Who knew who he really was in the end? Did it matter?

Rose pulled the phone plug out of the wall and crawled around until she found the second outlet in the kitchen. It had been such a long time since she'd been to her parents' cabin. Selling it would be on the horizon for the next year. Sentimentality was fine until she needed to pay bills.

The second outlet didn't work either, so either the phone company hadn't been keeping up with the line, despite her monthly check, or...

Was it possible? She stood, a layer of dust coming with her, and tried not to think about where her mind wanted to go. Could someone have cut the line? The person after Kent...

She bit down on her lip and put her hands in her pockets to stop from screaming. Had she made things worse by bringing them here? Were they rats in a cage?

"Oh God, Kent. I don't have the faintest clue what to do. I really don't."

They didn't have food, and it was going to become cold very fast unless she could make a fire. How was she to manage when she couldn't open the door?

Unless Eli left some the last time they were here. She rushed to the hall closet and opened it up, only to find herself frozen in her spot, staring at a black coat she'd never thought to see again.

He'd left his soft cotton blazer, the item he said he hated and wore everywhere when it got cold, despite his disdain for the garment. Rose pressed her nose against it and inhaled. The material still smelled of him.

The floodgate of her memories opened, and she knew she'd not be closing it any time soon.

～

Two years earlier

Mister Hottie waited at their bench again. Five weeks in a row. It couldn't be coincidence anymore. He knew she'd be there—she always was.

She smiled and clutched the bagel she'd bought him tighter in her hand. He never ate anything, except a boring turkey sandwich with nothing else. When she'd questioned him about it, he'd shrugged, which was the way he answered a lot of inquiries she made.

Eli was either completely unused to talking about himself, or he was hiding from the mob. She suspected it was the first option, because mob informants were probably not enrolled in Columbia Medical School.

Today was the day. She'd have to find out if he wanted to

see her somewhere other than their bench. Her Monday classes would be ending, and she wouldn't be leaving her classroom anymore during the day. Today would either be goodbye or a very different kind of hello.

He'd made that single sexual innuendo the first week and never again. Had he changed his mind or somehow gotten scared off?

Maybe all her talking finally wore him down to being completely uninterested in pursuing it any further. Either way, she would put on her big girl panties and find out. She'd left off her science fiction clothing for the occasion, choosing to dress herself as a woman who didn't spend all day getting pawed at by adorable five and six year-olds. Black pants and a white fitted blouse, which—she hoped—tugged at her in the right places and didn't make her look fat.

He looked up when she approached and didn't smile. Then again, he never did. Elijah was serious, almost all of the time they were together. Since she'd always been a sucker for the tough cases, she couldn't help but see the sadness behind his blue eyes. Who put it there, and could she find a way to ease some of it?

"Hi." She smiled and sat down. "How are you?"

"Fine." He nodded at her. "You look different."

He'd noticed? "I changed. I mean, not today, I've been wearing the same clothes since I got dressed. I mean, I decided to dress differently today. The kids love my t-shirts and the principal likes to foster a community of creativity, so they dig the science fiction. Except, you know, I'm a grown woman. And you really don't want to hear all about it. Here," she handed him the bagel she'd bought, "I got food for you."

His eyebrows shot up. "You did?"

"It's nothing exciting. Just an everything bagel with cream cheese. I might have picked a different schmear, only they're very personal choices, and I didn't want to guess yours. So, plain cream cheese it was."

"No one has ever brought me a bagel before." He stared at it, still not having taken it from its paper wrapping.

"Too many carbs?" He was so fit. Maybe he never, ever ate white sugar or starch. He'd always remember her as the weird girl who tried to feed him poison.

"No. I don't…"

"Well, you don't have to eat it. You can throw it out."

He shook his head and set down his book on the bench. "I'm not going to toss it. Are you crazy?"

Elijah actually looked disgruntled. His face kind of scrunched up, and a muscle ticked in his jaw. Was he really upset she'd suggested he could throw out the bagel if he didn't want it?

"I don't think so. I mean, I've never been told I am. I passed a psychological evaluation to work with kids. Kind of a big deal in the private school sector in New York."

He leaned back on the bench and shook his head, a small smile playing on his face. "You're funny."

"You didn't laugh."

Eli nodded, the smile disappearing. "I almost never laugh."

She gasped. Wow. There was a proclamation she'd never heard before. "Why on earth not?"

"I guess I haven't had a lot of amusement in my life. When I think about you, Rose, I envision you laughing."

"You think about me?" Here was the chance. She'd ask him. Before she could chicken out. "I understand you're busy. Med students have hellish hours. Today is my last day of class outside of school."

"Oh." He rubbed at his forehead.

That was it? She'd hoped for more of a startled, I can't do without you Rose sort of reaction. Well, she wasn't going to dwell. Time to push on through. In for a penny, in for a pound and all that. "I've liked seeing you. I mean, I kind of inserted myself into your life. Sitting down and talking the way I did. The thing is, I saw you sitting here, and you looked as if you needed company. So I said to myself, Rose, really, what's the worst thing? He'll tell you to go away."

"I didn't."

"Right." For Eli, he was being downright talkative. "And I guess what I'm saying is I think you've been okay with us meeting week after week because if you weren't, you'd not be here. You'd sit in some other park, on some other bench."

He didn't respond, which she decided to take as a signal to keep talking. Eli must know where she was going.

"I'd like to see you again after today. If you don't want to, then today is goodbye." She put her hands in her lap and waited. Cabs honked, people shouted, several dogs barked somewhere in the distance. Still, New York seemed silent. Rose had never asked a guy out before, always content to wait for the guy to do it or not go out at all. Confidence in her looks didn't prove easy for her.

Redheads were a type, and it seemed most of the single men in New York preferred another brand.

"You're asking me on a date?" He cleared his throat.

"Oh, God." She'd never asked him two essential questions before she jumped right in with both feet. "You're taken or gay. Which one is it?"

"Neither."

Wow. He wasn't going to make her job easy, was he? She stood up. "Okay, you don't want to go out with me. Fine. I tell my kids all the time there is a right way and a wrong way to tell someone you don't want to play. You can be nice about it or mean. Obviously, Eli, I misread our times on this bench entirely. You didn't have to be an ass and let me go on and on. It would have more polite for you to simply say no thanks and—"

"I do want to *play* with you." Elijah motioned to the bench. "Sit back down, Rose."

Her knees worked without any conscious thought from her, and she parked herself on the bench.

"I don't communicate well. In my previous...life...job... whatever you want to call it, I never needed to."

"What did you—"

He interrupted her again, which must be a record for him. "I'm never going to want to discuss the old part of my life. It's over. I'm in school, and it's all about moving forward."

"So, you're saying you don't want to see me again..."

He touched her arm, and a jolt of electricity moved through her body. It left her slightly breathless. "I would really enjoy going out on a date with you. I don't want today to be the last time I see you."

"Great." For a change, it was she who was at a loss for words. He continued to stare at her with his blond hair and blue eyes and perfect cheekbones and kissable lips, and she simply could come up with nothing to say. Nothing what-so-frickin'-ever.

Dizzy and kind of lightheaded, she fought to maintain her equilibrium as her world tilted slightly.

"I'm available tonight."

"Oh." She sat straighter and tried to gather her thoughts. Rose's imagining of asking Eli out never reached the part of the equation of getting together for the date. Having been so preoccupied with the asking, she'd never thought of the actual going.

She continued, needing to do better than oh. "I'd like to go tonight, sure, this evening would be fine."

"Great. Where would you want to go?" He regarded her differently. She couldn't explain it, only it was as if he turned all of his focus onto her in a way it hadn't been before. The effect left her breathless, and yet, she would gladly give up oxygen to hold his regard for the rest of the day uninterrupted.

"Well, you know I'm a teacher, so some of the fancier places are out of my pay scale. That being said, I know a really good Italian place where you can order—"

"Rose."

She stopped talking. He'd said her name, and it sounded akin to music. "What?"

"I'm going to pay. It's a date. I'll take you out."

"No. I asked you out, which means I'm paying."

He shook his head. "I can't and won't accept you paying for anything. You did the asking, I'll do the paying, and since it's clearly going to be an issue you'll worry about, I'll assure you I can afford to take you out. I'll pick the place. You stay dressed as you are."

She opened and closed her mouth several times. "Okay."

"Good." He unwrapped the bagel and took a big bite. When he finished chewing, he smiled and nodded. "It's delicious, and you're going to be late."

She jumped to her feet, and when she would have darted, he grabbed her arm. "I need your phone number so I can text you mine. And then you'll send me back your address so I can pick you up."

Five minutes later, what he described happened. Exactly as Elijah said it would. It kept a smile on her face the rest of the day. It didn't bother her—well, maybe only slightly—she'd made a date with a guy who called his previous job his life and told her he didn't want to talk about it. Wasn't everyone entitled to their secrets? How bad could it be?

~

Now

"Ms. Rose."

She jumped at the sound of his voice. So intent on listening for noises outside, she hadn't noticed Kent awakened.

"Sweetheart. Come here." She extended her arms, and he walked into them. He needed to stay close where she could keep him near. If he moved around too much or was out of range, and something happened, she'd never forgive herself.

"It happened, really? My Maw Maw, she's dead." He hadn't quite gotten rid of the lisp when he made his *s* sounds, although it was much better than when he'd been in her class. The act left the impression of his being much younger than his actual age.

She saw children two years younger than him every day. Still, Kent seemed very small to her.

"It did."

"The woman police officer, she came through the door. Shot my Maw Maw, and then she wanted me. I ran. I hid. And then you came."

Exactly the way he told the story earlier. Starts and stops, not much detail to hold onto. His Maw Maw started medicating him earlier in the year to help with his focus, which would have to be wearing off soon. The fact he'd slept at all surprised her. Trauma could trump anything going on in the body, it seemed. She'd never needed him to take medication when he'd been in her class. Since he was older, and the work was more taxing, the teachers complained more. Who was she to judge? She liked Kent focused or inattentive. Either way, he was a great kid.

"We're going to be okay." Lying to him seemed the kindest thing she could do.

"You always told us not to fib."

She squeezed his arm. "Smarty-pants. Don't you think I can figure out what to do?"

He was silent for a while, and when he spoke again, his words surprised her. "Maybe we can call my dad."

"Your dad?" The day must really be taxing him. "Kent, your father died before you were born. In Afghanistan. He was a Marine, and he didn't come back home. You've never met him."

"They were lying when they told me those stories. I've always believed my daddy's alive."

"I don't think they were." Nothing could be more heart-breaking than a child's wishful thinking, such as the father he'd never known swooping in and saving the day. Why not expect Prince Charming to show up and do it on his white horse? Or Elijah Jones to suddenly appear on her doorstep begging forgiveness with a completely acceptable reason for disappearing without a trace?

"I can always tell when someone is fibbing. Their voice sounds funny. I can't focus on some things, like History. Social studies. Blah. Only details make sense to me. I can hear things. See them. My Maw Maw used to sound different in the way she talked about my dad. She thought the money must be coming from somewhere. I heard her on the phone. She tried to find out. Recently, she hired someone to find out."

These were questions Rose couldn't deal with. If there were answers, she'd have to find them later. Distracting him and keeping him busy were important, as were basic necessities. "I found some wood in the closet where an old friend put it. Do you want to help me make a fire?"

If someone hunted them, they probably knew they were there anyway. Might as well be warm.

3

Now

"Usually, when someone calls me to ask to do something, they haven't already done it. I should bust your balls for coming to me after the fact."

Frustration edged Steele's voice. Plat didn't usually incur his team leader's wrath. He actually liked to work for Steele. He was fair, and he took care of his guys, which went a long way to inspire loyalty.

"Do you know the expression it's better to ask for forgiveness than permission?"

A cab blasted his horn, and Plat winced. A year since he'd been in New York City, and he'd forgotten the sheer volume of sound on the street. The noise used to be unbearable, until he'd met Rose. She'd quieted everything.

Only he didn't expect to see her on his trip. Or if he did, she'd probably be more interested in yelling at him than making anything easier. He would let her.

"Is that what you're doing? Asking for forgiveness?"

Now would be a good time to really start explaining,

except saying ten words when four would do didn't work for him. Well, with anyone except Rose. "Do I need to?"

"We'll talk when you come back. You've never done this before. It's gotta be serious, or you wouldn't have gotten on a plane and left. I'll trust you to handle your personal shit. But I expect to see you as soon as it's over. Be less than a week. If you don't come back, I'm activating that GPS chip in your shoulder and coming after you. In that case, Platinum, you'd better have some hell of a stout reason to be radio silent, or I'm going to be pissed."

"Right." *Fuck.*

"And good work on the Rodgers situation. We were all surprised by how fast you took care of him."

Another car horn blasted, and his ears rang. "Thanks."

Plat disconnected the phone.

Steele's mention of Rodgers boosted his confidence. He could actually accomplish his task. The only time in his career had he been given the opportunity to go against another sniper one on one. His most recent target worked for the enemy doing Plat's exact job for the other side. Two of them got up in the morning, and only Plat returned. *Oorah.*

Give him a mission to rid the world of trash any day over what he needed to manage on his current task. He was going to have to go lie his way through the door of The Boy's school, resist all urges to go stare at Rose from a distance, and find out what was going on. It was a good thing he held the paperwork to show he managed Kent's scholarship money. The papers should at least help him through the door.

In the year he'd dated Rose, he'd never stepped through the door of Coleto Academy. When he'd met her after work, he'd waited outside.

He buzzed the bell and went inside. The building looked old and well-kept with the walls colorfully decorated. Smiling children darted around him, and he moved out of their way. Making a quick note to avoid the hallway with the label Kindergarten for obvious reasons, he went into the office and nearly collided with a woman running down the hall.

He caught her before she fell over, and he watched as she ran down the hallway he was determined to avoid.

"I'm so sorry," the secretary sitting behind one of the desks called out to him. "We're in crisis mode here. Are you part of the police force?"

She looked like a nice woman—her desk held a nametag saying Nancy—and she smiled brightly. Her hair was blonde with grey roots, and she'd kicked her shoes off beneath her desk. The school might be in some kind of crisis mode, although Nancy did not seem to be. And seeing as he wasn't sporting a badge or a gun or any kind of cop paraphernalia whatsoever, he wouldn't have pinned himself as a cop

It might be interesting to play at it for a while, except he needed answers on Kent. He didn't have time for anything else.

"It's so awful about Kent. Do you think you'll find him?"

And she talked because he didn't answer. Happened in his life more than anyone would believe. His son went missing, the school knew, the cops were involved, and there was some kind of crisis going on.

"You can count on me finding him, Nancy." He walked toward her desk and smiled, making sure to show some teeth.

"Oh." She clutched her chest. "Thank you. His grandmother's murder is such a shock. And one of our kindergarten teachers, Ms. Rose, has gone missing. I have so much I'm worrying about."

Whatever else she would have said he missed. Ringing echoed in his ears and wouldn't stop. Grandmother dead. Both Kent and *Rose* missing.

Plat never considered himself a narcissist. He did not believe the world revolved around him, yet there was no earthly way both The Boy and His Rose—The Rose disappeared at the same time, without it having something to do with him.

Some enemy fucker found what he'd taken such pains to hide. When he discovered who had taken his son, killed The Boy's grandmother, and kidnapped the only woman he'd ever loved, he would destroy them.

Everyone left clues behind. He was a sniper, details were his specialty.

～

ROSE HAD REDECORATED HER APARTMENT. Wishing away his nostalgia, Platinum sighed to the quiet rooms. What had he expected? She wouldn't change a thing? The entire overhaul of her environment threw him. If her pictures weren't still in their frames, he'd have thought he was in the wrong apartment in her fifth-floor walkup. Where had all her science fiction nick-knacks gone?

Though her perfume still clung to the walls too, he refused to dwell on her vanilla scent either. No signs of struggle. Despite the fact she'd gone missing from school, it didn't appear the cops made it through her place yet.

If Rose had been snagged here, she'd have put up a fight. He suddenly envisioned her hands gripping the silk binds on her wrists, and the way she playfully pulled on them the last time they'd been together. Rose Smith was as tough as anyone he knew.

She'd be screaming, kicking, and...

He walked over to her dry erase board. She'd changed the color of the walls and the fabric on the chairs, yet she still kept her dry erase board. Nothing went into her Google calendar without also making it on the old fashioned scheduler, which belonged more in a college dorm than her quite-sophisticated redone apartment.

Where had she been recently? He scanned her handwriting and stopped when he read the notation detailing The Boy. It looked as if she made a weekly stop with Kent. Huh. Why? She'd liked all of her students. Did she work with all of them after they moved on from her class?

What if...

An idea formulated in his mind. Kent's grandmother died, shot, if the reports he'd stolen off the secretary's desk were to be believed. The day his Rose—The Rose since he placed *the* word in front of the name of everyone he loved—went to see The Boy. His love would never have shot anyone, certainly not an old woman trying to raise a child on her social security checks and anonymous donations.

No, she would have taken Kent and run, maybe even gone into hiding if she'd witnessed the tragedy—if she'd been scared.

And he knew where she'd go—her parent's cabin—he'd been there with her, once. Rose's version of the middle of nowhere illustrated her true innocence, an innocence he'd treasured. He could be there in a few hours.

And fuck if he'd ever be letting her, or The Boy, out of his sight again. Even if he needed to explain a lot when he found them.

Platinum knew he was right about what happened and

where they were, because the other options weren't stomachable.

He glanced once more around the room. Why would she have decided on black and white plaids? She was a bright color girl. If she spoke to him enough for him to ask, he'd find out. His heart clenched, and he ignored the emotional pang. Not hearing her voice while she happily chatted? Not ever getting the chance to, somehow, explain to The Boy how he couldn't be in his life, although he thought of him constantly? Those were the worries keeping him up at night.

Their deaths would not be added to them.

Two years ago

"This is my place."

Rose whirled around her small living room as though she welcomed him to a palace and he couldn't help but grin. A single glass of white wine, and she chatted more than ever. He loved it.

"It's nice." Should he say something else? "I admire your paint colors."

She pointed at the dark red wall. "What can I say? I enjoy elemental tones, which speak to me."

Was it possible he could live as she did? He hadn't wanted the government to kill off his previous life, to tell him he would no longer be who he'd always been. Yet standing with Rose in her small living room, he wondered if he could live this way. Could he let what happened with Operation Phoenix go? Forget about the dirty bombs of the world? Of the Marines who hadn't come home?

Rose spinning in her living room made hope possible, if

not probable. Part of Eli would always be on that fucked up mission, wondering how it all went so bad.

Every time the beautiful redhead laughed at something he said, she offered him a glimpse of something pure left in a dark world. Maybe The Boy could have a shot at it. Maybe Elijah might...

"Are you going to kiss me?" He tuned in immediately with her question. Truth was, he never should have let himself become distracted. Every word she uttered fascinated him. He wanted to remember every single detail.

Elijah walked toward her and placed his hand on her cheek. Her skin was so soft. "I am going to kiss you." She shuddered beneath his fingertips. "Were you asking in general or requesting it immediately?"

She laughed, which was what he wanted. "I guess I'm kind of pushy, aren't I?"

"You're used to being in charge. You run your classroom, your life, and you arrange things. I enjoy those traits about you. Admire it. Pushy on you equates sexy." She blushed. Her pale skin showed her every emotion. "Only how about in this way, you let me? I'll give you what you need. I'll take care of you, beautiful."

"I'm not good at letting other people handle things." She looked down, and he tipped her chin to make her recapture eye contact. When he held her blue eyed gaze again, he smiled.

"I think you don't understand how good it can be. Let's not worry about it right this minute." He ran his finger down her nose. "You're lovely. So beautiful, I can't believe I get to touch you."

"Okay." Except insecurity continued to flicker in her eyes.

"What are you worrying about?"

"When you say let you be in charge, do you mean BDSM, dominance, submissive stuff? Is that what you enjoy?" Her voice wavered, and he tugged her against him, wanting to shelter her from whatever demons scared her.

"What I enjoy is you. I enjoy some of it, except I'd say it changes from partner to partner. I'm not living the lifestyle outside of the bedroom. At the moment, I'm not going to clubs. I have no issue with anyone who does. I used to. I guess I've always needed to do things my way."

And since he'd been forcibly reinvented, he hadn't exactly figured out what the new him would be about in any fashion. Rose was his first foray back into a life he hadn't exactly participated in fully the last time around.

"I had a bad time in college. My boyfriend. He hurt me with a flogger. I didn't like it, and the whole thing became really complicated. I hated it."

"Hmm." He kissed her temple, needing the contact. It wasn't the lips, though she gasped as though the contact were far more intimate. "I don't want to hurt you. He reminds me of a lazy sadist. It's not my kink. And you're not a masochist. He shouldn't have done those things with you without trying it out first."

"What is your kink then?" Her voice went raspy; she wasn't uninterested.

"I think we'd have to learn each other to figure out exactly what we both enjoy. We could start out very vanilla. I have no problem with anything you want. Fantasizing about you naked has gotten me through some pretty heavy-duty study sessions. Ah, and she turns red."

"I blush. I can't help it." She shook her head.

He kissed her other temple. "I wouldn't want you to."

"Go on. You were saying."

Rose didn't steer away from subjects, even if they frightened her. Another reason to admire her.

"Handcuffs, silk ties. Rope. Maybe a collar when we're alone. As I said, we'd figure it out. You'd have a safe word. The only thing I need from you is trust. We've only known each other two months. Once a week for two months." He tilted her chin up. "How about we start with this?"

He finally gave into the gnawing urge to take her mouth. Her breath was sweet, and the little mewing sound she made when he parted her lips thrilled him. For once in his life, there was no rush. All of the things he had waiting for him could do just that—wait.

Eli deepened the kiss, loving how she let him. Rose might have some trepidation brought on by an asshole who recklessly wielded a flogger. Still, she knew how to submit, naturally, and he was going to love showing her how much she loved it.

He pulled back from her. "Enough for today."

"Really? Why?" Her eyes were glazed. It would be easy to take her, to make her his to bind her to him. He knew she belonged to him.

He wouldn't do it, not yet. Rose deserved to be wooed, and although he was a man of few words, he'd give her the ones he could.

"Tell me something." He stepped back to adjust his pants. His cock had gotten hard startlingly fast. He wasn't sixteen years old. Patience continued to be his strongest quality. *Shit, tonight would be a challenge.*

"Ah...okay." Her eyes were looking less glazed.

"Do you have science fiction posters up in your bedroom? If I take you in there, am I going to see Hans Solo staring down at me?"

She twirled a piece of her hair. "Maybe."

"Hans specifically?"

"Maybe." Rose grinned, and he traced her lip with the pad of his thumb. He wanted to remember her as she was forever.

"Anyone else? I mean, I need to know who I need to compete with for your affection."

"Have you ever seen *Buffy the Vampire Slayer*?"

He couldn't remember if he'd watched it, ever. Not that he remembered. "Vampires? Really?"

Holding back from taking her was hard, but talking to her? Nothing had ever been so easy or so right.

~

Now

Whoever shot at The Boy and The Rose turned out to be a pretty bad sniper. Plat looked up at the building across the street toward where the victim—shot across the street from where Kent lived—had been gunned down. The roof gave easy access, good vision, plenty of places to hide.

And yet, whoever started such a private war with him missed the intended target. A clean shot wouldn't have broken off and hit the building next to it. At least not a mistake he made, which meant whoever this fucker was terrifying his people and killing old women wasn't up to snuff.

Plat took out his phone and dialed Copper. Steele's timeline notwithstanding, he needed some help before he lost his way.

She picked up on the first ring. "Platinum?"

"If I'm arrested, I'm going to need you to spring me out of jail."

Silence met his statement. After several seconds, she spoke away from the phone. "Merc, Platinum thinks he's going to jail." He couldn't hear the rest of their exchange, until she spoke to him again. "Where are you, and how much shit are you in?"

"I'm going to break into my old apartment. The one I lived in during the time after Phoenix and before we went Metal. It's in New York City.'

"Feeling nostalgic? Just can't stay away? What does your old life have to do with your kid?"

"Copper, some asshole with a sniper rifle has him. And... someone else too." She'd either figure out what he meant by his words, or she wouldn't. He wasn't going to explain it on the phone. Copper wanted to hear about his love life about as much as he wanted to hear about hers, which amounted to none at all. "I have an old M40A5 hidden in there. It's old, but it'll do." The team owned the newer versions thanks to Warbucks, only beggars couldn't be choosers.

He'd chosen to handle his shit alone and flown commercial. TSA tended to frown over firearms getting on the plane.

"You're going after the guy?"

"After I retrieve my rifle."

"And since you're not a burglar, you're worried you're about to be arrested doing it."

Time to fess up about what he really needed. "I think I can manage to extract my hidden property. If I can't, Copper, I need you to rescue my kid. He's with a woman, and I'm going to text you the address. If I land in jail, there's no time to waste. He's only eight years old."

"If you can't save him, we will."

"Thanks." He'd known she'd say what she did, because it's what he would have told any of his team if they'd asked. They were his—albeit dysfunctional—family, and they were why he still did what he did day in and day out. The Marines, and eventually his team, had taken a fucked up, barely ever sober, angry-at-the-world, twenty-two-year-old Timothy O'Connell, and made him a man.

"Don't get dead."

"Right."

He hung up. Someone would be dying, only it wouldn't be him.

Kill one man...terrorize a thousand. No one would be fucking with what belonged to him again.

Reconnaissance was always as much his job as point, shoot, and kill. For the current mission, he didn't have time for due diligence, not when he needed to retrieve the equipment. If he'd learned anything from his time in the field, it was a bad sniper could be more of a danger than a good sniper. Whoever shot the bullet missed. Badly.

He'd thank his lucky stars he—or he supposed it could be a she—hadn't made the shot. The victim's family wouldn't agree. He had to focus on his own people and see what he could do for the others later. The fact they'd tried in broad daylight on the street in New York City, and not been sure they could actually do it? Those actions spoke of stupidity or desperation.

In either case, he needed to get to Rose and Kent fast. Bypassing the front door didn't prove any problem. He possessed his old key, and the building managers hadn't bothered to change it.

Unfortunately, his luck ran out after that. The locks on his actual apartment door *had* been changed. He knocked and waited longer than needed to see if they answered. Plat pulled his hoodie up, a move he wished he'd made earlier. Elijah the medical student hadn't garnered a lot of attention in the building, which was fine. Still, he didn't want to draw anyone's notice.

Picking locks wasn't a skill they'd taught him in the Corps. His early days getting into trouble after his mother's death paid this particular talent forward. A credit card and a twist of a screwdriver helped him disengage the lock.

Unlike Rose's apartment, he didn't really care how the current renters decorated. Four walls and a roof were all he required. Rose made her living space home, and although he'd gotten close during his time in New York, Plat wasn't certain he'd ever really had a home.

His residences were always a place to sleep, shower, study, and hide his rifle. Fortunately for him, the current tenants hadn't noticed their closet's false back wall. If only his luck could hold out a little bit longer.

4

She lay on the floor in front of the fire with Kent—asleep once more—on her left. What must it be like to be able to close her eyes and forget everything the way he seemed to be able to do?

They'd eaten the can of beans she'd found in the back of a cabinet. She'd let him have the majority of it. Her stomach was in knots anyway. How could she sleep when there was somebody with a gun looking for Kent and her?

Was she being ridiculous? What was the likelihood she'd been followed all the way up to New Paltz? She should run to the car and take Kent to the police station. Rose drummed her fingers on the ground. Okay, that was exactly what she would do. In the morning when he woke, they'd seek help. And hopefully, they wouldn't charge her with kidnapping. Someone was bound to understand. Weren't they?

∾

THE SNIPER GREW tired of waiting. It wasn't the same as

when her husband lived. Sitting in silence and waiting seemed much more pleasurable when he'd been with her. Her darling had been The Sniper and she his spotter. Since the fool calling himself Platinum murdered him, she needed to be The Sniper to avenge his death.

Rose Smith wasn't making things easier. Why wouldn't she come out? She must be hungry, cold, and terrified. Since The Sniper would never again be able to use her police costume and have Kent believe it, she needed to wait Rose out.

By morning, if Rose and the child hadn't come out, The Sniper would go to them. Smoke encouraged exits. Setting the cabin ablaze would mean they had no choice except to run right into her line of fire.

ROSE HADN'T MEANT to sleep. She certainly didn't intend to rest so deeply she dreamed, yet she did, as if her mind needed to drop so completely out of the real world for her to be able to function.

The funny thing was, she knew she wasn't awake, because seeing Elijah only happened in her unconscious.

Lying on the floor of her cabin, she saw him exactly as he looked two years earlier. The first time they'd been together, when she'd thought they might have a chance, when she'd been certain she fallen smack into almost-perfect boyfriend territory.

Two years earlier

She leaned against the door of her apartment. They had a great date. Or at least, she thought it was fun. Rose could never be sure whether Eli enjoyed himself or not. He said so little.

How many other straight men liked Broadway shows? He'd spent more of the show watching her than what was going on during *Guys and Dolls* on the stage.

Still, he'd bought tickets. Coupled with the dinner he'd taken her to the week before, she felt more and more he wasn't some poor medical student living on student loans. It was rude to ask about money, so she wouldn't. Elijah never talked about his past. Could she ask him how he'd come to be a med student at thirty-five years old?

If it weren't for the complete lack of information, he'd be perfect. So, she wouldn't complain. Who wanted perfection anyway? How boring.

"What are you thinking about?" He leaned forward, invading her personal space. He exuded warmth, and she'd love to roll around in the gravity of his heat. Should she invite him inside?

They needed to talk about the things he'd brought up the last time they were together. The topics which kept her up and squirming, sometimes wet and desperate for relief her own fingers couldn't provide. Not when she craved his cock inside of her.

Sheesh. He was making her a sex addict, and they hadn't done anything yet.

"Do you read minds?" He smelled clean, like soap, and maybe a touch of some kind of aftershave. It didn't overwhelm her as some cologne did. In fact, it made her feel lightheaded in the best possible way. She didn't remember brands of scents. This one she would think of as Eli's smell for the rest of her life.

He shook his head. "If I did, I wouldn't need to ask, would I?"

"Did you enjoy the show?"

His mouth twisted in an upward, sideways grin before he spoke. "That's what you're contemplating? Whether or not I enjoyed the show? Okay, you're avoiding the question. I'll play along. I enjoyed watching you like the show."

"Why did you take me if you don't want to watch musicals? Or did you simply not think tonight's was any good?"

"You said you liked them."

She had? "When did I tell you?"

"Second time we met on the bench."

"Oh." She'd forgotten she'd babbled on about Broadway. "You really listened."

"To every word you say."

Rose melted. Nothing he could have said in the world would have made her fall harder for him than the words he'd spoken. *Every word she said.*

"I'm nervous, Eli. What if I really don't want any of the stuff you suggested?"

He bent over to whisper in her ear, "I know you, sweetheart." She loved the way his warm breath made her shiver. "I shouldn't have said anything to you about it. You make me forget the things I've learned. I lose all my good sense. Tell you what? Invite me in for the night. If you don't like things between us, you'll tell me to stop. We'll figure out a safe word for you. And I'll be totally vanilla. I don't care about any of it as much as I want you, Rose."

She fumbled with her keys using shaky hands. "Come in."

"Thanks." He took the keys from her hand and opened the door for her.

"I guess I'm—"

Whatever she would have said was immediately cut off. His mouth came down on hers, and not in the light gentle joining of new lovers' kind of a way. No, when Eli kissed her, she held no doubt of what the rough conquering of her lips meant, he laid claim to her.

And she loved it.

"Eli," she gasped when he let her breathe, and he nuzzled her neck. Her knees buckled, and he caught her.

"I think I'm a little worked up."

"Good."

He scooped her into his arms, and they were in her bedroom in no time. She still wore her coat, her shoes, and her purse swung over her body. Rose didn't care at all. Her whole body buzzed.

As if he only then realized how clothed she remained, he dropped her bag onto the ground. A grin crossed his face. "Guess I'm a little bit excited."

"Me, too." And nervous, except she didn't want to vocalize her concerns. He'd given her no reason not to trust his word. If she said no, she believed he'd back off whatever she didn't enjoy. They could be together in the ways she was more accustomed to.

"Coat." He stood, allowing her to strip. He did the same, and when she'd removed her coat, he took it from her and placed it on top of her desk chair with his own.

Eli had a way about him, a steadiness, which made her feel like he could handle anything thrown at him. Testing her theory, she tossed her scarf. He caught it in one hand, and she admired his bicep as he flexed.

"Rose," he said her name, and her insides melted, "put your hands up on the headboard and hold onto it."

It seemed simple enough. She could handle those instructions.

"Good girl." He winked at her, and her heart stuttered. "Here's how tonight is going to work. You should think of our evening as the negotiation round. Usually, you wouldn't be gripping the headboard, except I want to look at you all spread out for me. You can let go if you feel you're not in a position of power to have such a conversation."

She wasn't strapped down or tied up. Worst case scenario, she'd let go and send him on his way. He liked looking at her this way? Okay, for now, she'd remain where he directed her.

"I'm good here, I think."

Elijah rubbed at his chin. He held the look of a satisfied man. It must be the glint in his eyes and the cocky upturn of his mouth.

She raised her eyebrows. "You like that I want to stay this way."

"I do."

"I can tell."

He smiled. "Honey, if you could feel how hard I am, there'd be no questions. Hard as a rock."

"You've never been so chatty before. Talking about your erection makes you open up?"

He shrugged and walked toward her. "Guess the thought of getting you naked brings out the need to speak. Shall I continue?"

"By all means." Rose never particularly longed to be naked. She didn't love her nude form. Ten pounds too many made her hips too round, her breasts saggy, and her waist rounder than she'd want. Okay, maybe it was fifteen pounds.

Only the way Eli looked at her didn't make her feel flawed in any way.

By contrast, he looked at her as if she was the most desirable thing he'd ever seen.

"You need a safe word. For tonight, however, I'm going to suggest we keep it simple. I want to understand what you enjoy, what you don't, and what you think you might desire, even if you're not sure."

"Sounds easy. I'll tell you to stop if I don't want it."

"Perhaps. Only maybe one of the things you crave is to say no. To feel as if you're being forced. It's a kink."

When her ex flogged her back, hard, there had never been a discussion akin to the talk they were having. He'd suggested she would enjoy it, and when she hadn't protested, he'd gone for it. Hard.

Her crying and begging him to stop hadn't made it cease either.

"I don't think I have a kink."

"Maybe not. I personally happen to think everyone has them, even if they're small. Some people want to be spanked during sex or having their hair pulled. It's all kink, albeit smaller than my own."

The words he used should make her uncomfortable, only they didn't. Eli never lost her eye contact. With his eyes holding hers, she'd answer anything he wanted to ask.

"I never thought of those things as being exactly...kink."

He nodded. "I don't know if most people do."

"What's your...kink?" Since he'd said his was more pronounced than simply pulling her hair. She suddenly saw the flogger in her minds' eye and a sour pit formed in her stomach.

"Ties. The way you're holding onto the bedpost, I'd enjoy roping you up the same way. Or maybe with silk scarves. I'm a Dom, honey. I want to give you what you need. If you have a kink, and it's something I can give you and think you should have, which won't harm you, I want to give it to you."

Her mouth watered. Millions of women read *50 Shades of Grey*. She hadn't. What was the point? She'd hated the flogging. Lying on the bed in front of Eli, she wished she'd read the book or something akin to it. Never had she felt so out of her depth.

Tonight was new...and she liked it.

"For tonight." He kicked off his shoes. "We're going to be really simple. Red. Yellow. Green. I'm going to ask you periodically if you're okay and you're going to give me a color. Green means go. You're happy. Red—"

She nodded. "Not happy. Stop."

"All stop." He placed a hand on her thigh. "Yellow is you're unsure. You can also call out at any time. Red. Yellow. Green. Whatever you want. Tonight, you can speak without permission."

Rose gulped. "There might come a time when I can't?"

"Unless not talking turns out to be a red."

"I don't know. You remember how I enjoy speaking."

He kissed the top of her clothed knee. "And you know how I enjoy listening."

"So then the not talking bit..."

"Not for tonight." He was a towering figure of male hotness standing in front of her bed. "What are your words? What instructions did I give you?"

"Red for no, I hate what you're doing. Green for good, let's go on. And yellow for I'm not sure how I feel."

Those hadn't been his exact words, except they would have to be good enough for their first time. This had to be the strangest conversation she'd ever engaged in. Yet, her heart beat rapidly in anticipation. She couldn't deny her excitement.

"Great." He moved over her, and she guessed the conversation was over. His mouth met hers, and although she longed to lower her arms and stroke the back of his neck, he told her to keep her hands on the headboard. She'd obeyed.

Rose lost herself in the heat of his mouth on hers. She squirmed from the need to do more than stay still, and he raised his head to look at her.

"Color?"

He wanted to be told how she felt about kissing? "Green. Definitely green."

"Good." He rubbed his thumb over her lips. "Because I really enjoy having you like this."

"Totally at your mercy?"

Eli shook his head, the side smile she'd come to think of as both happy and sad crossing his face. "As you'll soon understand if you don't already, I'm entirely at yours."

He kissed her again. She had no idea how much time passed. Elijah seemed to have no interest in hurrying things along, and since her hands were holding the headboard, it left her with her legs free to run against him.

Over time, they seemed to find a rhythm where he would kiss her and grind his still clothed hips against her still wearing too much fabric pussy. Every time he did, a jolt of pure pleasure travelled up and down her spine.

After a bit, he lifted his head again, his eyes heated. Not that she was surprised. She could feel how excited he was, his bulging cock pressed against her with each rub they made.

"Color?"

"Green and frustrated."

Eli actually grinned, no sad smile to be seen on his face.

"Frustrated is good. Green is better. I'm going to have you let go, only for as long as it takes you to remove your shirt. Okay?"

She nodded. Anything to put his hands on her. Besides, the longer they kissed, the more comfortable she'd gotten with not having control over her hands. It was kind of... amazing. The way Eli kissed her with her hands on the headboard, it made her feel worshiped.

Rose got her shirt off, and he took it from her before throwing it aside.

"Eli?"

He raised an eyebrow. "Yes, darling?"

"Green." He hadn't asked, yet she'd wanted to tell him just the same.

~

Now

Rose sat up fast. Her heart raced. When was the last time she'd dreamed of Eli so vividly?

She rubbed at her eyes. It was still black outside and darker in the cabin, except for the slight embers still burning low in the fireplace. Kent breathed deeply—the sleep of children.

Despite almost being killed, he trusted her enough to go deeply into dreamland. Kent expected her to take care of him the way kids did before they knew better.

It was why she decided to teach elementary school and not high school. In ten years, without the world being so unkind to him as to murder his grandmother and shoot at him, he'd learn better than to trust every person around him.

"Enough, Rose," she spoke aloud and rose to her feet.

Dreaming of Elijah, something she managed to stop doing for about a month, had thrown her off more. Then again, she'd holed up in her parents' cabin with Kent. The last time she'd been here was with her vanished lover. In a weird way, Kent reminded her of Elijah.

There weren't many people walking around with the platinum blond hair they both possessed. Kent was too young to be bleaching his hair, and Elijah would have scoffed at the idea.

He'd been very basic when it came to grooming. Soap, toothpaste, aftershave, razors, deodorant, shampoo plus conditioner. No dye anywhere in his bathroom.

They were both lucky when it came to hair color genetics. Very unusual, very beautiful. Although Eli always scoffed when she told him how attractive she found his hair. Silky, too. He'd told her once how much he hated the color. It made him stand out.

She sighed loudly, breaking the silence of the cabin. Once upon a time, she'd run her hands through his hair for hours while he'd slept on the same floor.

Until he'd woken up in a cold sweat, a bad dream darkening his eyes and his mood sour. For a fleeting moment, she tried to reach out to him, but as with any subject touching on his past, he hadn't wanted to talk about it.

Her ex possessed demons and wherever he disappeared to, she hoped he managed them. People should not have to suffer alone.

Or maybe her cabin simply brought out the worst. The walls were cursed. Her parents had loved it, and they were dead. She'd brought Eli here, and then he'd vanished. She'd taken refuge with Kent and...

No. She refused to go down such a dreadful path in her

thoughts. Nothing could happen to him. Rose would simply not allow it.

The sound startled her, and she whirled around. Someone tapped on her door, then tried the doorknob.

Her heart rose into her throat. Oh hell, what was she supposed to do? She had no weapons and no idea how to use them. Why oh, why had she counted on the four walls of her parents' old place to do anything at all?

If the person after them wanted to come in, they'd simply open the door and enter. Of course, they would.

Well they'd have to go through her to Kent.

She rushed forward at the same time as the door opened. With her hands out in front of her, as if she were some kind of banshee, she launched herself at whoever the lunatic after them turned out to be.

"No," she shouted. If it woke Kent, so be it. He needed to run.

"Rose." The man grabbed her hands before she could successfully claw at him. "Rose, stop. I knocked first. Someone here to hurt you wouldn't."

It took her a second to recognize the voice. Funny, because she'd been dreaming about him. Yet it did take a full second for her to realize she launched herself at Elijah.

"You," she breathed out, yet relief didn't fill her at seeing him. What were the chances he'd show back up? Slim to none.

"Me."

She pulled back, and he let go of her hands. "You're involved. I should have known. My crazy boyfriend who vanishes would be shooting at me on the street. Coming after my student. I'll...stop you. I'll kill you, Eli, before I let you hurt him. I swear I will."

In the still way only Eli could pull off, he didn't move at all.

Finally, he spoke. "Few things. If I were going to shoot you, I wouldn't have missed. I realize you don't possess knowledge about this part of me, and for good reasons. You have no reason to trust me. I get it. More than you'll ever imagine. I'll tell you a single thing. I'm here to protect you and The Boy."

With so many horrible things happening, she couldn't make sense of any of it. "Why did you say it the way you did? The Boy? As if you're putting capital letters on it?"

"It's a thing I do."

"You." Kent's voice caught her attention, and she whirled around to see him. He pointed at Elijah. "I used to see you on the street. Sometimes. You look like me. I told Maw Maw. I told her, and she laughed. You're my father."

Her ex nodded. "I am actually."

Oh, hell.

5

Now

Platinum expected anger, rage, and accusations. Dreaded telling his son the truth, who he was, and why he'd been absent from his life. Walking in the door detonated an emotional IED inside.

He met his son's wide eyes. Eyes he recognized, because he saw them in the mirror every day.

"Look, Kent. I understand. No one understands how shitty a bad father can be better than I. And some day, you and I will talk about how we got here. The only thing I can tell you is I would have handled it differently if I could have. My priority is your safety. You and Rose. Okay?" He said the next sentence as much for Rose as for Kent, "The rest we'll figure out as we go."

He clenched his jaw so tightly, his ears hurt. In a kinder world, he'd have been able to see Rose again under far different circumstances, to hold her in his arms, to explain to her his disappearance had nothing to do with her at all.

In a better existence, he wouldn't be a stranger to his son.

Plat dealt in facts. Not fiction. Truth, he'd chosen to join Elite Metal, albeit having been kidnapped to have the option to do so. Truth, his conscious decision to do so cost him the only two people he loved in the world.

The whys would have to wait.

"We have a very sloppy would-be sniper after you. I'm going to have to ask the two of you to be patient while I get control of all the factors involved here. I only came in because I don't want you panicky if you hear gunfire. I have no idea if sloppy shooter out there has a silencer on the gun he or she is using."

He glanced from Kent to Rose. Her eyes were huge. She didn't seem to be looking at him, not really—shock. Still, she spoke to him through trembling lips. "How do you propose to deal with the sniper out there? What are you going to be able to do about it? Shouldn't you call someone, and how do you know about this anyway?"

Plat held up his hand to silence her, and she stopped talking. He'd missed the sound of her voice so much. The pleasure and soothing he took from the lyrical quality of her tones were too much of a distraction. A temptation.

"I learned about the present circumstances because I hired a private detective to keep an eye on Kent. When Kent went missing, I started trying to find out what happened. I don't know how long it's been since Kent went to school. Was he missing before you went on the run?"

The timeline bothered him. Rose hadn't been missing very long. Why had Tony lost Kent if they'd only been in the cabin for what seemed a very short time? The sniper only missed shooting them the day before.

"He missed a little school. His grandmother wasn't

feeling well. Why? It's not relevant." She put her hands on her hips. Rose wouldn't have yelled before he'd left. If he'd stayed quiet, she would have done as he asked.

Of course, he'd lost the right to her submissive behavior. His heart panged with the disappointment. Saving her life came first. Seeing if there was any possibility of fixing things could come afterwards.

And Tony clearly did not earn his retainer. He lost the boy because Kent's grandmother got sick. Utter incompetence.

"Eli?" Rose's voice held enormous frustration. He'd gone off into his own head again. Too long passed since he'd last worked on his communication skills. His team had a verbal shorthand. They didn't need a hell of a lot of words.

"That's not actually my name. It's fine if you want to call me Elijah. Only it was never real." She deserved to know.

Her eyes went suspiciously moist. No way could he deal with her crying. On his best day, women's tears befuddled him. Right then didn't count as his best anything.

"To answer your question, darling, I'm going to do what I do. I'm a sniper. I used to do it for Uncle Sam. These days, things are a little less clear. I am going to shoot whoever it is who is out there in the head."

Her mouth fell open. He supposed he really bumbled the exchange. Either he'd blown it, or there was no really good way to manage it at all. *How did you tell the woman you loved yet abandoned you were really a sniper, and not the med student you tried to be the whole time she knew you?* The simplest answer was the one he'd relied on before someone tried to kill his son. *You don't.*

"Keep your head down. Stay flat on the floor, you and Kent. Whatever crap we have to deal with, we'll sort it out. Everyone stays alive."

"Wait."

He paused. Being so close to Rose again and actually speaking to Kent played havoc on his nerves.

"Yeah?" She hadn't aged a day. The wariness in her eyes was new. While he was sure the lousy sniper who tried to shoot her played a large role in her hooded gaze, he'd bet money his presence was the reason for her guarded eyes.

"What should I call you? Since Elijah is not your name."

"These days it's Platinum."

"As in the metal or your hair?" She coughed, and he watched a shiver wreck through her body. They'd have been okay in here when the fire blazed, except the chill had won. The longer Rose and Kent stayed, the worse it would be for them.

"Both. One led to the other."

He wanted to leave, tried to again, this time nearly stopping when Kent called out. "Please be careful. No one is bullet proof."

Plat nodded at his son. He knew better than most. Likely, the person would miss. Then he'd be able to track their direction easily. The bullet didn't come, and he wasn't surprised. Oh well, he'd have to track the old fashioned way.

Of course, he might also take one in the head.

The nip of the night struck his cheeks. He processed the temperature as he did the direction of the breeze and the air speed velocity. Digging into himself, he sought the stillness vital to his job. The Silence. When he'd first been coming up in the Marines, his commanding officer described what it took to excel at his job.

Plat's ability to hit a target accurately notwithstanding, his skills with a rifle hadn't been why he kept getting promoted, and they'd not constituted the reason why Marine special forces wanted him along.

He blended, disappeared into his surroundings in a way which simply couldn't be taught. If he really wanted to psychoanalyze the damn thing—and fuck, he did not—he could take it back to the days he'd needed to vanish because his abandoned and divorced mother entertained her male friends in the apartment he'd been too young to flee.

Better to simply disappear. If they didn't notice him, he could pretend the whole thing wasn't happening.

He needed to perform his inner checklist. More than his life was at stake. He wouldn't lose the two souls he'd left behind in the cabin. *Ever.*

He was good at his job. Plat sharpened his focus. He'd find the fool, and with a single pop, the whole mess would be over.

~

Two years earlier

He never thought about the night everything went sideways and got completely fucked. Elijah couldn't let thoughts of Operation Phoenix cross his mind.

So of course, the memories visited him when he slept.

Vulnerability didn't work for him. Not even a little bit. Which was how he found himself lying in the dark next to a sleeping Rose with his arm flung over his eyes, as if he could block out his dark thoughts as easily as he could the light from the street.

Operation fucking Phoenix.

Rose murmured in her sleep, and he let his arm fall down so he could stare at her in the darkness. Her eyes were closed, and he could see small movements beneath her closed lids that indicated she'd reached a dream state.

He should leave her alone. They'd engaged in quite a workout, and she needed rest. His cock twitched at the memory of how they both came hours earlier.

Naked and trembling, only not with fear...

His Rose liked to hold on to the headboard. She'd come beautifully around his cock. His balls throbbed as blood pooled back into his dick, leaving him immediately erect again.

Would she want to be tied?

He'd not expected to reach such a place with her, not yet. The chance to find out made him put the silk ties into his bag, along with the condoms.

Elijah was always in control. Except he wasn't. He needed Rose, and though vulnerability should have scared the shit out of him, it didn't.

He wasn't a sniper anymore. Circumstances left him living a civilian life. Medical students got to fall in love. They didn't have to worry the fucking world was going to end the next day if the Iranians got plutonium from Russia.

Eli eased closer to Rose. With a swift move, he tugged her tighter against him until her mouth was close to his. Her eyes fluttered open, and he kissed her before she could speak.

This was how he wanted to wake her, with kisses for the rest of her life.

She moaned against him, her body squirming with impatience. He loved her small movements, and he loved how he was going to help her to control them. She'd come harder when he did.

He reached over the bed and pulled his bag closer.

"What are you doing?" she whispered, even though they were alone, and no one could overhear. Yet, he liked how it made the moment feel private, belonging only to them.

"Trust me." He pulled the silk ties out of the innermost pocket of his backpack. Holding them up, he let her study them for a moment. She'd learned the color codes earlier. They'd stick with them. "Color?"

"I liked everything we did earlier." She patted at his face. "Don't smirk."

He hadn't realized he'd done so. "What can I say? A man likes to hear his woman was satisfied."

She pointed at the ties. "Will they hurt?"

"They're silk." He placed one in her fingers so she could feel how smooth they were. "Shouldn't hurt much. And if they do, you can call red."

"They feel okay, I think I could enjoy the silk."

He did too and planned to dress her entirely in silk to be spread out beneath him as she was...draped and secured for his pleasure and hers.

She raised an eyebrow. "What are you thinking about?"

"Reading me?" An unusual development or merely another sign he'd adjusted to civilian life? Or maybe because he'd fallen over a cliff for Rose.

"Only when you're so obviously contemplating something other than the ties you put in my hand." She wiggled them in his face.

"I think I might have another kink. Don't worry. We'll figure it out later." He grinned because he couldn't help it. She made him happy. He nodded toward the red silk. "Color?"

"Green."

Awesome. He pushed her hands up against the headboard. He took the ties from her, and carefully—not wanting to hurt her, only restrain her—he knotted them and secured her to the headboard.

She gasped, and he needed to learn if it was a good

sound or not. "Color?" He'd repeat the question as many times as necessary until he learned her well enough, he could have a PhD in the subject of Rose.

"Green." She tugged at her restraints, and they didn't budge. "I guess you mean business."

"Always."

There had never been a time in his life where he hadn't been entirely serious about what he was doing. His focus amounted to making Rose come. Hard.

He scooted down until he positioned his mouth on her pussy, and he licked his lips. Getting women off while they were tied up made him hard as hell. With Rose, it was even more so. He didn't want the satisfaction of knowing he made her come, any fool holding a dildo could do so. No, Rose needed to understand her immense pleasure had been provided by him and always would be.

She moaned as he licked her clit. This was the closest he would ever be to any kind of heaven. Elijah closed his eyes and lost himself in the moment. Making Rose squirm, making her moan, got him harder and harder. His pleasure didn't matter. Not yet, anyway.

When she was panting, he pulled back and pressed two fingers deeper inside of her than his tongue could manage. She was so wet, and his balls hardened tighter. Any more hardening and they might actually fall off.

"Eli."

He loved her breathy moan. If he could, he'd keep her doing it every hour of every day.

"Here's how tonight is going to work, sweet Rose, you aren't going to come until I tell you to."

She nodded. *Good*. His little submissive who didn't realize what she was yet. Still, she gave herself to him beautifully, as if she'd been born to do so.

Eli loved the way she tasted. He'd never been with a woman who reminded him so much of honey. He breathed it in before he bit gently on her clit.

Her legs wobbled, only she didn't come, and her obeying him made him smile. "You listen so well, beautiful."

She groaned. "And you're tormenting me."

"In the best possible way." He looked up at her wrists. She gripped the ropes tightly. "Color?"

"Green, but getting frustrated." She cocked an eyebrow at him, and he laughed.

"Fair enough." He pressed on her small bundle of nerves again, and she gasped. "You can come around my cock. When you're ready, and I'm inside you."

He moved until he was close enough to press into her. First, he grabbed the condom wrapper he'd left earlier on her bedside table. He'd always take care of her in whatever way he could, and it didn't frighten him he wanted to.

Eli sheathed himself and then pressed deep into her trembling body. She sighed his name, and he bit down on her shoulder. He might never stop having the need to taste her, to lick her, to have the essence that was Rose on his tongue, in his body.

They might never enjoy a full night sleep again.

Slowly, he moved. With her hands where he wanted them, he let his own roam her body. Her breast filled his palm, and with every thrust of his hips and jolt of her muscles against his cock, he squeezed them.

"Eli." She gritted her teeth.

"Why are you holding back?" He couldn't help his smile. Rose felt so right, so completely perfect the way she welcomed her into his body. And it seemed she actually liked what he did.

How had he gotten so lucky? "I told you to come when I was in you. Anytime you want to, you can."

"It feels so good." She strained her neck. Rose was close. Another few seconds, and she would explode around him. Then it would be seconds. Jesus, he was so close himself. "I don't want it to end."

"We can be together again and again. A million different ways. Until neither of us can move. Sweetheart, I need you to come because it's the most beautiful fucking thing I've ever seen in my whole ridiculous life."

He'd never been more honest. If her hands were free, she'd be able to feel how fast his heart beat, and it wasn't only because she gave him more physical pleasure than he'd ever known before. No, it was because when he was with Rose, all he wanted to do was speak the truth.

His gorgeous woman, who the universe shoved in his direction, although he'd never in a million years have expected her.

"Ah, Eli. Yes. I'm coming..." Her words stuttered, and her muscles spasmed around him. Wetness drenched his cock as she shattered around him.

His ears rang and he held off, breathing through the push to come inside of her hard. He wouldn't, not until she'd reached all her pleasure. Rose's needs came first, because indulging her carnally was the only thing he could give to her. The rest of his life, he'd always have to hold back. Together in the bedroom, he'd make sure she possessed all of him.

Maybe it would be enough.

His body shattered, and he thought maybe his soul did too.

~

Now

The other sniper fled. *Fucking coward.*

Stalking a woman and a child, killing a grandmother—those things were easy. Facing him *mano a mano* would have taken some goddamned courage, and clearly, his target was a pansy ass.

He shook his head. Now would have been a useful time to have a spotter. When things had gone to hell in a hand basket during Operation Phoenix, his spotter ranked among the casualties.

Never again.

Plat wouldn't lose someone else who was his responsibility...

He stopped moving. The hair on the back of his neck didn't stand to attention the way they did when someone stared at him. The cold air move over his skin. What caught his attention?

It wasn't something in the present...no, a memory played with his mind, and for once, it contained nothing to do with Rose.

The memory of his dead spotter made his pause. He very rarely gave Jack much of a thought. Not because he hadn't liked the man, he had. They'd been on the verge of being friends, and he didn't have many of those. Dealing with anything to do with the fuck up of Phoenix gave him a horrible headache.

He'd never done emotions well.

Spotters...he'd not used one since he'd agreed to become Platinum again, to leave Elijah behind, to put Rose into a past he'd never visit again.

Plat squatted down. He ran his hands through the cold ground.

Rodgers. It had been his only solo assignment since Warbucks brought them all in. A single sniper against the other. He'd taken the son-of-a-bitch and loved every second of bringing the evil motherfucker down.

Only...why had Rodgers been alone?

He grabbed his phone and scanned through the note-book where he'd jotted notes about the assignment before he'd done it. Months had passed, and it took him a minute to find the old notes. Fortunately, he never deleted anything, or he'd be royally screwed.

There in black text with a question mark next to it was a random piece of information he'd forgotten, because it hadn't applied the day of the hunt. Rodgers always used a spotter—his wife.

Dora Rodgers. She hadn't been there. Bernardo Rodgers died alone. Hadn't he?

His spidey-sense tingled again. If his guess was true... and the more he sat with the idea, the more it made sense.

He'd killed her husband. She knew how to use a sniper rifle—albeit badly—and how to conduct dirty business.

Plat killed her family. She wanted his. Rubbing his chin, he stared at the cabin where he'd left the two people in the universe outside of his team he loved, even if they both hated him.

Dora wasn't getting to them. They'd come back to Texas with him. And then he'd finish the job properly. Both the sniper and his spotter would be gone, where they couldn't hurt anyone anymore.

6

Now

Rose watched *Plat* pace the room. His movements were quite different than the Elijah she'd known for a year. Her boyfriend had been still most of the time, controlled. This guy, wearing her love's face, appeared really disgruntled.

She wasn't sure exactly where she was. In the hours following Platinum's invasion of the cabin, the strangest things happened. A private plane arrived, they'd been shuffled onto it, and despite the fact he'd remained eerily quiet, it'd been clear to her that Kent's discovered father seemed concerned for her safety. She and Kent must have been on the same page. They asked no questions and had been given zero in the way of answers.

After they landed, they'd been hauled off into a bullet proof—she'd actually asked, and the driver who had yet to be introduced grunted a yes—and eventually entered a compound she'd never dreamed she'd see in her life.

Someone was spending a lot of money on the facility, and she couldn't imagine Uncle Sam was footing the bill.

Since she'd calmed down, the lack of information needed to change. As soon as he got off whatever call seemed to be taking up so much of his time.

"So you can take care of it?" He tapped his foot on the floor while he spoke on the phone. "I won't have her arrested for kidnapping when she was hands down saving my kid from shit I—*we*—caused" Pause. "Uh-huh."

She looked down at Kent. He slept, only not easily, every once in a while throwing himself over as if he couldn't make himself comfortable. He was Eli, no Platinum's—she needed to think of his name right—son. How could she have not noticed?

They shared the same rare, white blond hair. Beyond the obvious hair connection, Kent shared his eyes and the same long face. In retrospect, there could be no doubt they were father and son.

She stared at both of their faces almost every day for an entire year, and she hadn't known. How stupid was she? Was this how Lois Lane felt when she found out about Superman? *Glasses on, glasses off...*

The blond hunk, whatever he wanted to call himself, disconnected his call and regarded her silently. And there it was, the silent stillness she'd grown to find so comforting.

"Did you date me, make me fall in love with you, use me, to gather information about Kent?" There were a million questions she should be asking. Danger, death, and violence were all around them. The truth. How much of a fool had she been? How pathetic?

"Did I ask you about Kent once when we were together?" He didn't move, didn't even seem to breathe.

"No." She choked on her answer. He hadn't. In all of the

days and nights they spent together, he never brought Kent or any of her other children up. Sometimes she spoke about them when she told him about her day. Never by name...

He pursed his lips before he spoke, as if he tasted something bad. "The first time you sat down next to me and I realized you were his teacher, I decided I would make you someone I could speak to, call up if I needed to. I wasn't outside of his school for the fun of it. Like a moth, I couldn't stay away from the flame that was Kent."

"Why go through such a ruse then? Why not present yourself to his grandmother and be part of his life?" She stood up. Yes, her new line of questioning was much more on track. Rose could focus on something other than her broken heart, and the strange disparity between her desire to throttle or kiss him.

"If only it were simple." He shook his head. "I let them know I was going to explain our situation to you. They ran a quick background check on you, and you're not a risk. I wish you being safe made understanding what happened somehow easier."

"You're not making sense." Yet her heart beat rapidly as if he confessed truths, which floored her. Or maybe it was anticipation riddling her with anxiety. She'd wanted answers for so long.

"Long before you met me, I was a mixed up kid. My father was rich. Other than checks cashed every month, I never saw him. Occasionally, he got drunk and remembered he'd fathered a kid. He certainly never remembered my mother." He shrugged. "Whine. Whine. Whine. Bad childhood."

"Tell your story. I could do without the sarcastic avoidance."

Although, she did like hearing his voice again. Would it

always make her feel connected to the world more? Or was her need to hear him leftover because he'd been more than her boyfriend, more than her love? He'd shown her parts of herself she'd never known she possessed. The kind of woman who could come only when he told her to, who loved the ties he used on her wrists, the ropes he would eventually press against her body.

"Fair enough." He nodded. "I joined the Marines, and it turned out I possessed a real gift with a sniper rifle. I had the temperament too. I rose quickly through the ranks."

"And the whole time you pretended to be a medical student named Elijah was why?"

"I'll get to what happened during my strange year in New York. It wasn't pretend. To say so is to use the wrong word. And when I was Eli, I was a medical student. None of the things I told you were lies. I simply didn't happen to mention how once upon a time I had been called either Tom O'Connell or Platinum in the Corps."

"You're going to have to explain all of it." Her stomach turned over.

Plat put his hands in front of himself as if he shielded an assault. "I will. I swear it. Telling you would be easier if you let me talk."

"And that's all I want to do in life, make things easier on you."

"I deserve your scorn. Does it help to lash out at me?" He raised an eyebrow and rubbed his chin the way he did sometimes when he listened intently. She resisted the urge to stroke the slight dusting of blond whiskers there.

"No, actually. Go on." She did need to hear the whole thing. Interrupting him didn't finish this faster.

"Eventually, I ended up on an elite recon team. We were the best of the best. A mission came in. Not to become too technical about things, we were sent to stop a shipment of plutonium from Russia to Iran. The whole thing went belly up. We lost some really good men. An entire team, in fact." His voice hitched, and her heart bled, although she knew it shouldn't. Why couldn't she stop herself from caring? *Stupid, stupid Rose.*

"Elijah, Platinum. I don't know what to call you."

"Call me anything you want, Rose. Please give me your voice back. Not the same way you did on the plane or the car. I'll take anything, okay? Whatever you want. Yell, scream, and curse. No more silence. Your voice...it matters to me."

His words so closely echoed her thoughts, it was everything she could do not to start sobbing. If he cared as she did, what could have taken him away?

"Please finish, Platinum."

"Um. Okay. Right. Things went to hell on the Phoenix mission. Afterwards, things moved fast. Cover ups. Hidden agendas. Those of us who were left were given new identities, our old ones being declared dead or we never existed. Tom disappeared, as well as his nickname Platinum. Elijah was handed a new life and the ability to do what I always wanted to do only never admitted."

"To be a doctor." The very idea blew her mind. How could people simply disappear? Maybe her disbelief made her naïve. She thought what he spoke of was the stuff of movies.

"Yes. I started to daydream about it about two years before I could do it. When I retired from the Marines, I'd apply and go. My time table got moved up. Anyway, it wasn't until then I knew Kent existed. His mother had been a..." He stared at the boy, his voice drifting off.

She rubbed the boy's hair. "I think he's out."

"I'd known his mother for a single night. She wrote me, and I never got the letters. Someone must have wanted me not to leave my job. I still don't know exactly who sent them to me, except I got them my first week here. I couldn't introduce myself to him. His father was gone. I did what I could to help him. Thought I covered myself pretty well."

"His grandmother started trying to find things out. Maybe she opened some doors she shouldn't have."

He nodded. "In a million years, I wouldn't have predicted discovery. Maybe I should have. I thought they were sure I was a dead-beat dad."

"Kent thought you were out there in the way only kids can think, and his grandmother got confused by the money."

"Right." He nodded, his eyes distant. "Then after our night at your parents' cabin, I was kidnapped."

She gasped. "Kidnapped?" His story got more and more unbelievable.

"They call them the Ghosts. I have no idea who they are. They pulled me off the street, hood over my head, the whole nine yards. I was fairly sure the reaper had come for me. My only two regrets were you and Kent." He cleared his throat. "When I was next allowed to see, I was here. With all my former teammates. And we were given a choice. The chance to take down the people who killed the others in Russia. The opportunity to undo what happened as best we could. All I needed to do was be Platinum again."

"And what happened to Elijah?" Her voice wavered.

"He had to be gone."

"Just like that?"

He cracked his neck, and the muscles in his jaw clenched. "Just like that."

There weren't words for her pain. She'd thought when

he'd first vanished, she knew what it was to hurt. Only nothing compared.

"I guess..." How should she say what she needed to say? How did she make her lips form syllables? "Did you think about saying no? Was doing so an option? Did they force you?" *Please let him say yes, they'd force him. Please let him...*

"It was a choice. I decided to stay. We all were given the option."

Everything inside of her went numb. "How could you do it? I mean, I thought we really had something. I loved you. And I believed you felt the same for me."

"Rose." His voice cracked. "What you've been through over the last few days, it's a touch of how fucked things are out there. I've seen things you should never have to imagine. You live in the world." He nodded toward Kent. "So does he. My job in life, it's not to be a doctor. I knew it every day when I studied. Today as you see me, it's who I am. Platinum. I put myself in the way. I say no, you can't blow up that city today, no the sun will come up tomorrow. It's not pretty. It's not nice. It's what it is. There was a man still out there who blew three teams halfway to hell, and only a handful of us crawled away. That bastard got away with nuclear material. I'm one of the men and women who says no more."

Her tongue felt thick in her mouth. She could barely get the words out. "And so it was bye, Rose. No word. No earthly idea of what happened to you."

He visibly swallowed. "I'm not going to make excuses. How it went was how it had to go."

"I see."

For the first time she really did.

Kent stirred, his eyes fluttering open. Aware of their connection, she compared their mirroring attributes. No doubt about it, the resemblance was there. She'd always loved Kent. She cared for all of her kids, but the lonely lost child with the attention issues touched her heart. Like father, like son.

"Dad?"

Platinum kneeled down. "Hey buddy. Did you rest?"

"I knew you were real. I saw you from the playground. You looked like me."

The then five-year-old proved more intuitive than she did.

"Kent." She turned to him. "Would you do me a favor? It's very important."

Her serious student nodded quickly. "Sure."

"Put your hands over your ears and sing very loudly. Don't stop till I point at you." She waited a beat to make sure he heard her. "Do it now."

The child started to sing the national anthem. Fine. That would work.

"Platinum," she spit out his name. He needed to hear her.

"Rose?"

"If you hurt this child, I don't care how tough and lethal you are, I'll kill you. With my bare hands." She kept his eye contact. He should see how serious she was. Eli had always been able to read her. Let Platinum do it now.

"Things have always changed. I mean...I'm not good at the sharing part. Rose, I need to tell you how the last year has been..."

She held up her hand. "No. Nothing has changed. Other than Kent. The rest of it, consider it—us over."

She waited for the pain to erupt. Nothing. No emotions assaulted her.

The numbness was a good thing...right?

1 year earlier

His apartment had been emptied out. She stood in the doorway and stared at the hollowness within the four walls. The sounds of Manhattan muted. She could hear none of it.

When the landlord told her Eli had left, she didn't believe him. Moving trucks? How was it possible?

Rose leaned against the doorway and tried to catch her breath. Why did it feel as if she'd run a marathon, when all she'd done was take an elevator to the fourth floor of Eli's building?

She grabbed her phone with shaking hands and somehow managed to click on his name in her contact list to dial him. It went straight to voicemail, and instead of hearing his sweet voice, a computer message told her she dialed the wrong number?

What? She tried again and could barely breathe when the same message happened. Where could he have gone? He wouldn't have moved without telling her? Had he changed apartments? Surprising her by moving in with her?

She bit her shaking fingernail.

The school—they would know where he'd gone. She rushed out and headed toward Eli's medical school. Somehow, she must have hailed a taxi, although she held no memory of doing so. The next time she cued in, she was standing outside of the admission building, crying with her head in her hands.

"Okay, Rose, pull it together."

She wiped at her face with her hands, making her palms wet. Another ten minutes, and she would be late for work. Whatever this mess turned out to be, she couldn't get fired over it. Elijah would be furious with her. He probably had a very good reason for where he was and why his apartment was empty and the school had no records of him. Yet the wicked coil of doubt wouldn't leave her alone. Who was Elijah?

Don't you trust me, sweetheart?

Yes, she did. She'd given herself to him totally the weekend before. Total abandon bounded within his ropes. Whatever he wanted, it had given her bliss to obey.

The woman at the front desk hadn't wanted to help her. Privacy laws meant they couldn't tell her if Elijah existed in their records.

"Ma'am." Rose actually took the woman's hand in hers and squeezed. She knew it was weird, her behavior broke a ton of social codes. "I love this man. I think he loves me. We connected. And now he seems to be missing. His apartment is empty. His cell phone is disconnected. I am not crazy. I need to find out. I promise not to stalk him or show up here every day, only please, please help me."

The woman's eyes were huge. She opened and closed her mouth twice before she spoke. "My husband left."

"Oh yes?" Rose tried to smile. "So then you understand. I mean, I don't have a clue what's happened here."

"I'll help you." She dropped Rose's hand. "They could fire me…"

"I'll never tell a soul." She felt as if she swore an oath on a sacred document. For as long as she lived, she'd never get —she looked at the woman's nametag, which read Lori —fired.

The woman typed furiously on the computer's keyboard as if she meant to punish it with her strong keystrokes. A piece of her dyed blonde hair fell over her face, and Lori blew it away with a gust of breath.

"What did you tell me his name was?"

"Elijah Jones." She bit down on another nail. So much for her not chewing all of her nails off anymore.

Lori's eyebrows furrowed. "Spelled the normal way?"

"Yes." She nodded. "Why, what's wrong?"

"Are you sure he went to school here?" Lori's kind blue eyes met her own. A lone tear slipped from Rose's eye before she could stop it.

"Yes." Or maybe she wasn't sure. He'd told her he'd gone here, she'd met him outside of class. Did she know for sure he went to school? No, of course not.

She wanted to sink to the floor, only she couldn't do so. This was neither the time nor the place to break down. Not to mention, she hadn't called in sick. She actually needed to go to work if she didn't want to be fired.

"Thanks so much for helping, Lori. I'll never tell."

Rose shoved her hands in her pockets and made her way outside. One day earlier, she'd been in absolute bliss convinced they would be together forever. How could today have happen? Could things really go to hell so quickly?

～

Now

Rose looked around at the room Platinum labeled hers. Neither of them managed to speak directly to each other since she'd pronounced nothing changed. They'd both spoken to Kent, who looked as if someone had taken all the color from his cheeks.

He must be so confused. She wanted to help him. Did they have psychologists somewhere around? Ones who could help children?

A knock on the door startled her, and she walked over. "Who is it?"

"Me," Platinum's voice called through the door. "I can show you some identification through the key hole if you want."

She snickered. "Like I'd believe any of it anyway." Rose unlocked the door and let the man who destroyed her and continued to confound her step through.

"It was a joke." He shrugged.

"I got it. So was my response. Sort of."

Wow, things were off between them. The ease they'd once had long gone, drowned by lies and the conspiracies she might never understand.

"Right."

He nodded, not taking his eyes off her. What did he see when he looked? Had she gained or lost weight? Changed her hair? Was he glad he'd managed to escape a destiny with her before things went too far askew?

Was there such a thing as too far? If they'd come for him two years later when they'd potentially been married, would he still have disappeared?

"Did you need something?" Because if he didn't, if he'd come simply to stare at her and make her hate her betray-ing-her body for still wanting him despite how shitty he behaved, then he could go to hell. And fast.

"I wanted to tell you what I did on the phone earlier. Warbucks, the man who set this thing up, he's obviously really connected. You're golden. The authorities aren't going to charge you with kidnapping or anything. They're setting up custody so he's with me. However it will end up working."

Her mouth went dry. "Thank you. I really was worried

about it. He doesn't belong to me. I shouldn't have taken him and run."

"Yes. You should have." The seriousness of his tone made her stare at his solid gaze. "I'll always be in awe of your bravery."

"Don't say things like that, Platinum."

He raised an eyebrow. "Why not?"

"They make me hate you less."

"Oh, Rose." He groaned. "You hate me, and all I can think about is getting you tied up and under me until I can figure out how I can make you forgive me for being a total ass."

Well then...what was she supposed to do with that?

7

Now

Platinum stood watching his opponent bumbling with her equipment, and if he weren't determined to blow her miserable head off, he'd actually feel sorry for the fool. Her husband had been the brains of the operation.

He shook his head. Dora took the bait left for her and arrived where Platinum wanted her. A few scattered addresses partially burned in the fireplace, and she thought Plat moved them all to another more remote cabin in Texas.

Foolish woman. Her husband would not have made the same mistake. He'd been a worthy adversary. One of Red Wolf's top men, Platinum hadn't been certain which of them would survive the night. He'd been glad to dispense the world from the evil of Bernardo Rodgers.

Even if delivering the final shot hadn't actually calmed the demon inside of him which threatened always to erupt from his very soul. No, there had only been a single person, one time, when quiet finally happened, and he'd chosen to leave her in New York City. She waited an hour away. Hating him.

His last foolish remark had been among the stupidest of his life. He'd told her he'd been imagining her tied up? *Brilliant, Plat.*

The woman he'd come to think of before he'd left New York as *his little love* shoved him from her room without the slightest response. He hadn't known she could push like that.

He sighed, and the beeper in his ear sounded. It was Copper. She was going to want to be informed what he intended to do, since he'd gotten the woman to their location.

Plat leaned against the tree. The fact Dora held no idea she was being watched...

No, she'd killed The Boy's grandmother and terrified both Kent and Rose. She needed to be eliminated. A quick bullet through the head wasn't enough. She had to know what was about to happen to her. Kindness be damned.

~

Three months earlier...

Bernardo Rodgers. At last in Plat's scope. Silence moved through the night. Other people didn't understand what he meant when he spoke of silence, as if it could be personified. All that meant to him was Silence hadn't spoken to them yet.

She'd been speaking to him his whole life. And now she moved. The hazy feeling he got when he knew the shot was at hand—the time when his senses moved in perfect coordination with his mind. The moment when the world fell to Silence.

His team might not understand it. He'd bet money Bernardo did.

The other man was six feet tall. Platinum towered over him. Not that they'd be close to each other on the field today to really judge.

A drop of rain hit Plat's head. This area, remote as it was in the middle of Nevada—ballsy for the other man to have picked a location in the middle of the United States—had been set out for training some of Red Wolf's operatives. Here, with little around to distract him, Bernardo could practice without chance of getting caught.

Only the other sniper had been, and he didn't know it yet.

Considering the role Rodgers played in the nightmare which been Operation Phoenix, and more specifically the picking off Bernardo did of part of Chrome's team—one by one—while Plat had been stuck behind enemy fire with a dying spotter and black smoke obscuring his vision—it was about time Rodgers got what was coming to him.

Beyond time...

The wind tickled his ear, and his vision sharpened. He needed to act. If Bernardo saw him, he'd be dead, and since the other man managed to singlehandedly take out a caravan of school children trying to go to a refugee camp in Uganda the year before, Plat didn't think he'd hesitate to blow his head off.

Revenge could taste so sweet.

Silence moved...and he fired.

Rodgers fell to the ground, pieces of his brain scattering on the desert sand beneath him.

Plat stood up, packing up his weapon in the way he'd

been trained. Every movement controlled, every action from muscle memory. Plat expected to have to kill two people that afternoon. Usually, Rodgers brought his spotter with him, though he apparently travelled alone to practice. If the intel was correct, the other man used his wife as a spotter.

They must have some kind of interesting relationship.

He shrugged. She was a widow. He'd follow up with Steele and see if he wanted him to track the spotter down or leave it. Without Rodgers to assist, she wouldn't be much of a danger to anyone anymore.

Silence retreated, and he could hear the birds chirping in the distance. A plane sped by somewhere in the clouds. The sounds of life, the sounds of normal.

He'd known a touch of that life. Nine months earlier with his Rose. For once, he let the thought travel through his mind. It had become a second full time job to not let himself remember her.

Usually, he would leave. The bullet he used to take out Bernardo would be untraceable by any authority looking into it. He'd taken great pains to not be seen by anyone when he'd come to the location. Certainly, Bernardo hadn't seen him.

He walked the mile to where Bernardo lay dead. Squatting down, he looked at the man who caused so much pain in the lives of his crew.

Dead bodies always looked the same. With the soul gone, the shells resembled something out of a movie set. Not real anymore, at least to Platinum. It didn't seem to matter where he found them. The battlefield, the dead homeless man on the subway in New York, his father at the funeral home.

The second they died, everything about the physicality of their bodies changed.

He'd wanted to help people for a change. Not continue to put them into the ground.

Except some folks needed to die for everyone else to live.

He shook his head, staring down at Bernardo's unseeing eyes. "You didn't even see it coming. You should have. Fuck, you should have."

Or maybe that was the way it was for people like them—even if he didn't want to put himself in the same category as the dead man—there were too many things in common to deny the comparison entirely. Perhaps they all took a bullet in the back of the head some day when they least expected it.

Would Rose be sad if she heard of his death?

He shook his head. "God damn it, Platinum, stop thinking about her. She's moved on. She has someone else. And it's better for her you left. She hates you the way you deserve to be despised."

By all that was holy, he needed to get out of there. His bones ached, and he felt a million years old. Maybe he needed a physical. Something could have gone terribly wrong with his endocrine system.

He kicked a rock as he stormed toward the exit path he mapped out to return to his car. Shit. Double shit. There was nothing physically wrong with him. He had a full work up every six months. No, this was some fucked up psychological breakdown because he missed his girlfriend.

Ached for her soft skin, the sound of her voice while she talked so he didn't have to, and the way her eyes met his in the bedroom when for a single second, they were completely as one.

He made his choice, and he lived with it. If he hadn't taken Warbucks up on his offer, something was going to have to change anyway. He loved medical school, except the constant nightmares and the inability to sleep when he wasn't with Rose made studying extremely difficult. There were only so many runs through Central Park and cups of coffee he could use to stay awake.

Maybe it should have surprised him—although it didn't —that as soon as he'd joined back up with the others to take down Red Wolf, he'd slept like a baby. Twelve hours straight sometimes.

Yet, he felt nothing except tired. Could loneliness actually be pressing down on his bones?

He should never have given in to the urge to go down and look at the body. It was maudlin and put him more out of sorts than he needed to be. What he required was a big drink and maybe a quick fuck.

If only he could jerk off. His own hand wasn't getting the job done, and not a single woman he'd laid eyes on had done anything for him since he'd left Rose. He wouldn't be surprised, always Rose, was the only lady who could do it for him.

Her image wasn't enough. The feel of her. The ropes on her wrists. The way she came around him. He needed those things.

He wanted his Rose back, and the chance to spend time with his son.

Kent—the constant ache, even when Rose was with him. Jesus, everything was so completely fu—

Silence hit the back of his neck, and he stopped moving. The random whining of his thoughts quit immediately. He whirled around. What caught his attention and made the Silence come back?

He waited, and the sensation passed. No one was there. He would have known, and certainly if someone saw him by the dead body, there would be yelling and screaming. Fury. Terror.

Only nothing happened, and after a minute, the sensation completely fled. Yeah, it was time for him to leave. Before everything went really down the toilet.

~

Now

He waited a beat, watching the woman arrange her equipment. Did she really think she was going to shoot him from her current position? Platinum was so close behind her, he could have reached out and touched her.

Instead, he pulled out his handgun. It was his personal revolver. He wouldn't use anything attached to the team. Of course if the weapon was traced, it would only lead to a dead man named Tim O'Connell.

Still, he'd inadvertently exposed all of his crew to danger by simply getting found in the first place. He wouldn't risk them—or Rose or Kent—again.

"I could shoot you in the head."

Dora jumped and spun around. Seeing her up close, he did a quick scan of what he'd seen earlier from a distance. She looked roughly the same age as her late husband. Mid-forties. Short and fit, her hair stopped below her ears in a cut which looked as if it came from another decade.

Her eyes were red rimmed, her mouth open in shock.

He took the chance to rip the rifle from her hands. She gasped as she took a step back, nearly toppling over.

"Tsk. Tsk." He hadn't moved from his spot. "You don't get to die breaking your neck. Not at least until I've had a chance to speak with you."

She steeled her spine, and he waited while she said exactly what he expected. "You killed my husband."

"And he killed hundreds of people... Probably more. Come to think of it, you were as culpable as he, weren't you? Both of you took paychecks from Red Wolf?"

She didn't move, except when she spoke, he wished he had already shot her in the head. "Red Wolf was a great man. My husband is a patriot and—"

He raised his hand, and she shut up. He really didn't know if he had it in him to hit a woman. Killing her constituted a different matter. Striking her? He didn't have the stomach for it. However, Dora didn't need to learn about his personal limitations. Let her be scared.

"Stop."

She closed her mouth, and he let her stand there silent for a moment or two.

"Did you see me the day of his death? Afterwards? When I was leaving?" When he'd felt the momentary prick of awareness. "Was that how you found me?"

"How I first discovered it was you who murdered him, yes." Her voice sounded hoarse. "Finding you after proved more difficult. Until your picture came up on a web search. An old woman looking for a man who should have been dead. You were in your Marine uniform and—"

"Got it," he interrupted.

When he got things settled, he'd get it all down. And anything the poor woman's search stirred up. She'd certainly paid for her questions with her life. He'd have to live with that. Another constant pang on his conscience.

"You shot my son's grandmother. Terrified him. You've left him in a state where he will have to recover from. I don't know if he can. Is it possible for an eight, almost nine-year-old boy to come back?" He shook his head. This woman didn't deserve so many words from him. They were Rose's to have. "You took a shot at my love's head."

"She got in the way—"

"Are you under the impression I care what you have to say? I don't." He stepped toward her. "I could have killed you the second you appeared. I have people watching you. So many eyes in your direction, and you had no idea. What kind of spotter were you? Did Bernardo do all the work, and you came around only to watch?"

"I—"

"Don't talk. The things I have to say to you don't require your response. I'd rather not hear the timbre of your voice." He held up his revolver. "This was my father's gun. I don't really remember the story of how he came to have it. You're going to kill yourself with it."

"I certainly am not." She gritted her teeth.

He hadn't expected an immediate agreement. It went against the very nature of people who did their jobs, ones who walked in the darkness to either hurt or protect the innocent. They survived. Like cockroaches.

"You are, because you have two options. Die by your own hand—one bullet through your temple will likely suffice— or I'll kill you." He paused to let his words sink in. "And I won't do it fast."

"What do you mean? I've seen how you can shoot. You and Bernardo. You can do the same as he could. A single shot. Don't act as if you can't." She rushed him and took a swing at his head. He laughed as he ducked out of her way and grabbed her wrist.

In under two seconds, he restrained against the tree. At least he had to give her credit for trying. "You should have been trained better."

She struggled for a few seconds, and he felt the second

the fight moved out of her. Death was in the air. She might not feel it the same way he did, but deep down inside, she had to feel her time was up. He'd seen it with patients in hospitals. The fight left.

"I'll shoot you first in the gut." He could picture the wound. "Gut shots hurt. And you don't die right away from them. From there, I can become downright creative. I'll—"

"Okay," she interrupted him, and he let her. Would he actually shoot a woman in the stomach? No. She'd terrified his people. That meant she got to suffer before she died.

"I could take the gun, and I could shoot you with it."

He whispered in her ear. These would be the last words he'd speak to her, one way or another. "You could try."

~

Now

Platinum knelt down in front of his son. Kent sat in a lounge chair too big for his small body and stared intently at a tablet where he must have been playing a game. His hand moved fast, tapping frantically.

"Hi."

Kent's head shot up. "Hello."

They stared at each other for a second, neither of them speaking. He supposed he should figure out something to say. It couldn't fall to Kent to take charge of their relationship.

"Where did you acquire the tablet?" He pointed to it.

"A lady gave it to me."

The woman in question must be Poppy. The face of Warbucks' organization. She was in charge of all the toys.

The big, dangerous ones, and apparently, the smaller fun ones too.

"Did you say thank you?" His response felt like a really inane thing to say. The kid hardly knew him. He wasn't really in a position to be giving lessons in manners.

"I did." Kent sniffed. "Did you give me the money to pay for school?"

"Yes."

"That's what I thought." Kent nodded, chewing on his bottom lip. "Ms. Rose says you guys take care of bad guys here."

"She's right. We do." Had there ever been a harder conversation in the history of the world? At least Rose wasn't calling him the devil to his son.

"Did you find the bad guy after me?"

In all the world, Kent should never have to ask such a question, and Plat's heart sunk into his gut. Never-fucking-again. "Yes."

He wouldn't elaborate, wouldn't tell The Boy the details. Kent never needed to learn it was a woman. The particulars of her death would remain with Platinum. The team with him hadn't seen the final moment.

The bang, and then the Silence. His friends wouldn't have felt it anyway, not the way he did. Hell, maybe he was crazy.

He was all Kent had left, and someway, he'd have to figure out how to be a father.

"Good. Ms. Rose, she took me and ran. Is she going to be in trouble?"

"No, son." He couldn't believe how easily the word came out. "The people who run this place, they're fixing it all up. Everything is going to be fine for Rose."

"Good."

"Yep. Real good."

Kent held up the tablet. "I'm playing Minecraft."

"Yeah?"

Kent patted the side of the chair. "Would you like to sit here and play it with me?"

"I can't think of anything I'd rather do."

Kent smelled of soap and icing. Maybe Poppy had given him more than the tablet. He'd have to find out all the things the child liked and what he didn't. They'd have to figure it out together.

It looked as if they had plenty of time.

ROSE STARED out the window of her room. Platinum would have to teach her to lock her door. He knocked on the side of the wall, and she didn't turn around when she spoke.

"I knew you were there."

That was surprising. "You did?"

"The air always moves differently when you're in the room."

Huh. "Really?"

She finally turned around. "Yes. Like tickles on the back of my neck."

He knew the feeling well. Of course, he had no idea she could feel it, or why she did when he was there.

It was time for the truth.

"I'll never be able to undo the hurt I caused you. I can't begin to try. What I can do is try to tell you, so maybe you'll understand some things I don't really get myself."

She crossed her arms over her chest. "Okay. I'll listen to whatever you to say to me, Eli. Oh damn, I'm sorry. I might never be able to stop."

"Don't try. I actually want it. I want to be Eli for you. I liked who he was. Either way, I need you to see me."

She walked toward him. "I'm so stupid. I should be getting out of here as fast as I can. Yet, I've found you again. I was going to be killed in a cabin, and you showed up. I don't want to let you go again. Although I am so mad at you..."

"Rose, sweetheart. Out there in the world, there are people who are trying to sell plutonium. There are people trafficking drugs. There are folks who have devoted their lives to destroying others."

She shifted her weight on her feet. A small movement. Still, a tell spoke volumes as to her discomfort.

"I've seen all of them, and I can't let any of it touch you."

8

She sat up on her bed, the moon shining through the window, and leaned her head down on her knees. Rose's head wouldn't turn off. She was safe, free to leave if she wanted. Yet, she hadn't lied to Elijah when she'd told him she didn't want to leave him.

Maybe her conflict made her sick in the head

Stupid, foolish heart.

Only now, things made sense. The parts of Eli's life which had always been distant—the bad dreams which were rare and potent, the insomnia which was much more common, the *I'm never going to talk about my past* attitude—all of it could finally be reconciled.

As she'd fallen in love with him, she'd known deep in her heart there were going to be things she needed to learn about him before there could be a real future. Of course, she'd been in such la-la land in love, she'd shoved it away from her day-to-day thoughts.

All of it made sense, at least to a point. She might never really understand it, only she could try to work with the fact she finally understood the truth. He was a hero, and given his proclamation about the threat after her having been eliminated, she assumed he killed the person responsible.

How did a person live with taking another life, when they were all alone in the dark?

She knew the answer to her own question. When he'd been with her, Elijah Jones, also known as Platinum—and apparently, another name too—hadn't slept very much at all. And when he did, he endured nightmares.

She jumped to her feet, and in a few seconds, got dressed to make her way to his room. Kent was asleep down the hall from his father. The child was sleeping a lot. His behavior was probably normal. She needed to remember to ask about the psychologists. They'd find him some help. Funny, how she was already putting herself into his plan.

Rose really had no idea if Eli wanted her in his life that way or not. He'd not told her either way. In all the time he'd stood in front of her and told her about the things in the world which were frightening and scary, he'd never once said anything about how he felt about her.

Well, other than the remark about being tied up, which made her a lot more hot and bothered than it should, considering she was determined not to be.

She scurried toward his room and knocked gently on the door.

"Yep," he called out, and she paused for half a second before she entered. There would be no going back after she did this. Her hand shook, and she stepped through the doorway anyway. Being scared never worked for her.

Eli stared at her for a moment. "You okay?"

"No." She spoke quickly, determined to only tell him the truth. "I'm not."

He lay on the bed, his legs crossed in front of him. Eli wore only dark green pajama pants, leaving him shirtless.

She took a moment to stop and look at him. Undressed, there were some obvious changes in him.

Elijah had always been fit. Lean and muscular. He'd run more daily than any other person she knew who wasn't training for an Iron Man or a marathon. He looked more bulked up, as if he lifted weights.

"What's wrong?" He raised his eyebrows in a questioning manner.

"You, Platinum." Hell, she might go crazy changing around names. It all amounted to the confusing male sitting in his bed, looking delicious and frustrating at the same time.

Caution be damned, she was still in love with the enigma of a man.

"What about me in specific?" He still hadn't moved. He'd definitely gotten into the not-moving zone he frequented. It wasn't as confusing as it used to be. When he got still, it was because he was a predator ready to pounce, if need be.

"I can't pull you out of my head." She cleared her throat. "Mostly because all the reasons why I shouldn't be withstanding, I'm still in love with you. And so I need to find out, if leaving me to go save the world for me, changed your heart. You never did tell me you loved me. I thought you might have. I guess I'm asking you, Elijah, should I stay, or go and finally move on?"

And somehow, she would. If all he wanted to do was tie her up because he liked to do so, she would go home and put him out of her mind. It would take years and probably ten pounds put on from ice cream. Still, she would do it. *Somehow.*

"Am I in love with you?" He moved, rising to his knees and edging to the end of the bed, close enough that she could feel the heat from his body. "Are you kidding?"

"No." She grabbed a pillow and whacked him with it. "Can you answer? Outside of running for my life, coming in here tonight is the hardest thing I've ever done."

"I'm so in love with you, every bone in my body hurts when I'm away from you for too long. You're on my mind the second I wake up, and I fall asleep thinking of you. I love you so much, I did something I've never considered doing before today, so on the off chance you ever let me touch you again, I wouldn't have torture on my hands." He stood up and backed her up until she pressed against the wall. Her heart beat so fast, it might explode. "I can never undo what happened. I have to earn your trust again. Don't go. Let me do it."

She threw her arms around him, and he caught her, pulling her legs off the floor. Their lips fused together. She didn't know who kissed who first, just that soon he was devouring her, and she loved every single fucking moment of it. His hands roamed her body.

Rose didn't fool herself. Tonight wasn't going to make everything okay between them, not by a long shot. The heat between them was going to explode. She needed it, and after his multiple confessions to her, it seemed he was in the same bad way.

Denying it only postponed what they both needed, each other.

He pulled back, letting her body slide down the front of his. She could feel his hard cock as she traveled the length of him until she hit the floor. Her mouth watered, and Eli took her cheeks in his hands.

"Do you remember your signals?" They'd always talked about a safe word. Only, she'd liked the red, yellow, green directions. Since she hadn't wanted to change it up, he hadn't made her. They'd always stayed with their street light instructions.

"Not likely to forget them. I see them every time I'm in the car."

He stroked his thumb down the side of her face. "You're funny."

"I know." When he moved his finger over her mouth, she nipped it lightly and he hissed, which quickly turned into a groan and a hard press of his hips against her own. Moisture pooled on her panties. Yes...

Her body tingled with anticipation. "Do you have your rope?"

"What do you think?" He leaned in to kiss her again, and she loved the way his mouth gentled against hers. She might never grasp exactly how much power he contained inside of him. All she could be sure about was the way his hands would never harm her.

Maybe she shouldn't ask the question, it would spoil the mood. Only she didn't want to keep things to herself anymore. They'd lived enough of those days. "Anyone else had those ropes around them since you took them from me?"

He stopped where he'd been making love to her neck. She missed the warmth, even if she didn't regret the question. "I hate you needed to ask me."

"Not an answer."

Elijah breathed against her neck. "No one. I can't think about anyone else. Imagining you is the only way I can jerk off, and still, it's completely dissatisfying."

"Well, that was vivid."

He laughed, and she felt it all the way to her toes. "You did ask."

"True. I'm going to. I'm going to want answers."

"Unless something is classified, I'll always make sure you understand what's going on."

She supposed his response constituted the best she could ask for. "Fair enough."

"What about you? Do I need to kill some bastard for having his hands on what is mine?"

"I think you're only half kidding."

"Sweetheart." He held her gaze in his. "I'm not kidding at all. I imagined you had moved on. Told myself you must have. But now I find I want to kill anyone you were with."

"*No one.*" And she'd never been so glad to be able to answer in the negative and really mean it.

He walked away from her to the closet and came back holding a purple rope. It had been her favorite, he'd bought it because she said she liked the color. The Eli she'd known was always doing things to make her happy.

Without a word, he took off her shirt, followed by her bra. Although his eyes gazed down for a moment with heat at her naked breasts, his attention was unsurprisingly elsewhere.

"Give me your wrists."

She did as he asked and extended her hands in the way he'd shown her many times. He folded the rope in half. It had always impressed her how meticulous he became when he handled the rope.

"You're so careful with it."

"No." He shook his head, not looking at her when he spoke. "I'm careful with you. The more I pay attention, the surer I can be you're fine. You trust me." He raised his eyes. "Don't you? Color?"

They hadn't done anything yet except look at the rope. "Green, tough guy, green."

He smirked. "Good."

Elijah continued on with his work, wrapping the rope around her wrist, twisting and turning it as if he was a man who knew what he was doing. She knew for a fact he did. He'd twisted it three times before he pulled it in the opposite direction to secure the rope.

His hands moved steadily. Was this way he handled his sniper rifle? Come to think of it, she'd never watched him do anything he hadn't completely invested in. Even making spaghetti.

Her man finally knotted it. She was fully secured. A calmness she'd forgotten happened when he tied her, filled her up. Her toes tingled, and she let herself take a deep breath.

"Color?"

She looked up at her face. He'd gone unreadable. Was he nervous? "Green, Eli."

"Good." He tugged her with the remaining length of the rope, bringing her over to the bed.

"Lay down, sweetheart. And close your eyes."

As he'd instructed, she did. He finished undressing her, and then she heard him removing his own clothing. It was weird laying there on his bed with her eyes closed. He'd not asked her to before.

Her face must have betrayed something she thought, because he questioned her, "Color?"

"Green, although I've never particularly liked antic-ipation."

"Then I won't make you wait any longer." He kissed the top of her knee cap, and she shivered. Who knew she was sensitive there? Well, Elijah, apparently. "Usually when I tie up your hands, I strap them up to the headboard. I think we'll try something else tonight."

"Oh?"

"Good girl, keeping your eyes closed."

She smiled. "You know me, I love to be compliant."

"Sure. Ha."

She shook her head. "Sarcasm, Elijah. It doesn't become you."

"Open your eyes." She lifted lids. He lay on the bed next to her, completely naked in his masculine glory.

"You're so muscular."

He shrugged, showing off a muscle set. "Lots of sexual frustration. I've been spending a lot of time at the gym."

With her hands tied by the wrists, she didn't have motion with them, even though her hands were free. She let herself touch his pecs. "Lots of hard work."

"Climb on top of me, sweetheart."

"What?" Did she miss a set of instructions because she'd been so preoccupied looking at the way his body looked sculpted?

Elijah put his hands under his head. "You. On top."

"We've never done it with me on top."

"I know."

Her hands were tied, yet she could still move them. He wanted her to be on top? "What's going on?"

"Trust."

"Oh, I see." She felt she actually did. Elijah was never out of control, and this time, he was giving it to her.

She reached for him with her hands, and although it was challenging with them tied, she stroked his hard cock. He groaned and closed his eyes. Knowing the chance to stroke him was a rarity, she let herself indulge in it for a while. His hardness lengthened more, and her mouth watered.

Eli opened an eye. "I'd really love to come inside of you.

Too much more of any of your gentle torture, and I'm going to be over before it gets really going."

"How do you like the rope rubbing against you?"

"Seeing you in it is my kink. On my own skin, it's an extension to how I feel about you."

His words made sense. "Elijah?"

"Yes, sweetheart."

He always asked her. It would be her turn. "Color?"

"Green, my Rose. Totally green."

"Good."

She climbed on top of him and rubbed his bare cock against the outside of her pussy. Shivers travelled through her, but she wasn't on the pill, and they weren't going to go there. "Condom?"

He leaned forward and grabbed a condom off the side table. In a few seconds, he had himself sheathed.

With exquisite torture in mind, she moved over him slowly, until she'd put him deep inside of her, balls to tip. "You're going to kill me. Aren't you?"

"Would be a great way to die."

She moved, inch by inch, until he was almost out of her, then she pressed back down. His hips danced with hers, and before she knew it, they'd started their hot caresses with his cock hitting her clit with each stroke, sending pleasure surging through her body. He'd said it wouldn't take much for him, and she could feel him lengthening inside of her.

"Shit, baby. So good." His words sounded strained. She looked down at his sweet face, the one she'd thought she'd lost forever, to see the muscles in his strong neck clenching.

Elijah was hanging on by a thread. She knew the feeling. Maybe it was seconds, or perhaps hours went by, and finally, she came in a surge of heat and wetness as she never had before.

He called out her name, his hips rising and falling in a spasm of movement which extended her own pleasure further.

She collapsed on top of him, and as the passion cooled, the tears she hadn't known she held back fell from her eyes. Rose couldn't have stopped them if she tried. Elijah wrapped his arms around her and curled his body around hers in a protection of love and security.

He didn't ask her to stop crying, which was good because she wasn't certain she could have if he'd wanted her to.

She closed her eyes and listened to his heart beat. "Rose? Can you do something for me please?"

"Sure." She didn't have the strength to do much more than breathe.

"Tomorrow, I want you to tell me all about the new season of *Doctor Who*."

His words were so surprising, she actually woke up enough to look at him. "What?"

"The whole season. Start to finish. Could you talk to me for hours?"

Rose lost him once, and though it might take a long time to really believe they were fine, she wouldn't trade a moment with this man for anything in the universe.

"Sure thing, Elijah. Whatever you want."

Always.

ZINC

1

From behind the hood he had worn for three years to hide himself from the world, Zachery 'Zinc' Daniels watched Adam Steele. The man had once been more brother than friend. He stroked Alayna Steele's face. The former spook had become the love of Adam's life. She smiled and laughed at something he said. Zinc narrowed his eyes, studying them. Funny what a difference three years made.

Once, it had been Zinc planning a wedding, touching the love of his life, and making future plans while his best friend laughed and denied he would ever have any interest in doing the same.

The dreams died the same way Zinc had—on an icy stretch of road in Russia when a hail of bullets and a detonation dropped him. Dying hadn't been so bad. Then Adam had left Zinc's body behind. And never looked back.

"It's time," Titanium announced.

Time? Zinc regarded the man who had been both his commander and kidnapper. Titanium had once been a commander in the Marines, although the same FUBAR night which had taken Zinc's life, had also stolen Titanium's legs and his eyesight. Yet Titanium, hidden behind the kind of power only the very rich enjoyed, still led men into battle, whether they agreed to be on his teams or not.

For three years, the former Elite Recon commander dictated all the terms of Zinc's life. Where he would live, how he would act, who he would talk to. And with no warning, he wanted them to reveal themselves to the friends Titanium's Ghosts left behind? To the people who thought them dead?

Time. It was a funny concept. Years could fly by in what felt like days, while minutes could become hours, seconds feeling as long as decades. Every minute Zinc had spent hiding beneath his hood on Titanium's command had been akin to centuries.

There had been a time when he had been young, filled with life, and sure of his place in the world. He'd known who he was and who would always be there for him.

And all of his best memories involved Adam Steele. His best friend. His brother. His fellow Marine. Oorah.

Funny really, if Zach hadn't pulled Steele from the wreck of twisted metal when they were fifteen, they probably wouldn't be standing in the room at all. They'd been out racing their father's cars. Neither of them had licenses. Though Steele's father hadn't been in love with a bottle of gin like Zach's, both men knew how to wield a belt on their son's behinds when needed. Of course, his punishments tended to go on a little longer, too. Not that he'd ever shared what happened at home. Men didn't whine about silly things such as pain.

The sound of Adam's car slamming into a tree echoed with the frame's unnatural crumpling and the shattering of glass—time had slowed as Zach rushed to the smoking pile of metal.

He didn't remember getting out of his own car and getting to his friend. Yet, there he had stood, in front of the wrecked vehicle. Blood flowed freely from the gash across Adam's forehead. Amazingly, his eyes had been open.

"Fuck."

"Yeah. That was bad. Shit, I thought you were dead." Adam lived. He could breathe again.

"I can't move my legs." Steele had grimaced. "There's glass everywhere, and I can't move to make it to the door. Pretty sure I'm screwed."

The situation was screwed, but not Adam. Although he wasn't going to tell his friend how bad he looked. Not then, not ever. "Don't worry, my man, we're good. I'm going to haul you out of the car."

"My dad's going to kill me."

"He won't." Adam's father would be mad, for sure. He'd also be relieved his son hadn't died. Steele's father was cool for a parent. He loved his children, put their welfare first. Someday when Zach had kids, he'd be the same way—take after Adam's father and not his own. No gin. No pills. No bullshit.

In the distance, sirens wailed. The cops were on their way.

"You should go." Adam groaned. "You don't have to be in trouble."

"I'll never leave you," Zach promised, and meant it. "Hold on. I'm getting you out of there. Take my hand." He reached through the window, cutting himself on some of the shredded glass when he did. "We'll make it out of here together."

His friend grinned. "You're my brother, Zach."

"Hold on, Adam. I've got you."

Zinc blinked, returning to the present. He was a Ghost. Every record of Zachary Daniels listed him as deceased.

Only he hadn't died. Knowing things had the potential to go FUBAR in Russia, and believing there was a traitor on their mission, Titanium had made arrangements to have his own men rushed out to a secret medical facility if things went to hell. Too bad Titanium failed to indicate to his hired mercenaries who was a member of his team and who wasn't.

Nearly dead on the ground, Zinc had been swept in by the so-called rescue without so much as a by your leave and woken three months later into a world of hell.

For three long years, he had been stuck. For three long years, he had watched his former brothers and sister-in-arms move on with their lives. Like Adam Steele. The man who should have stood at his side, been his best man when Zinc married. His brother. Buddy. Confidante. The guy who had abandoned Zinc on the cold ground in Russia to be drafted into a secret mission he would never have willingly joined.

Steele had a choice. Chrome had a choice. Copper had a choice. Platinum. Adamantium. Sterling. Silver. Hell, even poor dead Cobalt. They'd all had a damn choice. They might argue they hadn't, they'd been relocated, forced to move on. But Zinc knew differently. The second Poppy brought them in, she offered them a choice never given to Zinc.

No one asked Zinc if he wanted his hell. They'd left him to it while they all moved on with their fucking lives.

He gritted his teeth.

After holding him hostage to the mission, Titanium decided it was time for a reveal without giving any of the

Ghosts a choice to stay hidden. When did he ever give anyone an out?

"Does it bother you?" Tungsten asked him one afternoon when they patrolled the compound. Tungsten's real name was Brad, but Zinc barely remembered it most days. "Steele looks right at you. Last week, he bumped into you when he wasn't watching where he went. He has no idea who you are. Don't you think, sometimes, they should know, these people who loved us. Shouldn't they know?"

His friend had lost everything, and Zinc knew the feeling. Exactly the same as Zinc, Brad had been manipulated by Titanium when he'd not been part of his team. Together, he and Zinc were in their unasked for hell together.

Unlike Zinc, however, who had distance from the woman he lost, Brad had to watch Copper fall in love. At least Zinc had been spared that special kind of hell.

"No. We're under hoods," he'd answered at the time. Only he did, in his worst moments, think how fucked it was none of his team, his friend, the people he thought of as family, recognized him at all. Adam Steele should have known him anywhere.

And he shouldn't have left his body on the ground.

With his fists clenched and his breaths coming out in hard puffs, he took off his hood. Then waited. Gasps sounded in the room, and someone cried out. But not Steele. Copper took off running, and behind him, Brad tried to move. Zinc couldn't take his eyes off Steele.

Say something, he willed his friend, *tell me you understand what has happened here. What you did to me when you left me there on the ground, when you didn't bring my body home.*

Nothing. Not a single reaction from the man he would give—and hell—had given his life for in Russia. Steele didn't seem surprised. Zinc stalked forward. It was the silence which was his undoing, the non-reaction. Steele's woman let out a cry, and Zinc's best friend did nothing.

Zinc couldn't take it anymore.

"How could you have left me there for these fuckers to take?" His whole body vibrated as he waited for any response, any reaction. Nothing came.

Crack. He whacked Steele's nose, and the room exploded into sound. Who gave a shit? He wasn't done yet. He swung at him again, hitting him harder. "Why? Fuck you, why? Why did you leave me there, Steele? How could you have let them do what they did to me? I pulled you from the car. All I wanted from you was to bring my body home when it was over. Why? Why? Why?"

Blood sprayed Zinc, and the front of Steel's shirt went red.

Good. Let him bleed. Let him hurt. Let him...

Whack. Zinc punched Steele again, slamming Steele square in the eye. Zinc's hand burned. Training had taught Zinc years ago how to hit without hurting himself, only fuck it, Zinc didn't care. Beating the bastard who left him behind felt too good. Years spent waiting for his moment, keeping quiet, staying in the shadows while his whole fucking world fell apart.

Strong arms hauled him backwards, holding him still as only a trained operative would know how to do. He knew for damn sure it wasn't any of the Ghosts stopping him, they all had their own battles to fight, and it took him a moment to recognize Merc as the guy halting his much needed assault.

"Merc, you let me at him. You'll never know, man. You'll never get it." Steele lay on the floor, gripping his beaten face as he continued to stare silently at Zinc. Why the fuck didn't he say something? Why hadn't he uttered a sound? "Why? You tell me why you let this happen, Steele. Why you didn't make sure I was dead? Why would you have left me to my fucking hell when I would never have done the same shit to you?"

Merc hissed an answer instead of Steele. "Put a sock in in this shit, asshole. He's your brother, and you just came back from the dead. So you need to give us a damn minute."

His words were meaningless. Another indication they were never going to understand what happened to him for the last three years. Zinc quit struggling. If Merc didn't want to let him go, he wasn't going to be let go. "I'm good. I won't hit him again." He waited a beat, and still, he didn't receive use of his arms back. "I swear it. No more punching."

Merc released his arms, and he swung around to regard his old friend.

"I did die in Russia, Merc. I really am nothing more than a Ghost. Thanks to him."

HIS HEAD POUNDED, only the pain was nothing new. Zinc had an almost constant headache. Some days it was ignorable, others not so much so. The doctors all told him the same thing—head injuries had repercussions. He'd been seriously injured. For all intents and purposes, he'd died. So losing his gall bladder and having his torso covered in burn scars wasn't such a big deal, considering. The mind splitting headaches, well, he'd had to learn to live with.

Zinc took a swig of whiskey and swallowed his pill. The headache would dim in half an hour. Ignoring the ache in his hand, well earned after breaking several bones in Steele's face, he clicked on the Facebook profile he let himself look at no more than twice a week. Ally Norman. The girl he was supposed to have married stared back at him from her profile. In her arms, she held her first child, who would be six months old soon. A little girl she and her husband, Rick, had named Ivy.

He sat back in his seat and stared at Ally's new profile picture. Technically, she had restricted her profile to being viewed by friends only, so he shouldn't have been able to see her stuff. Then again, he'd never seen a website he couldn't hack if he felt like fucking with it, and following his fiancée's new life consumed him. A raw gaping wound which would never heal.

The pain of seeing her gap toothed grin didn't hurt as bad anymore. Following her daily postings about playground trips and post-baby dieting was more of a remote interest in the doings of a person he'd once believed he would love for the rest of his life. She'd told him he was her love, and he'd proposed on a beach with the wind blowing her white skirt while she'd cried her yes in his arms.

Her new husband had apparently proposed on the dock of his beach house in Santa Barbara. He was some kind of yacht maker.

His phone pinged, tugging his attention from his Facebook stalking and recalling him to the present. Titanium wanted his attention. Honestly, it surprised him the man had left him alone for the forty-eight hours he had. Attacking Steele had felt great at the time, even if he was bound to find his ass chewed for it. Steele was important to Titanium, and Zinc had learned early on his own importance to the man in charge was relatively miniscule. Titanium only cared as much as Zinc was useful.

Zinc supposed he should thank him some day for saving his life.

Except he really didn't see the heart-to-heart happening, ever.

Zinc stood and shut off his screen. There was no such thing as privacy on the compound, not for the former Ghosts anyway, and too much attention to Ally would trigger internal alarms, which might land him in either a cell or a shrink's office. Having endured both, he knew he didn't want either.

Locking up his place, he made his way to Titanium's office swiftly and ignored the slight shake to his right leg. Physical therapy had healed most of the damage from the explosion, only nothing would ever make it entirely right. Mostly his leg worked fine, but similar to his head, he never did know when it might flare and make his day miserable.

"Hey."

Zinc looked over his shoulder and chose to ignore Platinum's call as he rounded a corner. Some of his old team had tried to reach out, and though he liked the quiet man, he wasn't ready to talk to him—or anyone. Zinc had broken Steele's nose, and he wasn't sure he wouldn't start pounding on someone else if given the chance. Better to simply stick to himself for the time being.

Titanium waited for him when he walked in his office and indicated a chair for him to sit in. Without a word, Zinc did as he was told. Titanium couldn't see, not since the mess in Russia. And yet...Zinc would sometimes swear Titanium's eyes functioned better than Zinc's did.

"You all right?"

Zinc sat back in his seat. He'd never been the kid to be hauled to the principal's office. Getting beat by his pop wasn't worth the momentary thrill of doing whatever would have landed him there. However, he didn't think the conversations usually began with the person doing the lecturing asking after the welfare of the guy who got in trouble.

"Fine."

Titanium shook his head. "Liar."

"Whatever." Sometimes he couldn't believe he spoke the way he did to the person who was basically his commanding officer. Only, he'd never been able to think of Titanium with the respect he'd once thrown Chrome. Titanium would be more properly called his jailor.

"How are the headaches? You still taking pills?"

"Only the ones the doctors give me, Dad." His brief foray into recreational means to cool his head had passed. They'd not particularly helped, and his month of getting sober in Titanium's cell had been enough. He wasn't a drug addict. He'd simply not let himself become his father.

"Mentally? You've had two days to cool off. I mean you beat the shit out of Steele. We had to send him and his girl away for a while. He needed surgery for the bone under his eye."

"Is there a point to our little talk?" Zinc had really had enough. If he wanted to talk, it wasn't going to be to Titanium.

"A situation has developed, and I want to send you on a mission. I'm trying to figure out how fucked you are, Zinc. Can you be trusted by yourself in a situation which might blow to pieces around you?"

His pulse increased. A mission? All by himself. He'd not had a job, which didn't involve the other Ghosts, since the coma. The idea wasn't...unappealing. "That's not really for me to say. You're in charge. You tell me."

"It's complicated. I'm not unhappy Steele exited for a while. We've been tracking a lawyer for some time. A man named Walter David. He was on the payroll for Red Wolf, helped him move arms, laundered money, did whatever needed to be done to make Red Wolf's operations look legitimate where needed."

Zinc hated him immediately. Lawyers always had a bad rep in jokes, although most of the ones he knew were extremely ethical, following the letter of the law in order to not be sanctioned. Every once in a while, someone such as Walter David gave them all a bad name. "What do you need me to do to him?"

"Initially, we thought it would be a simple smash and grab. Break in, take his papers, bust out. Kill him if need be, although not necessarily a must do. I planned on sending Platinum in later to take him out. However, some intel we acquired has complicated matters. Mr. David, it appears, has a certain taste for women. He likes to capture unwilling ladies, keep them naked and restrained, watch them, and then eventually give them to his clients to do with as they please."

Zinc stood. "Fuck that."

"My sentiments exactly." Titanium shook his head. "Look at the picture." He pointed to the table. "Recognize her?"

He stared at the screen, and for a second, he couldn't believe his eyes. On her knees, with her breasts pressed to her legs as the only thing blocking her from being fully nude, was Sarah Steele.

Zinc had known her for years. She was Steele's little sister, younger by four years. Brilliant—Steele had always called her the smartest member of the family—she'd been sent away to school when they were young. Some fancy place where she had learned to speak ten languages and ran a marathon a week. She was also gorgeous and kind hearted. And had always been completely off limits to any romantic thoughts as Steele's younger sister.

Although he'd always thought she was gorgeous as hell. Dark haired with equally dark colored eyes, she had a long face with high cheekbones he didn't often see outside of magazines. She was tall, slender, athletic, and tough in the way the Steeles always were.

Zinc hadn't seen her more than half a dozen times over the last decade.

"How?"

"She's Agency. We didn't know either." Titanium held his hand in front of him to stop Zinc from talking when he would have exploded. How the fuck did the man know when he was blind? "Deep cover. The whole lawyer persona is real. She is a corporate attorney in New York City. And yet, it turns out she is so much more too. She's been asking the wrong kinds of questions for years about her brother's death —yours too, for the record—and David decided to have her taken. She's next to be his voyeuristic gift. If you're okay for it, Zinc, I want you to go retrieve her and do all the other shit we need, too."

Thank God Steele isn't here to see his sister in trouble. It would kill him.

"When do I leave?"

"You understand what you'll likely have to do, right? The man likes to watch. She knows you. Hopefully, her recognizing you will help. If you need to, break her out using whatever methods necessary. We need her alive, and we have to move now. Her time has run out, and you're all that's standing between her and a fate worse than death. You feel me?"

Fuck.

～

SARAH STEELE HAD ALMOST GOTTEN USED to the feeling of being naked all the time. Almost being the key word. When she got off the God forsaken island where the asshat David had kept her for the last month—and she would find her way out of there, one way or another—she'd dress in clothes for the shower, she might never be naked again.

Spending her days on her knees, nude, for the sexual titillation of a truly evil douchebag would not define her life. She simply wouldn't let it.

I am Sarah Ambrosia Steele. I am strong, tough, and brilliant. I spoke fluent Mandarin when most of my peers were still struggling through writing English papers. I know five different types of ways to kill someone without breaking a sweat. It took four fuckers to bring me, and they only keep me here because of the God damned electric collar.

Some day, she would look back at her captivity as a blip in an otherwise well lived life. Things could always be worse, and she knew it. She'd not been raped. Yet. Though if the screams around the hall earlier in the week were any indication, the other women were not being quite as well kept.

After her initial abduction, she hadn't been beaten. Stripped and spoken to through a speaker on the wall, yes, and there was no doubt it sucked. But she wasn't dead.

Unlike her brother and his friends who had died because of some operation Walter David had been involved in, she still breathed air. Adam would never see another day, and neither would Zach or any of their other friends. She was alive, and where there was life, there was hope.

End of story.

She was a CIA operative and had personally been responsible for foiling nothing short of two terror threats against the United States by following the money and the business transactions her role as a high-powered lawyer afforded her access to. Damn it, she would do so again.

Pencil pushers could get things done.

She would survive. Whatever happened.

And she had killer legs and could manage to orgasm one-two-three with the help of her fingers when need be or on a hard cock when the right opportunity presented itself. Sex was always good for her.

If she could hang on to all these things about herself and not become the whining, sniveling creature after too many days spent non-consensually nude on her knees with her head bowed, she could survive this.

Whatever happened, she would not beg, she would not lose herself.

"Ms. Steele." Walter David's voice thundered through the room, and she jumped. Day and night, she had to stay as she was, or she would be zapped until her fingers burned, thanks to his sick collar. He could call out at any time. He liked to watch her naked and on the floor.

She also suspected he liked to see her jump when he spoke over the speaker after days of leaving her in silence with nothing except her own internal voice to keep her company.

"We have a gentleman for you, Ms. Steele. You're to be given to him. He is on his way to your room. He will pleasure himself with you as he sees fit, and I will watch. When he is done, he will determine what happens to you next. Try to stop him or hurt him in any way, and I will electrocute you from the collar. Do you need a reminder of how the collar shocking feels?"

"No." She shook her head. Sarah really didn't, and acting as some kind of hard ass would prove nothing. She didn't need to be injured when whomever the man turned out to be entered. By contrast, she should be strong and ready.

Some way or another she'd break out. As long as she lived, there was hope.

Whatever had to happen—

The door flung open, and a man appeared as David kept speaking. "Meet Terrance Monroe. He's my new best friend. He's taken with you, my dear. Remember what I said."

She raised her head to study the man standing in silence. The room where Sarah had been held was totally benign. Other than her mat on the floor where she was to kneel, there was nothing to look at other than the white walls around her. Sarah had to squint to make out the new colors the broad shouldered figure brought with him.

He wore a black suit, shiny, expensive looking dark shoes, and a red tie over his white dress shirt, which was neatly starched beneath the matching suit blazer. With sandy blond hair and an imposing cleft in his chin, she almost didn't recognize him.

Why would she? It had been years since she had laid eyes on him, and according to all reports—and hers were excellent sources—he was dead. Was she seeing a ghost? Sarah forced her heartbeat to slow. She wasn't crazy, not yet anyway.

Her brother's best friend, Zachery Daniels, stood before her very much alive, despite all reports to the contrary.

He raised a finger to his lips, ordering her silence.

"I want my women to be quiet. You'll speak only when I let you, and there won't be any questions. Understood?"

She could read between the lines. He wanted her to hush so she didn't give away his identity. Zach standing in front of her was so far beyond the realm of anything she imagined, she could only hope his arrival would also bring with him miracle-like possibilities and rescue.

Sarah was happy to stay silent.

How is he alive? Did that mean Adam...No, she shut off her train of thought. She was a professional CIA agent. The what ifs would wait for later.

Zach sauntered toward her. She'd always been attracted to him—every woman who met him ended up either crushing on or lusting after the man. The way he walked, the slickness of his moves, wasn't Zachery. He was a man's man, he didn't do smooth showing off ridiculousness, he didn't have to. Women wanted him without him having to audition for their approval.

His presentation was all part of the show.

"As does my esteemed host, I enjoy watching. I don't necessarily wish to touch." He reached into his coat pocket and pulled out a pair of handcuffs. Her eyes narrowed at the device. Handcuffs? For real? She could break out of them with her eyes closed in under a minute.

He quirked an eyebrow, and she said nothing. Whoever the very much alive Zachery was, he understood handcuffs wouldn't keep her restrained. He knew she was Agency.

All at once, her nudity hit her as a ton of bricks. She shuddered, and goosebumps broke out on her skin. Her brother's best friend, the subject of many of her earliest sexual fantasies, looked at her naked and vulnerable as she knelt on the floor. Heat flooded her cheeks, and she shivered. She wasn't ashamed of her body. In the real world outside of David's island hell, she chose who saw her without her clothes on.

Sarah wasn't submissive, the contrary when she actually played, and she would never have chosen to be on her knees when Zach viewed her nude.

He knelt and took her hands in his, gently stroking her knuckles with his thumb before he locked the handcuffs around her wrists.

"Maybe I lied." He spoke loud enough for the speakers in the room to catch his voice. "Maybe I will touch. A little."

He smoothed a finger around the side of her skin and she shuddered. Shouldn't her present circumstances preclude lust at such a simple action? Heaven knew she had no interest in actual intercourse. Still, Zach brought warmth with him, and when he looked her right in the eye, he wasn't pretending, but showing her he was very much present.

She wasn't alone.

"Off your knees," he instructed her. "I want you on your bottom with your legs in front of you. Understand?"

Since she could follow basic directions, she didn't find anything he said confusing. Changing his movements, he used both hands as he smoothed her skin from her legs all the way to her neck. "You wear a beautiful collar."

She almost snorted, then managed to restrain herself. It was her prison, the only thing really keeping her from true escape.

When he ran his hands down her skin again, he placed something in her palm, gently closing her fingers around whatever it was. Zachery the magician. Yes, he'd done these kinds of tricks when they'd been younger. One summer at the lake, he had taught her how to cheat at cards and do a sleight of hand. She couldn't look to see what he'd given her, yet her mind followed his.

He'd mentioned the collar and then stuck something in her handcuffed hands. The cuffs he knew she'd be able to rid herself of.

Zachery was telling her to escape; he'd given her the means to lose her collar. Whatever his story turned out to be, wherever he had vanished to for the last three years, she owed him a hell of a kiss.

He stood abruptly, his eyes never leaving hers. "Sarah," he whispered her name. "Be fast."

Whirling around, he pulled a gun out of his pocket and shot the camera. A startled yell filled the room.

She had no time to stop and react. He'd warned her. Be fast. She unhooked her hands as the first jolt to her collar hit, blinding her for a second. The door banged open, and out of the corner of her eye, she saw Zach run for the hall.

Shit, he left her? With shaking, electrified fingertips she jammed the metal object in her hand into the collar. Immediately the electricity stopped. Later, she'd ask him how he managed to short the thing out. After she killed him for leaving her alone.

Sarah jumped to her feet by the time Zach re-entered the room. "Catch."

Her hands shook from, well too many things to name, still, she managed to catch the gun he threw at her.

"Sorry for the abandonment, sweetheart. I had to kill the guard in the hall." He shrugged out of his jacket and wrapped it around her shoulders. It was huge, and she managed to cover herself pretty well within it. Distantly, she also noted it smelled of him, a clean cologne which always remained her of the ocean.

"CIA, huh? Can you run? We're not done here, and we still have shit to do."

"Yes." She spoke the word aloud. There would be no falling apart. Later, she promised herself, after she found out what the hell was going on. Later, in privacy and fully dressed, she'd fall apart, where no one could see.

2

Zinc had to push away his anger. Losing his temper was only going to make the fucking mess of a situation worse. For two days, he had wined and dined David into trusting him. Less than a single minute with Sarah, Zinc threw all caution to the wind.

It should have been hours before he blew out the camera, after he lulled the man into a blissful state of voyeuristic hotness. Only Sarah had been on the floor, and for two days, he'd been forced to bide his time, when all he wanted to do was chuck the mission and get her the hell out of there. Fuck it. Her safety was his mission. So what if he had to improvise on their way out? David could be halfway off the island.

He grabbed onto Sarah's soft hand and tugged her along. "There's a room ahead, I'm going to stash you in it while I handle things."

"No." She let go of his hand. "I'm not hiding. There are other women here, I heard them. I'm going to go find them."

He admired her backbone. Most people would be shaking in their boots after the ordeal she'd suffered. "You're the only kidnapped victim here. David got rid of the girls before I got here, or I would have saved them, too."

She nodded. "I'm still not hiding in a room while you take care of business."

A noise around the corner warned him they weren't alone, and he motioned to Sarah to stop. She tugged his jacket closer around herself, and he wished he had more clothing to give her. They'd have to wait until they got through whatever happened to find her clothes, and have what he was sure would be a very intense conversation about exactly what was going on.

Walter David had a secure island home for his maneuverings, and it wasn't exactly Fort Knox. Including the dead guard outside Sarah's room, there would be four more armed problems and David himself. Although, having spent two days with the drunk, Zinc didn't think the fool would prove much of a problem without his guards to do the dirty work for him.

Zinc darted to the side as they rounded the corner, and a pop exploding the wall next to his head let him know how close he'd been to being shot. You never hear the one which hits you. He'd been lucky.

"Zach."

"Got it, sweetheart." He had full visibility of the shooter and took him down seconds later.

Sarah closed in on his left. "You almost got hit."

"Nah. I'm hard to kill. Trust me." He took her hand again and pointed with his gun. "Through those doors. They're locked on the other side. We'll have to bust our way in."

"No." She shook her head. "I've got it." She still had one cuff from the handcuffs around her free wrist. Damn, she'd really not had time to pull herself completely out. She'd had to dislocate her wrist to have managed to be out at all and popped it back in. They'd have to wrap it up later. But damn.

Impressive.

She picked locks using the end of her open handcuff.

Very impressive.

The mission parameters were simple. Open the doors. Eliminate the guards. Take out David. Find her clothes. Get the fuck out of Dodge. Although, he did appreciate seeing her long legs stick out of his jacket. God, it had clearly been too long since he'd had a woman if he entertained thoughts about her legs while mid-mission.

"Got it." She turned and nodded to him. "Door should open. Have at it, Zach."

"I will. Move." He nodded her out of the way, and she followed orders. "Still can't get over the idea you're Agency and can pick locks. How the hell did that happen?"

"Asks the dead man." She raised an eyebrow, a challenge in her dark eyes "Q and A will have to wait for later."

"Fair enough." He grabbed the door handle, twisted, then pulled it open. "Stay."

He put two bullets into the guard waiting for them, which turned out to be more than he needed—better safe than sorry when it came to it. Apparently, without Red Wolf around, his former people were getting slack in their security.

"You're a good shot."

"Started when I was a kid, shooting with your brother and our dads on weekend hunting trips." He preferred not to think of those times, and the pang of pain in his chest as he spoke the words reminded him why. Ouch. Good memories could suck as much as bad ones.

"I remember. I used to hear about them at school. Adam

would write me." There was a sigh to her voice, and Zinc wondered if she also hated thinking about the past.

He moved forward, confidant she would follow him as she had done the whole time. "A single guard left, then David himself, unless he wised up and fled already."

"He's a coward who hides out behind people with guns. Straps electric collars to women who don't want it, and keeps them prisoner."

"And then kills them."

Her little gasp confirmed she hadn't had access to that last piece of information. If he'd known she'd been unaware, he'd have kept it to himself. Sarah didn't need to know how close she had come to death.

They'd gotten lucky.

Shouts echoed from within the private office suite. Zinc recognized the voices from earlier. David and his last guard —Walter David was afraid, and he had reason to be.

"I pay you to handle crisis," David wailed.

His guard didn't seem to care. "You don't pay me enough to be dead."

Zinc rolled his eyes. "It'll take a minute, sweetheart."

"Don't act cocky. You're the cocky ass who'll get dead." She motioned toward the door. "Have at it."

Did he hear boredom in her voice? They were in mid-escape, she'd been collared, shocked, and they'd been shot at, and she was naked, save for his jacket, yet Sarah Steele hadn't broken a sweat. What had happened to Adam's little sister to make her so badass?

Zinc kicked open the door, the shock jarring his bad knee while he ignored the pain. Maybe his move had been a little showy. Was he trying to impress Sarah? God, he needed his head on straight. He'd known her since she was four years old.

Of course, she was a grown woman.

A press of his finger discharged the bullet from his weapon right into the guard's head. The man fell backwards with a jolt, his lifeless brown eyes staring at the sky.

"You should have hired better security." He advanced on David. "Do you know who I am yet?"

"No..." David was short and stout with a pig nose, which had probably gotten him teased in school. He wore a mustache, a la Adolf Hitler. "Although, I'm starting to suspect you are part of the group responsible for my problems with Red Wolf."

"I'm not going to educate you. I was curious to see exactly how far your intelligence went on the subject. Intel matters."

David shook, and he held his hands in front of him. "I'll tell you anything you'd want to know. Don't kill me."

"Maybe I should make you beg. All those papers you got moved for Red Wolf, all the things you did to make his illegal dealings seem okay. All the pain your actions caused so many people."

Zinc wasn't thinking about himself. All the nameless—the souls they'd never know, the ones they couldn't save, the blind eyes they'd been forced to turn. The man in front of him had played a role.

"I'll beg." David dropped onto his knees. "I have no shame. All I have is information. Money transfers. Who, what, when, where, why."

The bang from behind accompanied by the bloody hole in David's forehead startled Zinc, and he whirled around. Gun in hand, Sarah shook her head.

When he could manage words, Zinc spoke. "He might have known something."

"There's nothing he can tell us those papers won't

contain." She pointed to the desk. "He's a lawyer. We'll find more out of his paper trail than anything he'd know or invent. And he kept me collared in a room against my will for a month."

Staring at her for a moment, Zinc recognized the hard look of her eyes, had seen it in the mirror many times over the last three years. She'd been pushed as far as she was going to go.

"Let's get his shit together then and get out of here. Then I'm going to have some questions for you, sweetheart, about how your kidnapping went down. David wasn't the brightest bulb in the bunch. If he found you, someone helped him."

"Right. You can then start with explaining to me how you're alive and where you have been."

"Of course."

It was going to be a long day.

THREE HOURS LATER, Zinc sat back in his seat and stared out the window. They were two hours from Texas. Sarah had been in the shower of the plane for an hour, and he wasn't going to rush her out. She should take as much time as she wanted to make herself comfortable after her ordeal.

The woman didn't rattle.

Her brother would be so surprised.

He pushed thoughts of Adam aside. As it was, Zinc was entertaining some seriously inappropriate thoughts about Sarah Steele. Like how her long legs looked wearing only his jacket. His cock jumped to attention. The girl was so completely off limits. He took a sip of his water, wishing it were whiskey. Given his family history, desire for alcohol was not one he could feed. Shit, his head hurt.

Where had he stuck his pills?

"Do you know when the last time I saw you was?" Sarah's voice startled him, and he turned. She leaned against the wall, dressed in his pajamas. He hadn't had anything else to give her. It took him a moment to find his voice. How could she be both so hot and so soft in his flannel pants and Yankees t-shirt?

She'd asked him something. The last time she saw him? "You'll have to remind me."

"The last time I saw you, or I guess, didn't see you, was when I stared at your closed coffin being lowered into the ground."

Well, he had walked right into her justified response. "And you want some answers."

"Immediately."

"Okay." He stood. The plane was flying smoothly, so far, they hadn't had a bump in the air. It was all right to move around. Titanium's private fleet was nothing if not luxurious, and the pilot currently operating the metal box sailing through the sky had come highly recommended.

"Tell me something right off the bat. Is my brother still alive, too?" Her eyes widened when she asked the question, the only outward indication of the stress asking the question caused her. He waited a beat, watching. Three years of being a Ghost had improved his people skills. A muscle in Sarah's jaw twitched. She was proving to be a woman who could keep her cool, only her outward demeanor didn't mean she wasn't freaking on the inside.

There was no easy way to do what it fell to him to tell her. Damn you, Adam.

"Yes. He's alive."

She put her hands on her hips. "And the two of you thought it was okay to fool all of us? To let anyone who gave a damn about you learn of your death? Tell me you've been on some kind of mission, some kind of top government, national security, can't do without you deal."

"I suppose that's questionable, depending on how you look at it, and what I'm going to say will confuse the fuck out of you before it makes any sense. Please know it was not a decision Adam and I made together. We didn't plot." In fact, in his case, all he did was die.

His head throbbed, and he reached to rub his forehead. Sarah took a step toward him. She smelled clean, of the soap she must have used in the shower, and it wafted over him. He'd forgotten how a warm, sensual woman could fill all the space in the room.

"You're in pain."

He waved his hand. "It's a constant. Comes and goes." Pressure in his ears drew his attention. They needed to finish their conversation and also delve into the deal with her and the Agency. First...why the fuck was the pilot changing altitude so quickly? "Buckle yourself in."

"What?" she asked him as she made her way to her seat. "Everything okay?"

"Probably." He was no longer a guy who assumed all was going to turn out all right. If the pilot had encountered some weather and needed to adjust the plane, he should have let them know over the speaker. There were rules when on a mission, and Zinc's heightened sense of self-preservation was making all his warning signals blast right then.

He turned and charged toward the front of the plane. If nothing was wrong, at least he was going to have a five-minute break from having to tell Sarah why she had thought he and Adam dead for three years. And he'd take a breath while he tried to forget how awesome her breasts appeared in his t-shirt. Fuck, how hard up was he?

SARAH DIDN'T REALLY KNOW MUCH about flying. Though she'd always considered herself a smart woman and found learning relatively straightforward, the science of aerodynamics confused her. Truthfully, she still couldn't make sense of exactly why airplanes did what they did. As long as they took off when they were supposed to and landed safely, the progression was good enough for her. She'd chosen to leave the mechanics of air travel a gap in her education and never thought to fill it.

Pilots adjusted altitudes all the time. Maybe Zach was trying to avoid her questions, although he didn't set off her coward alarms. She drummed her fingers on her lap. Adam was alive. Her eyes filled with tears, and she pushed them back. When she saw her big brother, she was going to kick his fucking ass.

And then hug him to death. It had been everything she could do to resist rushing at Zach and throwing her arms around him in utter relief when she'd come out of the shower and seen him sitting there, proving she hadn't invented the whole thing in her head. He lived, he was real.

She wiped the lone tear slipping along her cheek. Her ears popped, and she rubbed at them. Zach was right. They were descending, and quickly.

Sarah looked out the window, and sweat broke out on her palms. They were still over the ocean, which meant they absolutely should not be descending.

Zach had told her to buckle in and stay put, only if she was going to crash into the Gulf of Mexico, she'd rather not be taken by surprise. Quickly, she undid her seatbelt and abandoned her seat to head to the cockpit.

I am Sarah Steele and I am not sitting on my ass when something is really wrong.

The door to the cockpit was open, and a body was strewn on the floor. She stumbled, narrowly avoiding stepping on it, then clutched the wall. Sarah forced herself to breathe. The body lying face down wasn't Zach. The person had dark hair, not light, as Zach's looked. The blood on the floor wasn't his. She kept repeating those facts for a moment before she calmed.

Other than herself and Zach, the only other person on the plane had been the pilot. She'd not met him, because Zach had brought her quickly to the back of the plane so she could shower and change.

Shit. The pilot was dead. So who was flying the plane?

"Zach." Her voice croaked. She knew she'd berate herself for it later. Sarah always credited herself on being steady in crisis. Only flying a plane was beyond her capabilities.

"I thought I told you to strap in."

"I'm not good at following directions." She stepped over the body. Zach sat in the pilot's seat, and seeing him there eased some of the tension in her jaw. Was he qualified to fly? "Do you have a pilot's license?"

"It's got to be similar to riding a bike, right?" He turned and winked at her. "The pilot was going to crash us into the ocean. I got something about Red Wolf and loyalty before I broke his neck. All would be well, except he programmed the autopilot to bring us down, and I can't seem to make it stop. Our plane is Titanium's. You don't know him, so trust me when I say he's a very rich dude, and we're in a very expensive plane. It has after-market upgrades Uncle Sam doesn't know about yet."

He sounded so calm. They were crashing into the gulf,

and he'd said it with a smile. "So I should make my peace and be ready to meet my maker?"

"Not yet." He shook his head. "Sit in the co-pilot's chair. I've managed to slow the descent. Bought us some time. And if I can continue to fuck with the electronics here, I should be able to very shortly convince the autopilot to give me back control of my baby here. I'm good with tech, sweetheart. Trust me."

She sat because really, what other choice did she have? Zach hadn't affixed his seatbelt, and she leaned over to attach it for him before she did her own. He had to take care of himself. If he managed to save them and then went through the windshield because he didn't wear a seatbelt, she'd kill him.

"Don't worry. I've already died once in a fiery explosion. Can't happen to me twice, so we're both golden."

"What do you mean?" He'd died in a fiery explosion?

"Later." He reached over and handed her his cellphone. "I want you to take my phone. I need both hands to hold us steady for a minute while I mess with things. If you press button three, it's going to dial a man I want you to refer to as Chrome when he answers. After you identify yourself, you're going to let him know you're with Zinc—me. He's bound to be a little upset with me. Still, he's a very good guy, and he's not going to let our personal shit get in the way of what's happening here."

"What exactly am I to tell him is happening?" Because she wasn't a hundred percent certain, and she didn't want to get it wrong. Details were important.

"We're descending, against our will, from twenty-thousand feet. Hold my phone against the computer in front of you. My phone will take the readings from it and send it to Chrome's phone after you call him. Go on."

"All right."

She did as she had been told to, and seconds later, she did hear someone answer on the other end of the phone. A male voice, fortunately, since she didn't want to have to wait while he was found.

"Am I speaking with Chrome?"

A pause. "Who am I talking to?"

"My name is Sarah, I'm with Zinc, and um, we're likely about to have a plane crash."

"Not a crash, exactly," Zinc corrected.

"Where are you Sarah?" Whoever Chrome was, he really cut to the chase.

"Zinc said his phone will send the information to yours."

"Hold on. Checking." A brief pause. "Yes, got it. What does he need?"

Zach actually hadn't told her what to say. She looked at the man piloting the plane. His expression seemed unreadable. Once, when they were young, she would have claimed she knew him extremely well. How true was it anymore? She hadn't even known he was still alive. *Well...does it matter right now, Sarah?* "What do you need?"

"Put me on speaker. You're doing well, Sarah."

"Don't patronize me, Zach." She clicked the button to change the phone so Zach could hear Chrome and vice-versa.

"The pilot Titanium contracted for the mission turned out to be working for what's left of Red Wolf's people. Titanium clearly has some problems on his end. I've eliminated the pilot, and in about thirty seconds, I'm going to have enough control over the plane I should be able to make our landing a bail out situation rather than a full on crash."

Chrome cleared his throat. "I didn't know you were on a mission."

"Yeah, well, Titanium likes his secrets, and he keeps them close to his chest."

Sarah couldn't help but hear the bitterness in Zach's tone. The sneer forming on his mouth did nothing to lessen the effect.

"Can't get full control?"

"I think an engine is totally broken. Whoever the pilot was didn't plan on a return trip. What concerns me is he waited until we got on the plane to begin with. Anyway, we'll deal with that shit after we're on the ground. Basically, I need a retrieval."

"On it."

"Chrome?"

"Yes?"

"Thanks."

Sarah disconnected the phone. She happened to have a degree in psychology, among other things. Only she didn't need the years of study to tell her there was much not being said between those two men.

Either way, if the man called Chrome was sending help, she'd be grateful for it.

"What do you need from me?"

"See the button right there in the center console? Above the GPS? It says bail out. Do you see it?"

She did. She also noted how the plane continued to descend. It had been at twenty-thousand feet when she'd called Chrome. It read fifteen-thousand now. She took a deep breath. Zach had asked her a question.

"I do."

"When I tell you to, press it."

"That's it?" She'd take on a whole slew of activity and responsibility if it would take her mind off what was about to happen. Whatever he'd said to Chrome, it boiled down to one inescapable fact. He was going to crash the plane.

"Yep."

"I..." What did people talk about when they were so close to death? There had to be things to be said. "I had a real thing for you when we were younger. You had to know"

"I didn't, actually." Zach smiled. "You were not someone I could look at in a physical way, even if I did think you were hot." He shook his head. "Adam's sister? He'd have killed me where I stood."

She'd always wondered if he noticed her. "Hot?"

"Totally. Hot. Smart. Quiet. Sweet. And off limits."

For real? All the time she had spent in the dorm room of her boarding school, alone, and thinking about Zach's blue smiling eyes, and he had thought she was hot and off limits. Well, that was the way the cookie crumbled, she supposed. Or the plane crashed, as the case turned out to be.

Goosebumps broke out on her skin. They were really close to the water. She hadn't considered she would die when she was on her knees at the mercy of a madman. In a fiery plane crash? There was a very real chance.

And Zach looked cool as a cucumber. What the fuck was the matter with him?

"Hit the button, sweetheart."

With a shaking finger, she pushed the button and closed her eyes. If she was about to die in the Gulf of Mexico, she didn't want to watch it happen.

3

Zinc watched Sarah as she sat silently on the wing of the plane and stared at the clear blue sky. There wasn't a cloud to be seen, which should have made for beautiful flying weather, had someone not had it out for them.

Totally exposed to the elements, they ran the risk of severe sunburn if he didn't find her shelter from the beating rays.

Sarah didn't seem particularly concerned. Her face passive, her eyes skyward, she seemed almost serene.

"You don't rattle." He made it a statement, not a question. He'd seen her in not one, but two situations which would leave most people shaken to their core, and she didn't seem to have missed a beat.

"I do. Back there when you were crashing us into the water? Then was me freaking out."

"Could have fooled me." A slight aura formed over her head, and he internally groaned. His fucking head. The pain was about to go from mild throb in his temples to full on migraine. Zinc reached into his pocket. He had a lone pill left on him, the rest were buried somewhere in the disaster inside of the plane. No matter, he didn't want to take any medication, which might make him loopy until whatever rescue Chrome sent arrived.

He stared at his phone. When they'd not died, he'd sent Chrome a text informing him they were floating in the sea. His former friend and commander's only response had come a minute later.

She's Sarah Steele?

Yeah, he must have finally been talking to Titanium. None of the stuff going on at the Metal compound was Zinc's problem. Keeping the brunette beauty alive until he could place her under cover fell to him.

"That's the idea," Sarah finally responded. "You can't tell what I'm feeling or thinking unless I want you to. It's why I'm good at my job. Or I was, until I got taken."

"Sweetheart, as a person who has practically earned an advanced degree on the subject over the last three years, you can trust me when I say your situation screams betrayal in every way I look at it."

She held his gaze when she spoke, "Zach, it's time for you to start explaining. Start with the most logical beginning of your story and move from there. You're alive, Adam's alive. I want to know how, and why it was kept from me."

"Okay." He nodded. "We got sent to Russia to try to stop a uranium and plutonium exchange with the Iranians. The whole mission stunk from the very beginning. Steele wasn't supposed to be there, and key members of his team were missing. I was there, with Chrome. And a third team led by a man we'll call Titanium."

"And you're Zinc. I understand it. Metal. Adam would logically be Steele."

For more reasons than he would share with her. "I'd

gotten engaged, and I actually asked Adam if he'd be my best man."

"I met Ally at your funeral. Your sisters introduced me."

He waited for her to comment more. Didn't women usually follow declarative statements with things such as 'I liked her so much' or 'she had beautiful hair'? He waited, and when nothing came, he continued.

"Things went really badly. We had bad intelligence, and for a long time, our leaders thought it was from a particular traitorous CIA agent, except we know better about what happened." Exactly who the person was didn't fall to him to explain. Adam could tell her what he wanted her to know about his girl when they reconnected. "Anyway, things went to hell fast. We were set up. I have some memory loss of the actual explosion that got me. I remember Adam screaming. I tried to move out of the way. Then I knew I was dying."

He hadn't spoken about his death aloud in a very long time, and the migraine increased. Yet, Sarah's steady dark gaze held his, and somehow, his mouth formed the words.

"We had a big goodbye moment. Very...final. I think I was brave. I only know what happened after because I've been told. I didn't actually witness any of it myself."

She reached out and took his hand. Her skin was soft in his. She was warm and alive, which reminded him he was as well. "I'm sure you were brave, Zach. It would be hard to imagine you being anything else after you rescued me from David and got the plane down safely."

"The island was no big deal, and the plane landed safely mostly because of the equipment and the money put in, which would make it mostly indestructible."

"Don't push away your role. I didn't give you the compliment to hear you become sheepish. False modesty doesn't become you. And I'm not easily distracted. Please, go on. The rest you didn't see firsthand."

"Right." He nodded. Yes, she wanted him to finish. If she kept holding his hand the way she was, he'd tell her whatever she wanted to know. God, he was really pathetic. "Apparently, Titanium had a bad feeling about the whole thing from the start. He paid for a team to be ready to pull his men out if things went to hell. Only, he wasn't specific with who was to be saved. To be fair, my team wasn't supposed to be there originally. And his guys grabbed me and a couple of others who shouldn't have been taken, because we weren't Titanium's team. I woke three months later in the hospital."

How much to confess? The hell of the headaches? When he'd not been able to find words correctly, saying banana when he'd meant television remote. Learning to walk again. Waiting for someone to tell him the whole fucking thing was a terrible nightmare.

"Keep going. Was Adam killed too?"

He scratched his head. "No, he and the others were sent away, their deaths faked, and they were given new lives by Uncle Sam. In the meantime, Titanium and his people went about figuring out who the traitors were. When I was healed enough, I was assigned a position as a member of his Ghost team. At first, we investigated the others, Adam, Chrome, anyone who might have been the reason it all went to hell. When they were cleared, we brought them in, although we hid our faces from them under masks. They called us the Ghosts. They got to have new lives, go after Red Wolf, make right the wrongs. We watched them, kept them in line."

"Hold on." She let go of his hand. "You're telling me I thought you were both dead, and so did everyone you guys loved. Adam was really running around somewhere for a while, having another life, until he rejoined with Titanium. And yet still, for all that time, he thought you were dead, and you let him think so? How fucked is that? It's bad enough the whole world thought you two were rotting in the ground. You couldn't have at least let him know he hadn't lost his best friend?"

"We were strongly prohibited from making contact. Although I did make an effort to try to stick out, to try to make him look and see me. It didn't work."

She waited a beat, then said, "And the person who strongly stopped you from making contact for what, three years, was the Titanium fellow?"

He could almost see her brain working. She tapped her fingers on her knee and pursed her lips. "That's right."

"The same dude whose plane you crashed."

"Bailed out."

"Whatever." She sighed loudly. "Sure you didn't crash it to find a little revenge?"

He snorted. She was funny. The very idea. "I wish I'd thought of it."

"I bet. Anyway, it must have been quite a reunion for you and Adam. Lots of manly not crying, and 'I missed you, my brother' going on?"

The light pounded on his head, as if someone took a baseball bat and whacked him over and over again. Yep, the full-on migraine had arrived. "I actually beat him pretty hard. Broke his nose. The bone right under his eye. He had to have surgery."

She didn't speak for a moment, and when he could manage to look—the sun was really a wicked weapon—it was to find her staring at him with a raised eyebrow. "Why did you do that?"

"Because he left my body there for Titanium's people to

do whatever they did to me. Because he broke his promise to never leave me behind. Forgetting that a Marine never leaves another Marine fallen to the enemies, we had an understanding which went beyond those rules. He was family to me. And he left my not-so-dead corpse to be taken. And then for three years, I had to watch him live his life, move on, fall in love, and make things work, while I stared at him from behind my mask. And he never looked. Never got it. Never...The whole world moved on, Sarah, and I had to watch it all."

He let his voice trail off. No one understood. Even his fellow Ghosts felt different about their situations. Zinc closed his eyes. The migraine was going to win.

A soft hand touched his forehead, and he winced, although he liked the human contact. He had so little of it. "You're in pain."

"Almost all the time. Headaches. I'm lucky. Some of the others are a lot worse."

She kissed the side of his cheek, and for a second, he forgot about the mind splitting pain bearing on him as if his brain wanted to explode from the inside out. He opened his eyes to squint at her.

"Listen, I get what you're not saying. It blows my mind to hear you say Adam fell in love. He was always so against the idea. And you had Ally. She thought you died, and although I only know her very remotely through mutual friends on Facebook, she's moved on. Fast."

Yeah, she had, and it burned. He'd really believed her to be the love of his life, had asked her to marry him. If she had died, it wouldn't have been months before he found someone else. Years, maybe, if ever.

Sarah kept speaking, "What you went through, it blows. Only, I'll always be grateful Titanium's people got it wrong and saved you, because you're here with me. Living and breathing. I got to say things to you I'd never have if you were really in the ground, Zach. I mean, you would have lived your whole life and never known how I crushed on you when you were a teenager. What a sheer shame your not knowing would have been."

He loved the slight laughter to her edge. "Actually, your teenager fixation kind of made my day."

"Ah, above saving us from bad guys and crashing the plane?"

"Bailed out."

She shook her head. "Whatever. You're alive, Zach. I'm so fucking happy about it."

Those were the most beautiful words he'd heard in a long time. Not a single person had cared he was alive. He'd woken from a coma and been a mistake Titanium had to deal with. His life had moved on without him. With the exception of his teammate, Brad, he'd not had a person he trusted with him. The people he'd given his life for were under suspicion. Every day had been a solitary struggle.

Sarah cared he was alive.

There had to be something to say, only he'd gotten so far out of practice in talking about himself. "When I was in the coma, for three months, I dreamed."

She brushed his hair off his forehead. "About what?"

"The summers we spent at the lake. One time after Adam and I had gotten back from hunting with the dads, we were sitting at the edge of the dock, and you ran over. You must have been..." He tried to recall exactly how old Sarah was then. She was so captured in his memory from then, from his dreams of the lake when he'd barely been alive, it was hard to put exact details to the images which had sustained him in sleep.

"Fourteen." She nodded. "I remember it well. Adam didn't tell me to shove off and leave you two alone. I sat next to you, and we all had our feet hanging off the dock."

"Dogs barking in the distance with an eagle circling above our heads."

"I'd forgotten about the eagle. I think I was more focused on how close I got to sit to you, and whether or not you thought I looked pretty in my bathing suit."

He tweaked her chin. "I wasn't allowed to. Except I did."

Her voice was soft. "Awesome. I'm glad we kept you company when you slept."

"Or maybe it was my own version of heaven."

The sound of a helicopter caught his attention and brought with it his headache, which rushed back on him. The 'copter was unmarked, yet he recognized it as one of Titanium's birds.

"It's a friendly." He wobbled to his feet. "Ours."

"Good. We're really not prepared to defend ourselves from anything else."

She made a valid point. He'd pulled off a couple of impressive near misses in the last twenty-four hours. Three might be pushing his luck.

A voice came over a loudspeaker directed right at them, "Look at what you did to Titanium's plane."

Brad—also known as Tungsten—called to them, and Zach shook his head. "Can never trust me with the expensive machines."

Sarah squeezed his hand. Even with the aura radiating around her, thanks to his brain injury, she looked solid, real. His. He gasped at the thought as it hit him. The world seemed to shift around his feet. Sarah Steele was all grown. Beautiful, capable, and strong in a way most people would never be. The day he died, rules had stopped applying to anything.

So why couldn't she be his?

A ladder lowered from the hovering machine above their heads.

"Seriously?" Brad called again. "Titanium is going to kill you. You crashed one of two airplanes in his collection which can't be seen on radar. He's going to have to commission another."

"Wasn't me who set it to crash." No, the betraying ass Titanium had sent with him for the mission had been responsible.

"Man, he's gonna be pissed." Brad sounded almost gleeful about it. Then again, the man had his own issues with Titanium. "Wouldn't want to trade places with you this time, brother."

Bring it on.

SARAH WATCHED ZACH. He struggled against what had to be a nasty headache, blinking rapidly and rubbing the space between his eyes every few seconds before once again, shifting in his seat. They'd been airborne for a few minutes when Brad had passed a note from Chrome back to him. For the sake of transparency, he'd explained, he'd shown it to her.

Don't bring her back here yet. Not sure what's happening. Titanium looking into the contractors. I'm looking into other things. Steele blew a gasket when he found out he wasn't informed. Likely Agency betrayal, again. Throw your phone out the window. Brad knows the drill. He's going to leave you somewhere and lose you.

Find a way to contact me every two days.

Zach had immediately thrown his phone out the window, and presumably when Brad dropped them off, they'd be on their own. Agency betrayal. Zach had told her she'd been betrayed, and it seemed his people thought the same thing.

He'd died and come back. Her brother was alive and in love. It was hard to wrap her head around any of it. Only, Zach sat next to her very much alive and twitching in agony.

"Do you have any medication you can take?" Her college roommate had migraines. Sarah used to whisper, and it had been too loud. Still, she had to make herself heard over the helicopter noise.

"The only pill I have left makes me kind of loopy. Sometimes, tired."

"Either of those options would be better than you currently are. No offense, you're not good to me as you are. Take the pill, pass out if you need to. I've got you for a while. I can handle the next couple of hours if you're so out of it you can't be consulted."

His blood shot eyes bore into her soul. "I don't know."

"You know you can trust me." And she had to believe he did, because she had made a decision about her future when she hadn't died in a plane crash, and it had involved Zach. He needed her, and she wanted him to. The all but neglected boy had grown into a tough, thoughtful man. One version of him had died in Russia. Whomever he'd become since, they would discover together. Maybe while she sucked on his cock and let him go down on her at the same time.

Or maybe they'd save the discovering and get each other off simply for fun.

"Take the pill, Zach."

He reached into his pocket and pulled out a small pill case. "Is it bad I wish I had some whisky to wash it down with?"

"I understand the sentiment, only in your case, yes, it's bad."

His father had destroyed his liver from gin. Zach's father had been a bitter drunk, who had gone in and out of rehab his whole life. Her own father had finally cut ties with him after Adam and Zach died. Or not died, as the case turned out to be. People had to want to be better, and she had enormous respect for people who got sober and worked to stay on track the best they could, even if they relapsed. Only, Zach's dad was nasty, and the booze was the excuse, not the problem. He'd barely seemed to care when the boys were gone. He ignored his daughters, who in turn, pretended he didn't exist—total dysfunction from top to bottom.

Although she had preferred the old man drunk when he'd been around than the version he became when he spent short periods sober. There had been a time, when Adam had almost died being a jackass in a car race, and Zach had insisted it was his fault to spare her brother more punishment. His lying hadn't fooled her, she'd seen right through it. He'd made Adam drive in an imbecilic way, he'd claimed. As if anyone made Adam do anything Adam didn't want to do. Zach had taken the beating from hell for his saving Adam. And he'd never said a word. She doubted her then hospitalized brother had even known. But she had.

And being twelve at the time, she had no idea what to say or do.

Zach nodded and took a sip of water from the bottle next to him. The helicopter had been stocked to be comfortable and could apparently go silent, if Brad felt it necessary to hide their approach. She hoped they weren't about to face the kind of trouble which warranted his making a go silent decision.

She took another look at Zach when he'd put down the water. "No more drinking for you, if you have been. Not for a while."

He silently affirmed her statement again and leaned back against the window. "Shit."

"Come here." She patted her lap. "I can rub your temples. It will help."

She expected him to argue. Tough guys didn't care to appear needy. Zach surprised her when he gave in without an argument. Or maybe it spoke to his level of pain.

His head rested on her lap, and she immediately felt the sheer warmth she always associated with him. He could rival the sun. She ran her hand through his hair before she let her fingers rub in a circle on his temple. "What have you been doing besides the pills? Acupuncture? Massage? Any dental treatments? Vitamins? Herbal supplements?" He'd had an injury cause the migraines, which meant changing his diet would likely not offer much relief. Or maybe it would...

He said something she couldn't understand before he shook his head. All right, he didn't want to talk, and she understood perfectly. They'd be silent, and she would see if she could give him some pressure point relief for his discomfort.

Minutes later, he was out cold in her lap. She didn't know how she immediately knew the difference between Zach lying with his eyes closed and Zach fully asleep, except she noticed the second it happened. He didn't look any less pained in his sleep, yet his breathing evened out.

When he'd been nearly dead, he had dreamed of her and Adam. The thought softened her soul. Sarah had very few emotional triggers anymore. Zach was clearly still someone with the power to throw her off her game. Who was she kidding? He'd always been nothing more than a fantasy. His coma dreams had more to do with his brother-hood with Adam than anything relating to her. Yet, he'd had thousands of dreams he could have recreated with her brother and had chosen instead to include her.

"Hey," she called into the headset, which would grab Brad's attention.

"Need something?" he answered.

"You're supposed to be leaving us somewhere and losing us."

"Correct," Brad answered.

"Were you given any specific instructions about where, or is the destination decided by us?"

"I've been waiting for Zinc to let me know."

She looked at his out cold form. It was going to be a bit until Zach was giving orders to anyone, and she didn't want to be in the helicopter endlessly.

"How about Miami?"

"The place come from you or from him?"

She shrugged. Lying was always an option. She couldn't see his face, although his voice sounded curious, as if he asked for no other reason than his wanting to know the answer without an ulterior motive. Of course, tones could be deceptive, and if Zach's tale of the last three years proved anything, she was in the presence of very powerful people who could compel someone as tough as Zinc to do what they wanted.

Could hide the truth from Adam. Steele.

Zach said Brad was the other man caught in the web when Titanium had taken control of their lives. Tungsten.

And Chrome had sent him specifically to come retrieve them.

She needed to keep track of all the players so she could manage the conspiracy in her mind. Even her brother—who she had misled for years, and who had in turn, been lying to her—played a role.

Other than Zach and Adam, strangers were trying to save her life when her own Agency seemingly left her to die.

"Do you have a hard time taking orders from a woman? Will you only take us to Miami if I tell you Zach, who is out cold at the moment, told me to ask you?"

Silence met her query before a loud burst of masculine laughter caught her by surprise. She had no idea what he found so fucking funny. "Miami it is. Since Zinc showed you his orders, you know I'm to lose you there. I'll get you guys into a car, then I'm going to go find something to eat. When I come back, you'll be gone. I'd suggest out of Miami by tomorrow morning, at the latest. Keep moving until you're told otherwise."

"I have a little experience with how to survive. All recent captivity to the contrary."

"Captivity happens. Make sure Zinc takes good care of you. He's been on edge a lot."

She disconnected the conversation button. For the present, she would be seeing to Zach, and she knew herself well enough to understand doing so would be good for her too. She'd always been good at seeing others got what they needed.

Sarah stroked her hands through his hair, and his face relaxed a bit. He liked her touching him. Did he see her as a sister? He'd admitted he'd thought she was hot when he shouldn't. Did his confession mean anything? Probably not. Was she still hot to him?

His fiancée, Ally, who Sarah would admit at least to herself she hated on sight at the funeral, was her complete opposite. If Ally was Zach's type, he wasn't going to want to be with Sarah. She could pretend, when need be for the job, to be an Ally-type. Needy. Dependent. Fickle. No, the last word was unfair. How did she know the depth of Ally's feelings for Zach? Maybe she had settled for the new husband in a grief-ridden move to feel better.

Sarah had never had Zach as her own, had hardly seen him, thanks to her involvement with the Agency in the years before his 'death.' Yet in the three years since he and her brother had died, she hadn't stopped seeking answers. If he had been hers, there wouldn't have been a wedding six months later.

Could the reborn Zach prefer her type instead?

4

Zach sat on the dock, his feet swinging over. He knew he was asleep, having not been to this particular lake since he was eighteen years old. If he looked to his left, he'd see Adam, and to his right, in a moment, Sarah would join them, her feet joining his in the dangle over the dock.

Only Adam's feet were not dangling where they belonged. He quickly looked right, and Sarah leaned back on her elbows, her feet not pushed out in front of her, instead, tucked beneath her. She wasn't fourteen, she appeared older, beautiful not in the way of a teenager, instead, the gorgeous woman she had become.

"What's with the strange look on your face?"

His cock jumped to life, hard and straining in his pants as if she had been stroking him instead of simply speaking to him. "I'm dreaming. And my scene is different than I'm used to it."

Sarah reached out and brushed his hair off his forehead, as she had done when he'd rested his head on her lap in the helicopter.

The helicopter...

"Does it matter? If you're dreaming, have a good go at it. Pretty place. I'm hot as hell, obviously." She spoke with a twinkle in her eye. "Go wherever the dream takes you."

A blaring horn sounded, and it seemed so out of place. Where would a horn be coming from at the lake?

"What if the dream takes me to some place where you are on top of me with your legs spread, moving up and down on top of my erection, and making me come?"

"As I said, sometimes the dream needs to go where it goes."

Her words sounded good to him. He moved forward and...

Zach.

"Did you say something?" He ran his finger on the gentle slope of her nose. Sarah had such dainty features. Someone who could do her justice should paint her. Too bad he didn't possess an ounce of artistic ability.

"No." She smiled at him. "Well, I mean, you heard what I said."

Zach. I need you to wake.

Oh, right. He was asleep. Damn it. Of course, he'd never been alone with Sarah on a dock, and she had never invited him to put his hands on her. Although, she'd admitted she once crushed on him.

His eyes flew open on the thought. Disoriented, he braced himself for the blurry haze which always came on after a bad headache.

"You're okay." Sarah's soft hand stroked the side of his face. "I'm sorry I had to wake you at all."

"No. It's. Fine." His brain needed to cooperate, and it needed to immediately. Sometimes when he first awakened, it took him a while to find words, as it had been when he first came out of the coma. Although all of his problems were considered normal for his healing brain—the words a doctor used—he hated it and didn't want Sarah seeing him so laid out.

He cut his gaze away, pretending to look at his surroundings instead of giving his mind time to catch up with his alert state. They were in a car, a sedan by the size of it. Leather interior. Power steering. Four wheel drive. When he'd conked out, pathetically on her lap, they'd been in the helicopter with Brad piloting. How had they gotten into the car?

She watched him quietly for a bit before she spoke again, "Miami. We're at a Motel Six. I've rented us a room. Paid in the cash Brad gave us before he took off. He helped me maneuver you into the car. You kind of roused then, although I don't think you really woke."

Great. There was nothing he hated more than his brothers seeing him fall apart. Although he doubted Tungsten would ever tell a soul. Brad had seen him a lot worse, when he had first awoken in the hospital, when he hadn't been able to speak at all.

"Miami. Good choice." Easy to be lost in a huge city, and since he was coherent again, he'd take over keeping her safe.

"That's why I told Brad to leave us here." She winked at him. "I would have let you sleep some more, only I can't carry you inside the hotel room by myself."

"Yeah, no, you trying would be humiliating." He extended his hand. "Do you have the telephone to the room? I'll go check it out." She furrowed her brow, and he realized he misspoke. Zach clenched his jaw. Exactly how much embarrassment with Sarah was he going to have to endure? "Do you know what I meant, although I said the wrong thing? Probably if I try to self-correct over the next few minutes, I will continue to misspeak. So, I'm hoping you know what I..."

As an answer, she placed the key card in his outstretched hand. "Don't worry, I speak Zach."

He laughed at her response, the reaction catching him by surprise. "Then you'd be the only one. I'm not sure I speak me anymore."

Zinc exited the car. Maybe he couldn't always make himself understood—stupid brain—yet he could still check out a hotel room to make sure it was safe. Sarah was a very capable woman, and Zinc had known a lot of extremely tough ladies in his day, and if she'd wanted to argue with his protection, she could. The fact she hadn't fought him on that point, satisfied his need to protect.

The number of the room was on the key. The hotel looked old and in need of either a major renovation or a tear down. She'd been right to pick it. If ever there was a location where there wouldn't be video cameras, it was the motel she'd chosen.

He pushed the key in the slot and entered. The room smelled like it had been cleaned. Someone had at least sprayed air freshener, and he knew—unfortunately from experience—the air freshening might have been the extent of the sanitization. Zach did a quick look through. It seemed safe enough. He had no equipment to search for bugs, so his walk through would have to be good enough.

He crossed the room to the door and opened it before waving Sarah in. A few seconds later, she joined him. Her presence brought home a major factor he missed in his perusal. There was only a single bed in the room.

His mouth went dry.

Maybe they didn't have double beds in the hotel...

"How is your head?" She tapped her bag before pulling

out three medicine bottles. "I temporarily stole a phone off a man in the gas station and Googled migraine meds. Then I stole these three from a pharmacy. I left money they'll find, although I suppose it's really a moot point. No prescription, equals theft." She shrugged.

"You stole from a pharmacy? In my pajamas?" He took the vials from her hand. "How did you manage? And you temporarily stole a phone?"

"I gave it back. The dude never knew it was gone. I'm a CIA operative. I know I was held captive, and I mostly chase paper. It doesn't mean I don't have some skills. Maybe I have a trustworthy face? Maybe the guy liked the Yankees?"

Her answer did nothing to quiet his utter astonishment that she had stolen him medicine after Googling them from a stolen—sorry, borrowed—phone. He stared at her, hoping he didn't look like an idiot as she moved further into the room. Her hips swayed when she moved. Why hadn't he noticed before? Well, his head had been throbbing, and they'd been in deep trouble. Or maybe the movement was simply more pronounced.

"What do you think? It'll do, right? I didn't go in without you. I figured a small functional room was what I should expect."

He wanted to ask her about the bed, and instead, looked at his stolen prescriptions. One of them was right, the other two he had used and not found effective.

"You should take it round the clock. Stay ahead of the pain. It's really an autoimmune thing. Not letting the body find the pain again."

"Do you have a medical degree I don't remember?" He winked at her. The last thing Zach wanted was for her to think of him as some kind of patient who needed to be pitied.

She raised a dark eyebrow and walked toward him with those hips again. His cock hardened. "I care about you, so I'm going to level with you."

"Hold on." He held out his hand. There were things to say before she told him off. "You were held captive for a month by a sicko. Then you had to rescue your rescuer. I'm so sorry. It's inexcusable."

She blinked rapidly, and it took at least ten seconds for her to respond. "Are you out of your mind?"

"Always." She'd seen him in the car. Hell, she'd practically had to carry him.

"Zach. You rescued me from a psycho. You shot a bunch of people to do it. Killed a pilot who wanted to kill us. Managed to safely crash—if you say bail out, I'll kick you in the shin—the plane. Then you got a migraine headache, because you are three years removed from a head injury caused in an explosion, which killed you temporarily. I think I can live with what little role I have played in our adventure." She pointed her finger at him and poked it right into his shoulder. The movement actually hurt, and he took a step back. "Enough with the crap. Are you hungry?"

The abrupt change in topic threw him off his game. "I could eat."

"Great. Any residual headache? I'm asking because I want to know if we need to find somewhere quiet or bring take out here."

"I've always got a bit of a throb going on. I can manage in crowds pretty well if I don't let myself think about it."

"Okay. Then I know the place. It's quiet, and we'll blend in. I have some extra clothes for us in the car."

She did? What else had she been doing when he'd been unconscious? "Did you buy them or steal them?"

"A little of both. I don't want to use all our money today.

Oh, and I know you want to talk about what happened before I got taken. We'll do so at dinner." She nodded as if she liked the idea. "Another thing."

He crossed his arms over his chest. Had Sarah always been so bossy? And why did he find it so fucking hot?

She got and held his eye contact steadily. He had no interest in ever looking away. She was so...pretty. "I know I'm not your type."

What? "Come again?"

"I am not the type of girl you prefer."

"Ah." He rubbed his forehead. His head didn't hurt, the movement gave him something to do so he could catch his breath. Sarah Steele was every guy's type. "I don't think I have a type. If I recall correctly, my former dating life involved all kinds of women. Brunettes," although none of them had so many different shades in their hair as she did, "blondes, redheads, across the gambit for race and religion too. I enjoy women. Period."

"You misunderstand me. I don't mean physically." She smiled then. "I have killer legs, of course you'd want me." As if she wanted to show them off, she held her left out in front of her for a second. His cock jumped in his pants. Shit, she was so fucking hot.

Sarah kept talking. "I mean you go after girls who are needy. I'm not traditionally that girl. Other than being caught by Walter David, I can basically manage myself. For that matter, I can manage you too. I'm loyal as hell. I don't fall apart easily. I can understand you, Zach, in a time when I would bet a wimpy partner wouldn't. Something for you to ponder over dinner. Maybe you'd want to make the next few days more than running for our lives. I can make you feel good. We can attend to each other. Come on. You can help me pull the clothes out of the trunk."

His feet were glued to the ground. Sarah had propositioned him, and it hadn't been at all as he'd imagined it. Ever. His heart spun, and sweat broke out on the back of his neck. Shit. She was really, so completely hot.

"Ah. Okay. Right. Coming."

He chased her to the stairs. Would she never stop surprising him?

~

SARAH LOVED the sound of a steel drum band. She expected a different kind of music, she usually loved listening to Salsa when she was in Miami. The seafood restaurant they had fallen into had a small group of musicians in the corner, and she let the music drift over her while she sipped her red wine. Zach had ordered water, which he causally sipped while he eyed her.

They'd both finished their raw gulf oysters quickly and were waiting on the crab claws for their next course. For his part, Zach hadn't uttered a word since they'd sat.

"Have you slept since your abduction?"

She took a deep breath. Somehow, her lack of sleep would be his fault. Zach seemed to take responsibility for things when they didn't belong to him. Fortunately for him, she knew the feeling.

"No." She fingered the wine glass. "I think tonight will help. So will the music." And maybe sex, if she could talk him into it. "Don't start bemoaning my alert state. It's called adrenaline. I wouldn't have slept, even if you hadn't gotten a migraine."

A muscle ticked in his jaw. "Let's talk about how you got grabbed."

She'd rather talk about the sex idea. Although, she supposed his line of thinking made better sense.

My name is Sarah Steele and I am apparently obsessed with having sex with my brother's best friend. I'm in a 1980s romantic comedy movie complete with the music playing in the background.

"After you and Adam died, and by the way, it's totally strange to be discussing your death with, well, you."

Zach leaned forward. "Trust me. I get the weird."

"After you guys died, and we couldn't retrieve any information from Uncle Sam, I thought I'd be able to gather some information the other families couldn't. What good is security clearance if you can't use it to find out why your world is suddenly emptier?"

Zach furrowed his brow, yet didn't speak. He was so handsome backlit by the setting sun visible through the windows. In another, fairer world, she could simply sit and watch him for a while, pretend she was a girl he'd asked out. One of Zach's women, as Adam had once called them. Or as Ally—the lady he'd finally chosen—must have done.

She and Zach were old friends, and maybe they'd be lovers, if she could pull his head off the job for a few hours. She'd never, however, be the girl he simply chose.

And when she wasn't suddenly feeling melancholy from coming off an ordeal, she wouldn't care about not being the type of woman who sat admiring sunsets with hot men.

Sarah forced herself to concentrate. "The most I could find, and it took a lot of digging, were two words, Operation Phoenix. Afterwards, it all dropped dead, nothing. No trail to follow."

He nodded before he took a sip of his water. "I bet."

"I basically gave up for a while. Work was busy." She pulled at her sleeve, which itched her, or maybe her whole body found their conversation uncomfortable. "And I was grieving you guys. There were things to do, my parents did not take the death well. Neither did I, only helping them fixed me a bit. A few months ago, I went ahead and asked my handler if he could help. I didn't expect much. A tiny drop of understanding maybe. He said he would. Then, I got taken. Four guys. Hoods, drugs. I kicked a little ass, although clearly not enough."

Zach drummed his fingers on the table. "Fuck, you were so set up. Your handler. Who is he? Where is he?"

"He lived in New York City. When I wanted to see him, we had a signal." Like out of a movie. She'd drop a red grocery bag into a particular garbage can, and the next morning, he'd be on a bench waiting. "His name is Thomas. We kept it first name, although he clearly knew more about me."

"We're going to New York tomorrow. If I have to, I'll stick a gun to his head and find some answers."

She figured as much. Who else could have set her up, except Thomas? Funny, he'd always looked so unassuming. Small, non-descript, glasses. Her own job was always done to perfection, he'd never had to deal with her other than an occasional meeting, and then—boom—sex slave kidnapping. She shook her head.

I'm Sarah Steele. I am not lost to what happened to me. I'm in Miami, drinking red wine, listening to soft music, and wanting to give Zach a blowjob. Life is much better.

"Right."

"Sarah." Zach reached across the table. "Your color is changing. Despite the food, you're getting paler by the moment. I asked you about sleep. You've been through hell. We're in a great restaurant and sitting here, watching the light play on your hair? It's the best thing to happen to me in three years. I think, however, it's too soon for you. My suggestion is we take the food to go and eat in the motel room, so you can sleep."

"Hmm." He made sense, and she hated how true his words were. "I don't fall apart. I'm Sarah Steele. I keep it together when the rest of the world loses their collective minds. I didn't cry once on the island. I'm not going to here."

He motioned for the waiter, and when the man came over, he asked for the check. Was Zach really not going to say anything about her statement? Suddenly, the music wasn't so romantic, and the wine tasted bitter. She felt as though her skin might have become too tight on her body.

After throwing a few bills on the table, he stood and walked to the waiter. Zach's movements were always so precise. Nothing about how his body related to gravity had changed since the explosion. And how obsessed did it make her she knew such a detail about him?

Dinner bagged and retrieved, he returned and extended his free hand. "Come."

She stood, wrapping her fingers in his. "I only fall apart when I'm alone."

"Is the world going to end if you do it in front of someone else? You forget I've already seen you cry."

They walked hand in hand out of the restaurant, and she paused on the sidewalk as she digested his words. "When? You've never seen me cry."

"I think you were sixteen. Adam and I were home on leave. You had a date who stood you up. I remember it because after you went to bed, Adam and I went to the kid's house, dragged his stoned ass out, and beat the shit out of him. Twice." His mouth quirked as he remembered.

"You two beat him up?" Was it possible for the world to actually spin off its axis?

"Twice." He nodded. "Come on."

How was it possible she didn't know the roughing up happened? "I actually had sex with him years later in New York. He tried to be an actor. And I have no memory of you being there when I was crying. All these years, I thought I hid my tears."

"Hey, don't tell me about your sex life. I absolutely don't want to know. And I want to beat him again. If it makes me a Neanderthal, so fucking be it. The ass should never have gotten to touch you after hurting you. As for the tears, I may have caught you doing it for only a second without you knowing when you walked from your bedroom to the kitchen."

"Sneaky, I see. What can I say? I have a forgiving nature. Think of it as a revenge fuck. I walked away before he'd even woken."

Zach snorted and opened the car door. "Come on. I'm driving."

They rode to the motel in silence, and if she was a sulker, she'd probably give in to the urge. Any chance she'd had to see Zach between the sheets had flown out the window in the restaurant. The look in his eye? The way he had taken back control from her? Zach wasn't going to see her as anything other than a victim he had to protect.

After they arrived at the hotel, he checked the room once more before he let her inside. It was a sweet trait, although not necessary. With the gun tucked neatly in the back of her pants, she could easily get rid of anyone in the room as she did Walter David.

Had it only been the day before when she'd shot him?

"At least it makes sense why the guy you beat kept asking me if any of my family was around during the brief day we were together," she spoke to fill the silence.

"Seriously. No more about him. Unless you want me to Google him and reacquaint him with my fist."

He motioned for her to enter first. The buzz of the air conditioner in the window filled the room with a loud white noise, which would either keep her awake all night or help her sleep. She'd requested a king bed, hoping they'd be sharing it. Only since he'd already noted the beginning of her meltdown, she doubted he'd be interested.

"Go shower. Ten minutes at least. More would be better."

Had Zach given her an order? "Do I smell?"

"It'll relax you. I have something to do, and then I'll be back. I won't be far, and I'll be within range to eye the room." He pointed his finger. "Don't argue."

Well, okay. She walked toward the bathroom and heard him click the door shut. Zach had ordered her to the shower, and though he'd told her not to argue, she hadn't intended to in the first place. What was her compliance about?

She wasn't submissive, or at least she'd never been before. The few times she played at her friend's private dungeon in New York City, she'd practiced the dominant role. She had much to learn before she would ever call herself a master.

Except she had a feeling if Zach wanted her to do almost anything, she would, and really because she wanted to make him happy, see his bright blue eyes gleaming with approval and kindness when he gazed at her.

Those thoughts occupied her when she got in the shower and bathed herself under the hot stream.

She'd managed to work in a good lather when the bathroom door opened, and she jumped backwards, nearly stumbling in the shower when she did. A strong hand reached out and steadied her. "Easy there. It's only me. My fault. I should have knocked. I did tell you I would be eyeing the room. No one was getting in here."

"Did you need something?" She wiped the water out of her eyes. He'd busted in the bathroom. Had something happened?

"Desperately." He pulled off his shirt and threw it behind him. "Unless you've changed your mind. You can, you know. You can tell me tonight's all too much, and you want me to leave you alone.

Zach was built akin to some kind of Greek God. His abs were well defined and strong, his arms shaped as though he worked out regularly. When he'd been young, he'd been long and lean. The Marines made him stronger. He was pure muscle.

Her mouth went dry. He'd come in the bathroom because he wanted her. Desperately.

"I..." She wasn't sure what to say. Instead, she launched herself at him, and he caught her in his strong embrace. She was soaked, and he was half dressed. Whatever, it all worked for her.

His mouth met hers, and he kissed her, hard. His lips were unrelenting. He didn't ease her in, wasn't gentle.

Zachery's embrace was a claiming—the exact claim she'd been waiting for her whole life. Even if tomorrow she pretended she hadn't been, if she was disconnected, acted as if tonight meant less than it did, she knew it right then. She was Zach's girl. He'd always had her heart.

5

Zach should leave Sarah alone. She'd been through hell. The last thing she needed was him taking her up on an offer she made when she couldn't be expected to make sane decisions. And yet...

She'd told him she wanted him for a long time. He'd be lying if he pretended her words didn't make him feel as if he could strut for the rest of his life or never come off from the cloud her words had put him on.

The shower beat on their heads, and his cock strained against his zipper in his rapidly soaking pants.

"Hold on." The wetter they got, the worse it would be to remove them. He backed up a step, nearly tripping out of the shower when he did. *Smooth, Zach, smooth.*

"One of us is going to topple over." She laughed, covering her mouth with her hand.

"Won't be you." He finally got the rest of his pants off and discarded them to the side of the room. "I'd never let you fall, sweetheart."

She pulled him closer, and since he had his clothes off,

he could appreciate the beauty of being in the shower with such a hot woman and the warm water on his back.

He trailed kisses down her cheek toward her neck. Sarah smelled of cherries, and he wanted to bite her. When his teeth grazed her pulse point, he gave in to the urge. She sighed, and he forced himself to stay gentle.

"Harder," she whispered. "Sometimes I like the pain."

So his lady had some masochistic tendencies? Damn, it made him harder.

"Sending you in here was an elaborate plan to make you wet and warm. Didn't you catch on? I got some condoms from the front of the motel."

"Really?" Her eyes were huge. "I didn't guess. My radar is really off. I'm not usually fooled. I thought you weren't interested."

Zach shook his head. How could she possibly have thought he didn't want her? "Sarah, you tell me you want me between your legs, and you think I'm going to say anything except 'yes, please'?"

"I could make you say please, Zach." She kissed his chest, running her tongue around his nipple. "I could make you want to."

He lifted her by her bottom, taking them both out of the shower and back into the motel room. Somehow, he managed to grab a towel on his way out, which he quickly wrapped around her. Sarah's statement required an answer, so he gave her the truth. "You could make me do about anything you want. For tonight, why don't you let me take care of you?" Zach pinched her ass through the towel, and she shuddered. He had to double check. "Still like a little pain?"

"As you see."

"Good." He yanked back the towel. Zach had wanted her

dry, although not being able to see her naked left him bereft. Fuck if he was going to deny himself anything when it came to Sarah.

She wrapped her arms around his neck. "Does that mean you're a sadist?"

He shook his head. "Not particularly. Let's say I'll get off giving you what you want. Eventually."

"Um." She pressed her forehead to his. "Zach, usually I want to play. In private, anyway. Do you understand what I mean?"

"Hmmm." He kissed her nose. "I do, actually. Half-naked in bed isn't the time or place for us to figure out what works for us, agreed? I'm going to make you feel good and then put you to bed. Tomorrow will be soon enough to figure out if we match in kink."

If she really needed to have sex in public, he'd find a way to go there, although it had never worked for him in the past. He'd tried to get into it when her brother dragged him in and out of the clubs years before. For Sarah, he'd give it another go if it was a must do.

He laid her on the terrible bed, which would forever more be among his favorite locations in the world. She stared at him, running her hand across the side of his face. "I enjoy vanilla too, Zach. Being with you seems close to heaven for me. I never thought it would be you and me in an old hotel room getting sweaty. The stuff out of a fantasy."

He quieted her with a kiss. Her words did things to his equilibrium, and he couldn't let it throw him. Her lips were soft, her skin hot, and her body—for the moment—all his.

Zach ran his hand down the length of her until he reached her pussy. She shuddered when he pet her thighs, and it made his mouth go dry. How did he get this lucky? Sarah was strong, athletic, and her legs were those of a runner. He traced a circle around her pussy, but didn't dive closer. Tormenting her for a moment was much more fun.

The soft curls covering her pussy beckoned to him in the dimness of the lousy motel room. "I wish I could take you somewhere better. Make love to you on satin and roses."

"I'm not the kind of girl who needs those things." She shivered beneath his touch.

"Need, maybe not. Should have? Absolutely." He would do his best to make the old hotel room place good in her memory.

"Zach..." Her voice drifted off when he pressed his finger inside her pussy.

"Want me stroking you, do you?" He grinned. Foreplay was his favorite part. Well, maybe second favorite. The warm up before the actual entrance meant he got to show his woman—and the term fit her to a 'T'—he could make her body purr.

"More." She arched her back as he stroked her.

"Think I can manage." He found her clit and pinched it. She moaned and closed her eyes. "Ride with me. I want to see you come in a little bit."

And he'd had enough talking for a while. He wanted to live in the moment and let himself enjoy being with her. She thought being with him was a fantasy? Sarah had no idea how much the opposite proved true. A month earlier, he'd never have let himself imagine being with her could be more than a dream, let alone getting to touch her spectacular body.

Adding a second finger to the mix, he teased her clit some more until he could feel her juices on his hand. Yes, he wanted her wet and out of her mind.

"Spread your legs for me, sweetheart." He tapped on

each knee until she did what he said. "Good. Exactly what I want."

Having her come from some clit play would rock, but on his tongue? He'd fucking love it. Zach bent forward, loving the sweet manna smell of Sarah aroused. An urgency to have her made his balls ache, and he knew when she touched him, it wouldn't be long until he spent. But he refused to hold anything back in giving her pleasure.

Sarah would find release more than once if he had anything to say about it.

He leashed his desire and set about making her tremble. Zach replaced his fingers with his tongue. She tasted sweet and the bundle of nerves came out to play more as he savored it.

Sarah reached forward and stroked the top of his head in time to the swirl of his tongue. He stopped his movement, only to replace his tongue with his teeth. Gently, yet firmly, he bit, hoping her previous reactions to slight amounts of pain proved true. She cried out his name, her body bucking while wetness coated his tongue. He drank her deep, loving he got to share an intimate moment with her. His cock hardened to the point of pain.

When she seemed to slow, and her panting quieted, he pulled back to regard her. She stared back at him, her eyes hooded, passion in their dark depths.

"You have the look of a guy who knows he got a woman off. I think of it as male smugness."

Huh. He grinned. "You're funny. You know that?"

She sat, her long dark hair falling forward over her shoulders. "I know I want you between my thighs."

His pulsing cock reminded him he wanted it too. Big time.

Zach reached to the side of the bed for the condoms he

had gotten from the front of the motel where they had a machine. His hands shook, reminding him of his desperate situation. Sarah grabbed the foil from him. "Let me."

She grinned at him while she tore open the condom wrapper. "Over here, Zach. Lay next to me. On your back."

He scooted over to where she indicated, on his back. His heart rate picked up when she rolled toward him, condom in her outstretched hand.

"Wow, Zach, you're fucking huge."

"Ah...thanks."

It had only been his own hand for so long, stroking himself, getting himself to really unsatisfying conclusions. Should he tell her? Probably not. A confession of his desperate need wasn't hot.

Her hand stroked his cock once, and a moan sounded from deep inside his throat. Every nerve ending in his body flung to life.

"Careful." He sounded hoarse and was surprised he could manage to pull air at all. "I'm close."

"I can see that." She winked at him before she rolled the condom on his shaft, sheathing him completely. "Don't move."

"You want to ride me, sweetheart?"

She raised her eyebrows. "I want you to hush, Zachery Daniels, and let me take care of you."

"Tonight is supposed to be about you."

She placed her finger over his mouth. "Part of me is a care taker. Particularly in bed. You stopping your arguing with me and actually doing what I say because it'll make you feel good, is how you make tonight about me."

If she wanted to take care of him to make herself happy, he'd be glad to go along. "What did you have in mind?"

"For tonight, how about we keep it simple?"

She moved until she was mostly on top of him. Her breath was sweet when she pressed her lips to his. It was the sweetest kiss he'd ever received. She moved, kissing a trail down the center of his chest until she reached his sheathed cock. His balls ached. Was it possible he was going to spill himself like a teenager?

"Hold on there, Zinc." She smirked when she used his Metal name. "A big tough Marine such as you must be able to keep yourself under control."

Years of denial, and the simple disbelief at getting to be naked with Sarah, argued with her otherwise true words. "Oorah, Sarah. You're tormenting me."

"Because I know you love it."

With another wink, she stroked him hard in her hand before she straddled him, still not taking him inside of her. He moaned, his hips bucking. Fuck. With gentle fingertips, she tickled his leg. The strange sensation eased some of his imminent need to plunge into her until he came.

She inched forward, rubbing his dick around her clit before she sank down on him, taking him balls deep when she did. He grabbed the back of her ass, holding her still for a moment so he could really feel being deep inside of her. One perfect moment...

"You ready?" Her voice dropped a level, and God, it was so hot.

"Ride me, baby."

She took her own breasts in her hands as she slid up and down his cock. With no good place to put his hands while he enjoyed the show, he rested them on her thighs. It would give him easier access if he wanted to rub her clit and give her extra pleasure.

Anything for Sarah.

SARAH HAD NEVER BEEN SO TURNED on in her life. Zach had already gotten her off once. She would have loved to have gone down on him, to take him in her mouth and deep throat him until he called out her name over and over.

He'd been close. She'd seen the strain his face showed before she felt it on his cock. There was something really powerful about bringing a strong man like Zach so close to losing his cool.

So, she rode him instead.

In and out, she squeezed with her thighs. Every moan, curse, and groan he made was music for her soul. She was finding ecstasy with Zach, and right then, she owned him. He didn't belong to anyone else. The women she'd watched coming in and out of his life from a distance while she silently worried about each and every deployment didn't matter.

He was hers, and despite the horrific circumstances of their reunion, she had no intention of letting him go without a fight.

Zach pinched her. "Where is your head, hot stuff?"

She grinned at the endearment. "It's here with you, Zach. Where else would it be?"

"Good." He gripped her rear end before he flipped her over. His action shocked her. Wow, she hadn't seen his move coming, and her giggle took her by surprise too. "If I have to keep you under me to make sure your mind is where it's supposed to be, that is what I'm going to do."

He surged into her, a hand holding him above her as the other gripped in her hair. "Look me in the eyes, sweetheart. I want your eyes on me until you shatter into a million pieces."

Oh God, his words, combined with the way his cock rubbed against her clit every time he pushed in and out of her, drove her crazy. He'd told her to keep her eyes open. Although she might be tempted in other circumstances to tell him where he could shove his orders, she did want to do exactly what he said. In bed? God, yes she did.

Needed it.

Her body cried out, yes, please let her come. The pressure grew, rose, and travelled up her spine. Her hips rose to meet his, and she was so wet.

"So fucking beautiful, Sarah. You're something out of a dream. Squeezing my cock as you do, fitting me so fucking perfectly."

Yes, hell, it was as if she'd been made to have him inside of her. He let go of her hair and reached between them. "I'm close, Sarah. And so help me, you are going first."

Zach rubbed her clit in time with his pressing inside of her. His moves were all the pressure she needed. Yes, her body exploded around him. Liquid surged from her core, and she closed her eyes, finally letting her gaze leave his blue eyes.

She couldn't breathe, couldn't think, couldn't do anything except feel. Did she leave her body? She didn't know, didn't care. Fuck. Yes.

Distantly, she heard Zach call her name. She squeezed her legs around him tighter as her body milked his, pulling him deeper, wishing she'd been on the pill and they'd been blood tested so they could be skin-to-skin. She had Zach deep inside of her.

At last.

She must have passed out, because the world kind of drifted away on a pleasant haze of sex and Zach.

"SARAH," Zach's deep voice called to her, and she groaned. They'd had sex, and she had conked out.

Hot, Sarah. Great. Zach must be so thrilled to have a sexual partner who fell asleep with him still inside of her. I'm Sarah Steele, and I can do better than I did. She'd show him. Several times for the rest of the night.

She stretched, opening her eyes. "Sorry, I guess I dozed off."

"Oh, you did more than that." Zach leaned over her, his whiskered cheeks rubbing hers in a delicious jolt before he kissed her right beneath her eyes. "You've been snoring for six hours."

Snoring? Six hours? She sat and then had to stop because dizziness threatened to overtake her. "I so don't snore."

"Oh?" His blue eyes danced with laughter. Other than a lamp he turned on across the room, the motel remained bathed in darkness. "Then it must have been someone else lying next to me in the bed sawing wood. My mistake. I'm sorry I had to wake you. We need to be out of here before the sun comes out."

"Right." Her body felt tight, not the languid ease she should feel after coming the way she did. "Give me a minute. I'll be ready in two."

Zach stood. She noted he was fully dressed, and he smelled of soap. Had he been awake so long he had showered? She'd slept through all the noise?

"I knew you were the kind of girl who could be awake and gorgeous in two minutes."

"I don't know about gorgeous. I will be ready." Silly man. Being teased by Zach could become an addiction.

She got out of bed on unsteady feet, yet managed to make her way to the bathroom where she found her clothes had been hung on the motel's hangers. Zach again. Add considerate to the list of traits she admired about him. Had he gone to bed at all, or did he spend the night fixing everything? She'd have to ask him, she could offer to drive.

When she had reassembled herself into some manner of presentable—after their hell was over, she was getting her hair done, and a facial too—she walked out of the bathroom. Zach shot her a heated glance, which left her wishing they had more time.

"When we're on the road, I'll order you a crowbar and maybe some donuts."

She paused. "Am I going to need a crowbar with my donuts?" Had she missed some part of a plan?

"Shit." He closed his eyes before opening them again to go with a tic in his jaw. "I can't find the word. I obviously don't mean what I said. Let's go."

Her lover turned on his heel and walked out of the room, pausing outside the door to look left and right. When he'd moved a distance away, he stopped and waited for her. Just enough space between them to show how uncomfortable he was.

Shit. She had stumbled onto his soft spot. Sometimes he said the wrong words, leftover from his brain injury. He'd told her, and he'd done it once in the car when he first woke up from his headache. The tightness in his jaw, the way he tensed. Zach wasn't okay with it any more than he was with the migraines.

Her heart turned over twice. He was here, he was alive, he was incredible, and he beat himself up constantly over things which were in no way his fault. How could he not see how incredible he was? Where most men faltered, Zach stayed strong. Even through dying.

Hello morning, time to be totally insensitive. When they were giving out lessons in not being a complete ass, I missed the day.

"Zach." She fell into step with him.

"Don't. Okay? Don't."

He took her hand, only the teasing from earlier was gone. Instead, stony silent Zach—probably the way he behaved when he was being Zinc—took his place. It was fifteen minutes until he spoke again, and only then because he pulled into a coffee house drive thru to order. When the woman spoke over the intercom, he looked at her.

"You should tell her what you want. I don't want to say the wrong thing." He looked at the steering wheel.

Not the time to argue with him, especially since she really didn't feel like letting the complete stranger on the other end listening in. She did as he asked, getting herself a latte and a scone before she looked at him. "Hungry? Thirsty?"

"Black." She noticed he left out the word for coffee when he said it. "Not hungry at the moment. Thanks."

Always polite. She had to lean over him to speak to the intercom, which at least let her place her hand on his arm. The strain between them, when everything had been so easy, threatened to make her head explode.

"And a medium black coffee and a croissant." She leaned back. "You're not hungry, fine. You need to eat something, you can eat it later if you prefer."

He nodded and didn't answer as he paid the woman in utter silence. They drove a few more miles while she sipped her drink and stewed about what to do.

Finally, she really couldn't take it anymore. "I'm really sorry. Okay? I totally didn't realize you were misspeaking, or

I wouldn't have pointed it out. I say the wrong word some-times, and I didn't survive a head injury. I can see now how it's a really big deal for you, and I'll be more cognizant with how I react in the future. How long are you going to punish me for an honest mistake?"

"I'm not..." Except, he gripped the steering wheel tighter. "I'm not fucking punishing you."

"Sure feels as though you are."

"How am I doing that?" The muscle in his jaw ticked again. Zach had a tell when he got really upset, and it was right there at the top of jawline. "I'm not upset with you. I'm...embarrassed and sick of it. Okay? So can we not?"

"There's absolutely no reason for you to feel in any way weird about it. Hell, Zach, you're doing so well, I practically forgot you'd been exploded."

He didn't answer for a moment. "The scars on my body didn't remind you last night?"

"Oh, you're talking about a vanity thing. Funny, I thought you were too tough for such trivial crap." His eyes flashed, and she knew she'd gotten on the right path. Let him at least express his anger, better than the resigned nonsense they would never push through. "I saw the scars. I didn't comment because they are what they are. You're alive. I care a lot more about your heart beating than marks on your skin."

"Do you have any idea how frustrating it is to go through every day wondering if I'm going to say something wrong?"

"No, I don't. If it were me, I'd put it away, deal with it if it happens, and not spend so much time obsessing over some-thing clearly out of my control."

He stopped speaking again, and she also shut up. What the hell was the matter with her? She was dishing out advice she had no earthly right to be giving. How the hell did she know what it was like to be him? What he should and should not be doing?

I don't know how to keep my big mouth shut.

The sun rose while they were on the road, and she stopped obsessing enough to actually let herself enjoy the colors as they rose in the horizon. The earth around them woke. The sky looked blue and clear.

"Another day, another chance to do things better." He didn't look at her as he uttered the words, and she wondered if he spoke to her or to himself.

"I never see the sun rise. I'm either desperately trying to find a few more hours of sleep, or I'm already at my desk working."

"I haven't taken a lot of time to enjoy them lately, either." He cleared his throat. "Listen, when we stop for lunch, maybe we could talk terms. About the things you want to do in bed, and what I'm absolutely not cool with."

Well, his words constituted quite an abrupt shift, if nothing else. Was he offering her an olive branch? She decided to accept it as thus.

"All right. Sounds like a plan." She sipped her coffee again. "Never got kinky with any of the women you were a serial monogamist with?"

His mouth formed a smirk, and some of the tension in his jaw eased. "A serial monogamist?"

"As far as I could tell, you didn't do causal. You went from a serious relationship to breaking up to another until you ended it again. Lots of posing and smiling on your Face-book page." Until the bitch, Ally... She shook her head. No need to be cruel, even in her thoughts.

"Spent a lot of time focused on my dating life?" He full on grinned. "Honey, I'm so flattered. And to answer your question, I gave kink a go by following…a friend…to some of the kinky clubs he liked to frequent. Wasn't my thing."

She let his words digest. "Did you pause over the word friend because you were about to say Adam?"

"Thought that might be a little TMI for you, sweetheart."

"Shit. Yes. Never again. I don't want to know anything about Adam's sex life. No."

She rubbed at her eyes as though she could purge the image of her brother doing things she didn't want to know about from her imagination. "Blah. I need a shower."

Zach's laughter filled the car. She took a large gulp of cooling coffee. At least she'd found some way to improve their morning, although she might never be able to look at Adam again. After she hugged him to death for still being alive, of course.

6

Zach ordered his lunch without incident, getting through all the wording without screwing his speech. He really shouldn't be surprised, his dysnomia was always made worse when he was tired. The therapists at the hospital had been shocked he could speak at all. Maybe he should figure out how to let it go and be more grateful. Certainly, the last day with Sarah had helped. When had he been so happy? Maybe there was some point to his being around still.

He needed to drive them to New York the next morning so he could check in—as per his instructions—on time, which meant they had tonight to push through. He had some ideas of where he wanted to spend it, if Sarah was game. Of course, maybe it was better to surprise her.

Zach drummed his fingers on the table and regarded the dark beauty waiting silently across from him.

"You're going to make me talk first?" He watched her play with her straw in her mouth, and his cock got immediately strained again. Fuckity fuck. How could he still be so hot for her so instantly? Sarah was making him some kind of sex addict.

"Not necessarily. Maybe I want to look at you and was enjoying the view."

To his utter horror, his cheeks got hot. "Women don't say things like you do. What are we supposed to use to impress you, if you do?"

She sat straighter, her lips in a mock pout. "Sexist."

"Probably a little bit." Although back in the day, when they'd been speaking, before he'd been dead, Copper would have beat him to death before she put up with his open the door for a lady habits—of course, Copper wasn't a lady. She was a goddamn Marine. He grinned at the memory. There had been a time when things had been really fun, when being with his team had meant every day was damned good.

At some point, he'd stopped thinking about it because it had hurt too much to know they went on without him, as if he'd never existed. Maybe the time had come to try again.

"You told me you don't enjoy the dungeons. Or at least the, to quote you, kinky places you and a friend used to play."

If she wanted to avoid the word Adam then so would he. Her face in the car when she'd figured it out had been priceless. Zach had to bite his tongue to stop from laughing.

"I really didn't. Being out in public like that? It felt... wrong." He'd tried three times. Adam had loved the play, taken to it as though he'd been meant to do it. And Zach had run home as quickly as he could. It wasn't as if he had a problem with any of it. People got off however they got off. Picturing some of it could make him hard. Only when he'd been there, his anxiety had been so ramped up, there was no way he was getting off.

Sarah nodded as though what he said hadn't been

shocking, as if she was totally unfazed by the whole talking about sex and dominance thing. They might as well have been discussing dinner or the weather, for all it seemed to bother her.

"I don't have any trouble with vanilla sex, as you noticed last night." Some color finally hit her cheeks. It was nice to see she wasn't as immune to their sex talk as she seemed. "I do want to play. Sometimes. Or all the time, if that is what my partner wants. I've never been in a relationship or a sexual encounter where it's been all vanilla, all the time."

He'd already figured her preferences out. "I know, which is why I brought it up. I want to make you happy."

"I know you do." She took his hand in hers. Her fingers were so tiny against his own, so soft. Although he knew she could be deadly, and it took a tremendous amount to truly rattle her. Sarah was an amazing combination of both soft and hard, both on the inside and out.

She spoke again, "I don't have any particular need to have sex in public. Or behind closed doors in a public space. Or behind closed doors in a private club."

"I understand the general idea." He appreciated her being clear, only he wasn't entirely clueless.

"Do you have any problem with exploring some kink when it's the two of us, at home? In a hotel room or wherever we are alone." She rushed through the last sentence, and he had no idea why.

"You okay?"

Her eyebrows raised. "Fine."

Had he misread her sudden discomfort? "Good. No, I don't. Although there are some things I'm never going to be cool with."

"Like..." Her voice drifted off, indicating the question. Then the food arrived. He'd never been so grateful to see a hamburger in his life. The delivery of their meal at least gave him a chance to collect his thoughts. She was the most amazing woman he'd ever known. Fuck, if he couldn't make her happy.

"I don't want to be a constant disappointment to you." She had shoved a potato chip in her mouth and choked when he spoke. "Shit." He jumped, only she waved him off. When he'd convinced himself she wasn't about to choke to death, he sat back. "And I almost killed you."

"You caught me on the down chomp. That's all. I'm fine." She sipped her water and then rounded on him with her outstretched pointer finger. "If you ever say anything so ridiculous as disappointing me again, Zachery, I will beat you within an inch of your life."

He believed her. Sarah could be a scary lady if she wanted to be. "Sorry?"

She narrowed her eyes at him. "You were going to tell me what things you are not okay with."

"Right. I don't..." Days earlier, there was a whole list of things he would have said he didn't want. And yet for Sarah...maybe the nos altered slightly. He lowered his voice. "I don't want anything coming near my ass. I mean ever."

"Okay." She waited a second. "Is no ass play it?"

"Well, no. I mean, I'm never going to be your sub."

"Huh." She took a sip of her drink, and he eyed her plate.

"You've yet to have taken a single bite of your sandwich. Don't want it?" He refused to let her waste away during their hiding. People forgot to take care of themselves during heightened stressful experiences. She'd noted he hadn't eaten breakfast and insisted he have some for later, which he'd appreciated when he calmed.

Without a comment, she picked up the main portion of

her lunch and took a big bite. And then another. The lunch negotiation had to be the strangest conversation of his whole life, and Sarah managed it as if it was another day in the office. Well, maybe the second weirdest. The first had to be when he could finally think past the pain in his brain and form some semblance of words and a blind, amputated Titanium had told him what his future would entail.

Those conversations had been downright surreal. Chatting about sexual kinks fell short of those life altering words.

When she finally swallowed, she spoke again, "What does it mean to you to be submissive?"

"I'm not going to be calling you ma'am or letting you come at me with a switch. Waiting for you on my knees is off the table too."

"Zach." She grinned. "Let's not be too hung up on wording. There are lots of people who are switches. Sometimes they're on top, sometimes they're on the bottom. I'm not usually submissive either, yet when you took control in bed last night and made me shatter as you did, I liked it. I think you actually enjoy it when I tell you to do certain things too." She wasn't wrong, although it made him slightly uncomfortable to think about. "You're a caretaker. You want to make me happy. I want to let you. I also crave a little pain, you clearly cued into my kink."

He had, which was why he had done small things, such as tug on her hair when they'd been having sex.

Sarah wasn't finished. "Almost everyone has a little kink. I don't care so much about the Dom-sub role as I do about getting us both what we need. When life isn't crazy, let's visit a store, and figure it out together. And I'll say another thing." She leaned forward. "It takes a really strong man to submit to a strong woman. Some of the toughest guys I've ever known, really want to fall to their knees and give their girl their total submission." She winked at him. "I'm going to use the little girl's room."

He stared at her open mouthed as she walked away. Falling to his knees and giving her what she wanted...he could manage.

~

SARAH DOZED the rest of the afternoon in the car. Zach loved seeing her peacefully leaning against the window, her mouth slightly open, her breath calm and steady. She'd been chatty after lunch, talking about the radio, the weather, reminiscing about the ice cream stand near the lake where they used to go, and then she'd fallen silent, out like a light, all of a sudden.

He was glad she could rest. Although it wasn't the same as back home in northern California, Lake Lure in North Carolina was remote, only slightly out of their way, and he knew it from having spent some time fishing at a friend's house years earlier. Since he clearly jonesed to spend some time with Sarah at a lake, spending the night there would take care of his Sarah by the water craving too.

They'd left the hotel at four in the morning, and with only stopping for lunch, they were going to be at the lake by six o'clock-ish. It might take a while longer if he couldn't find a house for them to squat in for the evening. Zach banked on it being off-season and finding some empty lake houses to spend the night.

If not, maybe another cheap motel.

Sarah roused as he pulled down a driveway toward a house with no lights on, no cars in the driveway, located right where he wanted to be. "Wait in the car. Please."

She nodded, rubbing at her eyes. "Where are we?" Her

voice trailed after him, only he didn't respond. When he re-conned an area, it brought him back to his years with the Marines. He'd been a lifer, then Ally had come along. She hadn't wanted him to reup again, and he'd agreed to go civil-ian. Then everything had literally blown to pieces. As a member of Titanium's Ghosts, he still used his skills.

Although he hoped breaking and entering—like flying and crashing a plane—was similar to riding a bike, and he'd never forget how since it had been a damn long time for him.

Zinc took the stairs quietly. The crickets in the distance didn't stop chirping, which was an old trick he had picked up hunting with Adam and their dads. If the crickets stopped, he had been spotted by something.

The house was a two-story log cabin connected to the water by a long set of stairs. With the sun setting in the distance, it looked like something out of a movie. The cabin seemed rustic, yet the wood wasn't splintering, and the stairs themselves seemed well maintained. A private property sign had been nailed next to the front door.

Oh well...Zinc wanted off the grid, and doing so meant he was going to limit the amount of cash spent and the way they could be tracked. If all went well, the owners would never know they'd helped save a CIA agent with use of their cabin.

He looked through the window. Everything appeared closed. Someone had covered the furniture in blankets and unplugged all the appliances. There was no sign of any alarm system or video surveillance. A property management company could monitor the cabin, checking on it periodi-cally. A risk—but one worth taking.

They'd have to be on their way in the early morning to once again avoid detection. Their stop would also mean he'd miss his call in. He'd been told to check in every two days. They hadn't specified at what time of day his call needed to be.

"Perfect," he muttered to himself before he turned around. They were quickly losing sun, and he had plans for the house beyond hiding them. He made it back to the car faster than before, since he no longer worried about detection.

He opened Sarah's car door, and she stepped outside. "Where are we?"

"Come on." He took her hand, and she didn't resist. "Let's go look."

The awesomeness in Sarah not questioning him—but grinning at him while she took his hand and followed him to the lake—was not lost on him. If it was possible, Zach's heart came to life for the first time in three years.

"I want to look at you in the sunset by the water."

They rounded the corner and took the stairs to the dock. "Oh, Zach."

He stared at the lake spread out before them. The setting sun illuminated the ripples of slight waves. "It is beautiful, isn't it?"

When he turned, she wasn't looking at the water, instead at him. Sarah had the strangest expression on her face. She pursed her lips before she threw her arms around his neck. He caught her in his arms and was glad when he didn't trip.

They were having an out of a movie moment, and the hero never fell on his ass.

"You okay, Sarah?" Maybe bringing her to the lake had been a mistake. "Continuing on to New York made the most sense, and yet I knew these lake houses were here, or well, I hoped something similar would be, and I wanted to sit by a lake with you."

One more time in his life where he knew he would have to eventually give her back.

"I'm so happy you did."

He closed his eyes and held her tighter. The time with Sarah when he'd gotten to be Zach again was going to come to a close. They'd arrive in New York, he'd find her handler, end the douchebag. If there was anyone else involved, he'd take care of them, too. Then he'd go back to his life, and she would return to hers. Long distance from Texas—or wherever he got sent—to New York? In the past, he could have imagined it. He'd become enough of a cynic to know for him, it would never work.

The explosion, which shattered his life, had finally made him see fairytales didn't come true. Not for him.

Only he had her by the lake. Sharing the sunset was enough.

SARAH WANDERED through the house with a specific purpose. She'd never stolen a residence before, and while she knew it should be tweaking her conscience, like the pills, clothes, and phone, she felt no immediate remorse. In other circumstances, she knew Zach would have brought her here and paid for the rental.

She was learning to roll with the punches. He'd wanted to see her by the lake. She shuddered, warmth filling her all the way inside.

He was so...sweet. She sighed. And she'd been in love with him her whole life. No other man had ever measured to her fantasy Zach. The real version made it worse. He really was everything she wanted, wrapped in an occasionally grumpy and disgruntled package. If anything, his flaws only made him hotter. Sarah liked the touches of imperfection.

The closet of the master bedroom upstairs had what she wanted, and she grabbed the sturdiest tie she saw. She grinned as she looked at the design, a cartoon character giving a thumbs up. Somehow, the irony wasn't lost on her. She hoped Zach gave her a similar signal at the end of the night.

They were going to start out slow. He didn't want anything near his ass. Yes, fine. Although, maybe he could eventually be persuaded, ass play could be fun. At least, for her. He didn't want to call her ma'am. Fine, she actually preferred he not. They were figuring out bedroom kink and being completely private. If she never saw another dungeon because she was entirely with Zach, fine by her.

He stood in the living room staring out at the black lake. They'd closed all the blinds except the ones at the back of the house, and he'd told her as soon as it was full dark, he was going to close those too. When she suggested they not sleep upstairs because of ease in escape, he'd agreed. The downstairs guestroom would do, if not as comfortable as the main bedroom upstairs. The bed was slightly smaller; they would have to sleep closer together.

After they got done with finding out what play Zach liked in the bedroom.

Baby steps. And if all answered in no, if he liked none of it, then she'd deal with the new reality too. Vanilla sex with Zach was better than any other she'd ever had. She wanted kink with him, only she wanted him more.

"Can you wait for me in the bedroom?" She ran the tie through her hands and knew the second he noticed it. His eyes widened, and his stubborn chin raised a notch.

"Sure." He nodded and turned to walk down the hallway

towards the guest room. Sarah walked to the window where he had stood and closed it the rest of the way, drenching the room in darkness. Candles were the only light they'd allow themselves. She crossed the room and struck a match to light the candle.

Her hands were steady, only her heart was not. It threatened to explode from her chest. Sarah had never introduced anyone to the lifestyle before. Her partners were always very experienced, usually more so than she, in D/s play.

Was her suggesting they try stuff okay?

All right Sarah, you're not forcing Zach into anything. He wants to get kinky with me. We talked about it at lunch. He wants to make me happy, he wants...

Her mind stuttered. Zach had a need to make her happy. He'd said as much. Needing to make her happy was his thing—his kink. She could have gasped with the joy of it all. He was going to be okay, because he knew it was what she wanted.

He'd enjoy it for her enjoyment of it, if no other.

They were on the same page.

She took a deep breath. Not to mention, he was a strong man who would have no problem telling her if he detested every second of their playtime.

Sarah entered the bedroom feeling as if she'd better found her footing. The candle illuminated the room in a dusky haze. The room was decorated in reds and golds, or so she had seen before it had gotten dark. Everything looked brown. There was a dresser in the corner and a small chair to the right of the bed.

Zach leaned against the wall, his gaze holding her own. He had taken off his shirt. Sarah's mouth went dry. He was quite simply breathtaking. She'd not taken the opportunity to admire him the night before. Things had gone very fast, and she'd been in a bit of a state.

There was no rush. She could be patient, except she craved him.

"Sarah?"

There was something she had to say. "You made fun of me at lunch for saying I liked to look at you, only I do. It's the truth. There's no other way for me to describe you, except I take absolute pleasure getting to stare at you in the world, Zach. You were dead. And for some inexplicable reason, I get to look at you again. It's a gift."

"Why didn't I know? All those years?" His voice hitched. "You were there, and I didn't know what it could be between us."

She had to find her footing before she really fell apart. "To be fair, I said nothing, and I'm not exactly a shy retiring flower. I didn't think I'd be your type. Now? I don't give a shit if I am or not. You were dead, and now you're here. I'm taking what I want. Yes, I get it. I was Adam's sister. Still am, except it seems to bug you less."

"Doesn't bother me at all."

"Good." She pointed to the bed. "Sit. Feet on the floor in front of you, hands in front of you clasped." She demonstrated how she wanted his hands, fingers linked together. "Like me."

He nodded and did exactly as she asked. His eyes met hers expectantly. "I'm allowed to talk, right? I mean, I told you no yes ma'aming, or whatever."

"You better, Zach. How else am I going to know what you do and don't want?" She stood in front of him, still fingering the tie. He was really going along. "We need a safe word."

"I actually thought of one. Well, I need three, right? One for yes, for maybe, for no?"

He'd been to clubs, he wasn't totally virginal at kink, she reminded herself. "Three is always a good idea. However, tonight I think we'll assume the yes unless you say maybe or no. I'm not going to be doing anything too pushy. So, let's be very simple. Yellow for maybe, red for stop."

A slight smirk crossed his lips. "Yellow. Red. Look, I can say those words."

"I kind of thought you could." She stroked the side of his face. "Give me your hands."

He raised them to her. "Kind of hot, you telling me what to do."

"Only kind of?" She took the tie. "I'm going to keep the knot loose today. Any panic, you take it off, except if you say red, I'll take it off for you."

"Not going to freak out about having my hands restrained. Not if it makes you happy."

She smiled. His words confirmed her thoughts. He'd never see it as a kink, and his thoughts were fine, only if Zach wanted to make her happy to the point he'd try anything for her—it was how he got off.

When she'd restrained his hands, she winked at him. "Lay back."

He obeyed without question, and her whole body softened. "You can't believe what your compliance does to me. Seeing you tied. With your hands wrapped because I wanted them to be. I think I'm going to reward you. We good?"

"Excellent."

When he'd gotten into the position she wanted him in, flat on his back, arms over his head, restrained, it was a thing of beauty. "I wish I could really capture our moment."

He lifted his head and glared at her. "Don't you dare."

"I won't. Making a mental photo."

Sarah tugged at his pants until they were off and followed with his boxers. She ran her hands on his strong legs to feel him shudder. The night before, she had conked out before she had gotten to do all the things she wanted.

She wasn't tired, and they had all night.

Sarah took his cock in her hands. He'd barely let her touch him the last time. Zach seemed more in control, and she certainly felt similarly. The rush, the need was different, slower, easier.

"Sarah," he whispered her name.

"Stay where you are. Don't try to touch me."

Zach groaned, yet didn't move from the position where she placed him. "You're so hard, and you're all mine."

She leaned over him, taking him into her mouth. He tasted salty and all male. Zach hissed, and she raised her eyes to look at him. He'd kept his hands where she put them. Good job.

His listening to her made very happy. So pleased, in fact, she took him deeper down her throat. He was long, thick, and all male. No way would she ever take all of him, and she wasn't going to try. Sucking on his cock made her wet and hot. Where she couldn't throat him, she stroked with her hands in unison. Bobbing her head, she moaned. Giving Zach pleasure fueled her own.

Minutes passed, lost in her own desire, she heard only the hiss of his breath and the moments he would moan. He got harder and harder, until she knew he was close. She increased her pressure, moving faster. She wanted heat for Zach, needed to give him pleasure as much as he wanted to make her happy.

He came hard in her mouth, and she moaned with pleasure, soaking her own panties as she sucked him dry.

When he finished, she lifted her head, swallowing the last of him. She met his eyes staring back at her own. They were hooded, hot, and filled with male satisfaction.

"Happy?"

"Damn, Sarah." He laughed. "You are so fucking cool."

She was.

7

Zinc's head throbbed. The pain started the second they drove away from the lake house. He'd been amazingly headache free for the hours they'd spent there. Coming three times in a night probably had something to do with the temporary relief from the pain. Not that he could count on orgasming as a remedy for what ailed him.

It was nice to have had the reprieve, although not having the pain made him more aware of the constant ache.

Sarah pulled at her drink. They'd been driving for nine hours, and the silence in the car—unlike the day before—felt comfortable. He hadn't done anything stupid to piss her off.

"What happened to your motorcycle?"

Her question caught him by surprise. What was the last thing they'd talked about before they'd fallen quiet? Oh, Great Danes. Sarah loved those dogs. How had she gone from there to his long gone bike?

"The thing about dying is all of your stuff goes away. I

imagine when someone stays dead, it isn't as much of a problem."

She shook her head. "I hate when you make jokes about it. You forget, I was at your funeral. I heard the words spoken and watched when they lowered what I wrongly assumed was you into the ground."

"Going to have to start checking coffins, aren't you, sweetheart? Opening it? Making sure the deceased is inside?"

She pinched him on the arm before groaning dramatically. How was it possible he could enjoy everything about her? Ally, who he had wanted to spend his whole life with, bugged the shit out of him sometimes. Sarah was so damn fascinating. He'd be glad to listen to her talk about anything.

Sarah asked a question, he'd give her an answer.

"I've remotely tried to locate some of my stuff or at least, to know what happened to it. As you know, after my parents split, my sisters went to live with my mom in Florida, and I stayed with dad in Northern California, where you guys were. Well, your brother anyway. You were in your fancy finishing school having experimental sex with hot girls in your dorm room."

"I was what?" Her voice squeaked. "Zach." She pinched him again. "I can promise you, there was nothing so exciting going on."

"Too bad. I kind of liked imagining you and the hot co-eds in your dorm room."

"Your bike..." She let her voice trail off.

He nodded and sighed dramatically. Teasing her was fun, and it relieved the ache in his head. "If I had known Ally was going to go so quickly on to her next fiancé, I would have left my stuff to Kerry and April in Miami. They stayed after Mom died. Dad never wanted anything to do with me, he wouldn't have liked getting left with my stuff. Ally and I were engaged, so I named her next of kin."

"She has your bike." Her voice sounded tight.

"I know she sold my house. I followed the transaction online fairly easily. My car went next, through an online reseller. I've been waiting on the bike to pop on the Internet somewhere. I have Google alerts. There aren't many blue 2005 H-D FLSTFSE Screamin' Eagle Fat Boy's on the market. I'd find a way to buy it without her knowing it was me. Nothing yet. So, she either gave it away to someone, did a cash deal in person, or is still holding on to my bike. She hated the thing. Told me it made her feel dizzy to sit on the back. I don't know why she'd still have it."

Of all the things he lost, the bike bugged him the most. Fucking missed it.

"I'm sorry." Her face fell, and he hated to see her unhappy. Reaching out, he stroked the side of her cheek.

"Don't worry. I'm good. My turn for the question asking. How did you end up in the Agency?"

"I'm really smart."

"I know, baby. Lots of really smart people out there are not recruited to such covert branches of the CIA. Titanium doesn't know they're Agency until he has to research them off surveillance video." Or one of the Ghosts did. Titanium couldn't see anything anymore. Although he still seemed to know whenever Zach rolled his eyes at him.

"I went to law school at Harvard. At every major law school in the country, there are professors who are paid by the Agency to seek out talent. Most years, they won't contact anybody. Something about me triggered their alert. I was approached and recruited. Spent a year at Langley while I was also clerking for a federal judge. I've never been so busy. Afterwards, as they say, the rest was history."

"And all that time, we had no clue."

She smiled, which he would swear lit the whole world. "You not knowing constituted the general idea."

"Right."

Another nine hours passed before they hit his target, Edgewater, New Jersey. The commuter town had a ferry boat, and the parking lot would be the perfect place to ditch the car, though it opened them to more security cameras than he'd prefer. The ferry terminal boasted a second plus —it still had payphones.

Zinc had spent time there when, in his role as a Ghost, he'd had to help kidnap Platinum from New York City to bring him to the Elite Metal compound. They'd transported him from the truck where they held him to the ferry boat, and then taken a whole other car to the airport before flying home. It had been a long day. None had been as awful as the mission to kidnap Adam. Zach had frozen, and if Tungsten hadn't been there to basically shove him into action, the whole thing might have gone to hell.

He didn't want them to pull up together, and they were blocks from the ferry terminal. The time had come to cue Sarah in to his plan.

"You're really exceptional, and I'm not going to hover over you. In fact, I'm going to count on you to manage when another victim in your situation would fall apart. It goes against every protective instinct in my body."

Sarah handled herself on the island, she'd be able to travel through New York City by herself.

She came alert, her attention turning to him. "What are we doing?"

"I'm going to let you out here." He pulled out his wallet where he had the rest of the money Tungsten had left them in Miami. "I'm probably being over cautious. Most likely no one is looking for us. In case, we're going to split up. Walk the half a mile down the road. Carefully, please." The traffic on River Road was busy. Zach eased the car into one of the condo parking lots lining the area and drew the car to a stop.

"I think I can manage."

"Good." He reached into the back. "Put my hooded sweatshirt on. Keep your face covered and your head down. You're really interested in the ground."

"I know how to be lost."

"Excellent." His pulse skyrocketed. Separating fucking sucked. "Buy a ticket. Go on the ferry. Be lost in New York for the next three hours. Then meet me at the Marriot Marquis Hotel in Time Square. It's huge, and they'll probably have rooms. I'll have gotten us one. Go to the front desk. Use the name Daniels. They'll have a key for you. Wait for me there. Listen, what I'm about to say is important, no matter what happens, you go there and wait. If I don't show, someone else will. Do not leave the fucking room, Sarah."

"What are you going to do in the meantime? I'm really more equipped to help than to simply get lost and go to a hotel."

"You're a target. They've taken you once. They either know you've escaped the island and everyone there is dead, or they don't. I'd hope for the latter, I plan for the former. I'm going to track your handler. I don't want you anywhere near him."

She shook her head. "How will you know where to find him?"

"I'm going to count on my people to have worked a lot of info. If not, I'll improvise." He shrugged. "I need you to be there. I need to know you will be."

"If the best way I can help you is to go lose myself in

New York City and then wait at a hotel, then I guess I'm going damsel in distress." Sarah leaned over and kissed him on the cheek. He turned his head because he needed to more than breathing and caught her lips. He felt her smile over his mouth before she closed her eyes and kissed him deeply. When she withdrew, she barely moved before she spoke close to his mouth, "Wasn't sure if we had moved into a zone where kissing you wasn't going to be allowed."

He brushed the hair off her forehead. "I plan to kiss the fuck out of you tonight in the hotel after I've dealt with the people who hurt you. If you see me by the ferry, on the payphone, or on the boat, don't acknowledge me, I'll try not to be on the boat with you."

"Got it." She stroked both his cheeks with her hands. "I'll be fine, Zach. All getting kidnapped to the contrary, I'm really good at staying alive."

"I know. It feels as if I'm slamming the car into myself over and over again. I'm letting you out."

She opened the door. "I've got it."

He was sure she did. Without looking back at her, because it might kill him, he pulled the car back into traffic and headed to the ferry. He quickly took a ticket, which would let him pay for parking later if he was ever to return for the car, which he wasn't.

After parking, Zinc jumped out of the car and headed toward the ticket office. He'd buy his passage across the Hudson River to Manhattan first and then use the pay phone to check in back at the compound.

There were three people in line ahead of him, which gave him ample opportunity to keep his head from view and make note of all the video cameras he was going to avoid. There were three he spotted right away. He should have made notes of the security system when they extracted Platinum. Of course then, no one looked for him. David had cameras on his island, and Zinc hadn't gotten to disconnect them before he got Sarah out.

Was his face on some machine where the enemy might be looking for him?

He paid for his ticket and meandered over to the pay phones. It had been such a long time since he'd used a pay phone, it felt downright surreal.

Zinc dialed Chrome's number. It rang once before the other man answered. "I've been waiting for you all day."

"Took me a little while to arrive where I wanted to be." He wasn't going to explain about the lake and the need to see Sarah by the water. Or the blowjob he'd gotten with his hands tied.

"Edgewater, by New York City. I thought you'd head there. That's where I'd have gone. We have some information on Sarah. Steele is going crazy, his lady called in favors, and we have the name of her handler."

He took a steadying breath. Talking to Chrome about a mission felt so damn normal. "I already have it. What I need is a location."

"You'll know it when your backup arrives."

Zinc took a moment to digest his instructions. "Are you fucking kidding?"

"No."

He banged his hand on the side of the payphone, of all the pain in the ass orders. He didn't need to wait, he wanted to get his job done. All he needed was an address. How fucking hard was it to give him what he needed?

"Maybe I should be talking to Titanium. I've been dead to you for years."

A long pause greeted his purposeful dig. When Chrome got quiet, it was never good news. "You and I are going to talk about your attitude and some truths you might want to consider when you return back. Shut the fuck up and wait for your backup. Are you headed for the Marriot Marquis?"

"Yes." Damn it. He wouldn't say sir. He had to take orders. However, his years of blindly believing were behind him. After he took care of Sarah, he'd have to figure out who was in charge. "All I need is an address. I won't do anything. I'll wait." He closed his eyes. "At least let me do what I do. Let me recon."

Chrome rattled off an address on the Upper West Side, and Zinc committed it to memory.

"Before you hang up, you know what you uttered was a shitty thing to say to me. We've all been scrambling around here to help you. Titanium blew a gasket. Two of his contract pilots are officially no longer a plague on the world. And we've all been pulling intel for days. Missed the fuck out of you. Put your head on straight." A pause. "I'm not done. We're going to keep our conversation going later. And if you think you're going to take a blow at my face like you did Steele, you have another fucking thing coming."

He'd missed the fucker too, although he might never be ready to say so. "Thanks."

He meant it, so he said it before he hung up the phone. All he'd ever wanted was a simple life. Serve his country, marry a pretty girl, raise a couple of kids, vacation in the sunshine. How he'd ended up as Zinc the Ghost on a payphone in Edgewater was beyond him.

Zinc only knew he'd see Sarah to safety. The rest of it he'd figure out. His head pounded, and he looked up in time to see Sarah heading for the boat. Good girl.

～

SARAH STEPPED off the ferryboat and pulled her hoodie closer around her head. It was a little hot and humid to be wearing such thick clothing. What the hell, safety trumped fashion and comfort at the moment. By the end of the day, she'd be glistening with sweat. Maybe she'd have to take a shower with Zach. Hopefully, they wouldn't almost fall on their asses again.

She grinned at the memory as she hailed a taxi and told it where to go. New York usually invigorated her, the sounds, the noise, the constant motion. She worried about Zach and what he had planned, which took the edge off her joy at returning home.

He'd not looked at all when she crossed by him to reach the bus. He'd been standing so tall and stiff while he spoke, it hadn't been hard to picture him in fatigues in a war zone. He appeared a man who could handle quite a lot on his broad shoulders.

Even being blown up and losing everything...

She shook her head. He hadn't lost everything. He had her. They'd figure it out. And hopefully, he'd put a bullet in her handler's head and be done with him fast. God, she was so bloodthirsty. Sitting on her knees for a month had changed her. Although, she'd always been able to see the benefit of a well-placed shot right between the eyes.

The cab grinded to a stop after a near miss with a pedestrian, and she realized she'd gotten downtown to the shop she wanted without noticing.

She was too distracted by half, and she had to pull it together. When she'd been aware of her surroundings, she'd still been kidnapped, so being out of it simply would not do.

Sarah paid the cabbie and walked into the store. With New York really gentrified, there weren't too many sex toy stores available anymore, and yet she'd found an upscale establishment downtown named Lovely. She'd pick some small things to tempt Zach, a celebration after the day he was sure to have.

While she wandered around New York as some kind of coward. The idea disgusted her, yet she had no idea what his mission parameters were, and she wasn't going to fuck it up.

She was paying for the few items she'd picked out—a flogger, a pair of handcuffs, and some real hand ties—when she saw the movement behind her in the mirror. Having been grabbed from behind and kidnapped, she might have developed a very healthy case of paranoia.

Sarah watched the mirror again as she took her change and the bag with a smile. The hairs on the back of her neck stood. So what if someone had stopped and stared in the store window? It likely had nothing whatsoever to do with her. She was in New York, the streets were crowded, people were on them all the time.

And what were the chances anyone would track her here? She'd gotten on a boat, taken a cab, and bought a flogger. Who could have spotted her already?

Yet...

Another movement caught her attention. Someone was across the street, and he stared right at her. A man, dark haired, tall, tattoo on his left cheek. She recognized him immediately. He'd been the head dude who had taken her the first time.

She clenched her jaw. He wasn't going to receive a second chance, and damn it, she wasn't afraid. Maybe if she said it enough, she'd believe it.

Unlike the last time, she had a gun in her purse. If there was more than one, she was only going to fire off one shot off before she took it back. The dying idea seemed less appealing.

She needed to stay alive, which meant she needed to run like hell.

They'd found her here, so they could track her. Maybe the second she'd come back to New York, she'd activated some kind of tracker.

"Do you have a bathroom?" She smiled at the clerk.

"Usually we don't allow customers..."

She clasped her hands as if she begged. "Oh, pretty please? I have to go meet my boyfriend, and I really, really have to pee." Sarah gave it her best damsel in distress smile.

"Fine. It's back there." The clerk rolled his eyes while he pointed toward the back of the store.

Sarah moved quickly as she made her way into the small powder room. She wasn't wearing any of her clothes from before or during the island. Stripping, she checked herself and didn't feel anything on her body indicating a tracker. No bumps, lumps, scars, or wounds she didn't have before.

What could still be on her they could be using?

Her clothes were new. She'd bought them herself. Her shoes were new. Damn it. What...

The thought slammed into her. For a really bright girl she'd been really stupid.

I miss the obvious.

Her hair. Washing it wouldn't necessarily remove a bug entangled in there. Not if it was embedded in her scalp like a tic. She had to move. The dudes on the street would not push into the store to grab her unless they absolutely had to.

They wouldn't wait forever.

She walked back into the main part of the shop and grinned once again at the sales clerk. "I think I want to buy more stuff. Outfits."

Sarah pointed at some of the leather getups in the corner. Stalking over she grabbed some clothes in her size.

She had no doubt it would fit except, damn it, she had to pull her act off. Her very life depended on it. "I'm going to go try these on. I guess I'm not ready to stop buying yet. My poor boyfriend and all the money I spend. Bathroom okay?"

"We have a changing room."

She pretended not to hear as she slipped a razor from the grooming section into her purse. If it didn't have batteries already in it, she was royally screwed. "Oh, the bathroom will be fine." She called over her shoulder heading fast back to where she'd come from.

Seconds later she made a lot of noise and turned on the sink on full blast. Hopefully, the clerk wouldn't hear her or she'd have a lot of explaining to do.

She had to be fast, and she couldn't let herself worry for a second about what had to happen. Her hair or her life. Well, shit. The hair would grow back.

Sarah turned on the razor, and with singular determination and steady hands, she shaved her hair off until she could see the scalp. The fucking tracker was going. Strands of her hair fell to the floor piece by piece. She'd leave some money in the bathroom for the clerk. He was going to have a mess and a half to clean after she went out the window.

SARAH ROUNDED the corner towards the Marriot Marquis with her head down. Her makeshift shave job had to make her look deranged, and she was afraid to look in store windows. Fortunately, everything was normal in Time Square.

She'd left her bag of toys when she'd gone out the window, so she wouldn't have the pleasure of introducing Zach to some fun play to get over her day. The lobby in the

Marriot Marquis was huge, and when she walked in, the comfort of anonymity suited her. She tugged Zach's hoodie around her head and looked around.

As far as she could tell, she'd not been followed, which didn't surprise her since the tracker—which had been dug into her scalp similar to some blood sucking bug, and had led those fuckers back to her—was thankfully gone.

She looked at the clock on the wall as she approached the front desk. It was late. Almost after eleven. Wanting to be a hundred percent sure she didn't lead them to Zach, she'd spent much more time than necessary running through the city and sitting on park benches.

Her lover was going to be frantic.

Since her new haircut made it unlikely a slight smile and a flirty gaze would maneuver her upstairs fast, she took another tactic. The second she reached the front desk, she started to cough. Nothing made someone more anxious to be rid of someone than the potential of germs.

"Hi. I'm here to join the Daniels party." She coughed. And then she coughed again. For good measure, she doubled over.

"Here you go." The key card slid across to her, and she took it. Twelfth floor. Room 1203.

She nodded at the poor desk clerk. "Thanks."

Maybe she didn't need the theatrics. Zach hadn't told her if the whole thing was set from his organization or not. The only thing she'd known was she didn't want to show an ID she didn't have.

She made for the elevators, each step feeling a mile. If she'd missed a tracker and led the fuckers here, she would never forgive herself. No way had she come so close to get taken out of the elevator. Or shot to death in it.

The glass elevator she was in would be beautiful, except

it stopped on every floor on its way to twelve. She took a deep breath and tried to center herself.

Externally, in addition to the current state of her hair, dark bags under her eyes caught her attention in her reflection. She'd never been in denial about being vain. If asked, she talked about her intelligence. Sarah had always been proud of her intellectual abilities.

Her long, straight dark brown hair was the icing on the cake for her. Sarah had always liked herself. Where other girls faltered in their self-confidence as teenagers, she really hadn't. Wherever she went, people commented on her gorgeous hair.

And damn it, she was growing it back.

The elevator dinged on twelve, and she walked off. Her ankle was sore, and for the first time, she noticed it. How long had it been aching? She'd slightly tripped on 6th Street forty-five minutes earlier. She was going to have to find some ice, and no way did she have the time to deal with a sprain.

Don't fall apart. She gave herself a pep talk.

Tracking the numbers, she finally got to the room and with, somehow, a still steady hand, she stuck her key in the door and watched it turn green. She turned the handle to walk inside.

Zach stood right in front of the door.

"Shit. Sarah." She was yanked into his arms. His hands were on her arms, and they squeezed. She didn't mind. "What the fuck happened? Where have you been? Why weren't you...?"

She knew the second he saw her, really got a look at what she looked like. Zach steeled his face, and the worried lover fled, replaced with hard warrior eyes. He kicked the door closed behind her. "Start talking."

8

Z inc had been prepared to cut a swath through the population of New York to find Sarah if necessary, when she failed to appear at the hotel. He'd had about another minute in him of waiting, and then he would have gone to her handler's apartment, held a gun to his head, and demanded answers. Orders or no orders

He tried to listen over the pounding of his heart as his eyes roamed her body for signs of obvious trauma other than her shaved head. She seemed okay. Tired, sweaty, and her pupils were a little more dilated than he would have liked. Most likely, she needed food, rest, and more than a single day without trauma to cool her.

A tracker? Why the fuck hadn't the thought occurred to him? It was how they'd found her in the first place. She'd had to shave her head to run away. His hands tingled, and he knew he had to calm. There was no one for him to go and kill.

"Zach." Her voice wavered. "I think I'm a little spent."

"Come on, beautiful." He took her hand. "Let's make you comfortable."

She laughed, a small sad sound. "Not at the moment, not beautiful."

He stopped moving to stare. "Don't you dare say that. Hair, no hair. I don't give a shit. You are the most beautiful creature the world ever created. Insult yourself again, and fuck our roles, I'm putting you over my knee."

Her face brightened, and some of the wariness left her eyes. "I thought asses were off limits."

"Only mine."

His head pounded, and he pushed the pain away. There was no time for his headache shit. She needed him and—

A knock sounded at the door, and Sarah grabbed his arms. "It's them. The guys following me. I'm so sorry. They must know you killed my handler, and they're after you. I led them here."

She wasn't being coherent. "I didn't kill anyone. Plans have altered." Although he might need to kill someone to know he'd done something to make her traumatic day better for her. She should never have been left alone. He was a big fucking idiot. "And those guys wouldn't knock. The announcement is our backup. Do me a favor, stand in the corner, just in case."

No more taking chances. He pulled out his gun as he approached the door. He'd not ordered any room service, and it was too late for the maids. So it was either his backup, finally arriving, or someone really had picked the wrong night to go to the wrong room. He was shooting first, asking later.

He looked in the peep hole and closed his eyes. Chrome had to be kidding. He'd sent two men, one of them was Platinum, a trained sniper and a good choice, the other was a black, blue, and bandaged Adam-Fucking-Steele. What had Chrome been thinking sending her brother here with all the emotion of their reunion plaguing everything, and his own issues with the man?

"I can hear you breathing." Steele banged on the door again. "I'm not going away, so you can open it, or I'm going to take out my gun..."

Behind him, Platinum shook his head, and Zinc opened the door. "Steele. Platinum. Won't you come in?" He extended his hand to welcome them into the room.

"Adam." Sarah gasped behind him, her hands coming to her mouth. He took a deep breath. Whatever his issues with her brother were, he wasn't going to spoil their reunion moment.

"Sarah." Steele paused as he looked at her across the room. "Jesus, what happened to you? What did those fuckers do?"

She raised her eyebrows. "I could say the same thing, but I know who did that to you."

Zinc nodded to Platinum. "Let's go, I don't know, somewhere."

The thing about the sniper was he didn't talk if he didn't have to. So how the other guy had managed to find a woman and at some point, father a child was beyond Zinc. Didn't women want to talk? Sarah certainly did.

Platinum nodded as they walked into the hall. Zinc checked to make sure his key was still in his pocket before he shut the door behind him.

"How's it going?" Zach leaned against the wall.

"Good." Platinum rocked back and forth on his heel to his toes. "You done being a jackass?"

"Maybe. I don't know." He was being a bit of a jerk. Whether or not he was able to adjust his attitude yet, he wasn't exactly sure.

Plat shook his head. "We fucking missed you. Like pain."

Zach didn't want to talk about his years away from them. Maybe not ever. "Look at you forming sentences."

The sniper grinned at him. "Miracles do happen."

❧

SARAH MOVED before she knew she was going to. In a rush of momentum, she threw her arms around her big brother's neck. He caught her, and for a second, neither spoke.

"Listen—"

She shook her head. "You don't have to explain. I've had it all from Zach. I grasp it. There were lots of reasons the last three years happened. Some of them are mind blowing. The only thing which matters, you're alive."

A tear slipped from her eye, and she wiped it away. If she let those flow, another would follow, and a big snotty mess would happen. A big mess she did not need.

She pulled back. "I hear you're in love."

"I." He shook his head before he nodded. "She's excited to meet you. Sorry, talking with you is so surreal."

Sarah nodded. "Good word."

"Tell me what's been happening." Adam took a step away. "Who did that to your hair? Are you okay? How badly are you hurt?"

She opened her mouth and spit out the story. Well, almost all of it. There were certain parts her big brother never needed to hear. Ever. The tying Zach part was going to stay neatly tucked away and between the two of them.

❧

ZACH GAVE THEM TEN MINUTES, it was all he could tolerate. His head was pounding harder, he and Platinum had done the catch-up thing as much as either of them would, and he needed to see Sarah again. The look on her face when she'd come through the door, what she'd had to do to her hair, and then Adam showing, he had to make sure she was okay.

He banged on the door before he opened it and strode in. Sarah and Adam both turned to look when he and Platinum entered. Sarah looked okay, there as some color back to her cheeks, and she had a smile formed on her face. He took a deep breath. She was okay.

Sarah walked toward him. "I'm going to give you two a little time. Come on, Platinum, you and I are going to get to know each other." She breezed by him, stroking his arm as she passed. Platinum raised his eyebrows and then followed her back out to the hall.

"Sarah, honey, that's not necessary." The last thing he wanted was time with Adam. They weren't going to sing kumbaya. There was nothing to say.

She blatantly ignored him and spoke to Plat instead. "Tell me, do you have a name other than Platinum?"

"Couple of them."

The door closed behind them with a click, and he steeled his shoulders. If he managed to make it out of the room without breaking the furniture in frustration, he'd consider himself lucky.

"The other day, before you put me in the hospital, you said something to me. A question. Want to ask it again?" Adam's face was unreadable. It wasn't because of the bandages, either. He'd hidden behind the military mask they all wore when on a mission, which threatened to take a left turn into seriously fucked.

"Why bother? You didn't answer it then. Why now?"

"Jeez-us, Zach. Passive aggressive was never your style. You pulled off your fucking mask, and it was liking looking at a ghost. I couldn't speak. Why the fuck else would I have not answered you?"

Zinc shrugged. "Maybe there was nothing to say."

"There's fuck lots to say, you ass." Adam stalked toward him. Up close, Adam looked even worse. Who had let him come on this mission? "Ask me again."

"Should you be out of the hospital?" Maybe he could send Adam home.

"Fuck you. Ask it again."

Zach's temper rose, and the throbbing headache—which had been a dull ache—surged to life as if it wanted to take him to the ground. He wouldn't fall apart, couldn't let it win right then. Gritting his teeth, he found the words again. "Why did you leave me there for them to collect me? To take my body? To destroy everything in my life I ever gave two shits about?"

"Because I fucked up. The world was coming down around me. You were dead. There were bullets flying everywhere. Titanium's whole team was dead. Tungsten. Gold. All I could think about was getting the rest of them home. And I left you, and you were dead, and I beat myself up about it every day after. You know what? I'm not sorry. Because you're alive, and so whatever circumstances took place so you could pull off your hood and beat me, then fuck yeah, great. You're here. I'd do it again."

Zach's whole body went numb. He opened and closed his mouth several times because there were no words to say to adequately express, well, anything. "I had to watch you for three years..."

"Yeah." Adam nodded, running a hand through his hair. "That's some fucked shit. No words. And if I could kill Titanium for keeping you from us, I'd do it. Believe me, brother, I would. We need him. The whole operation, Elite Metal, it goes FUBAR without him. And he is the reason you're still here, so there's that too."

Zach walked to the window. Time Square flashed bright lights outside. He'd been watching them for hours, although he could barely see them from the blur of everything around him, thanks to the migraine he couldn't avoid for too much longer. "I did die that night. Three months in a coma, I woke a shell of my former self. I've got shit to deal with which basically makes me useless."

"Nah."

What? Zach whirled around. "Oh, you think you know? You've been aware of my living for a little over a week."

"You crashed a plane successfully in the Gulf of Mexico. The Zach I knew was amazing, only I gotta tell you, I don't think you'd have done it before. We'd be fishing you and my sister out of the ocean."

He took a deep breath. "I didn't crash it. I bailed out."

"Semantics."

Was it possible? Whatever. He wasn't going to deal with word choice. "One thing you should know."

Adam crossed his arms over his chest. "What?"

"Your sister and I? We're together. The whole unsaid rule about leaving her alone? Long gone."

Steele raised his eyebrows, and his jaw clenched. "You're sleeping with my sister?"

"Totally am."

His old friend huffed loudly. "Did you screw with her to be even with me over something? Fuck with my sister as a dick move?"

Zinc's numbness passed immediately, and a red hot rage —the likes of which he had only felt the last time he beat Steele's face—threatened to consume him again. "I'm not that kind of scum."

"I was willing to forgive you for the beating. The sleeping with my sister? I basically want to pound you into the ground."

Zinc stepped toward him, knowing the move was aggressive, knowing what it would do. "I dare you to try. And insinuate I would ever hurt your sister again, and I'll make my first pounding on you look as though it was a walk in the park."

The door swung open, and Sarah stepped into the room. She groaned loudly. "Is the drama necessary? You both missed each other. Tremendously. You thought he was dead. You thought he should have somehow known you were alive, or he should have taken your body so you didn't have to watch him move on with life in silence. Ultimately, you missed each other. So hug it out instead of the theatrics, please."

Hug? Not likely. Adam shifted his posture and as much as he no longer looked as though he was going to hit him, he didn't seem to want to embrace either. Thankfully.

They'd never been exactly touchy-feely guys.

"And if you do hit him, Adam. Not in the face. He has headaches. If you make them worse, I'm going to knee you in the balls."

The shot to his kidney caught him by surprise. Adam had always been able to swing hard.

STEELE'S INTEL, which came direct from his woman, told him Sarah's handler, whose real name was Fredrick Jacobs presently—it had changed three times as far as the records went, sometimes changed by the CIA, sometimes not—was seriously in debt. To the tune of three million dollars. To Nevada gangsters.

They'd expected to only run into him, a little smash and grab the bad guy. Only they'd found him meeting in his apartment with the men who took Sarah off the street. Or at least it seemed he was. Through the open window, Sarah identified a guy who looked familiar. They'd not been able to acquire an adequate headcount. Four guys had grabbed her. With the addition of Fredrick, the number should have made five guys, if they were all there.

They'd hit the bad guy jackpot. And they had the van to manage a bigger job. Though it was taking hours longer. The hot noon sun hit Zach's head akin to a baking oven.

"Targets located. Confirmed?" Plat's voice spoke over the microphone in Zinc's ears.

Zach sat on a bench a distance away pretending to look at his cellphone.

Steele answered before he could, from his local across the street. On the off chance they knew Zach's face. It had made sense to put Steele closer. "I count four."

He raised his head at Steel's words. "There should be five." He spoke low.

"Confirm, Zinc. Only four. That's my visual, too." Platinum sounded no more than a whisper in his ear.

He would love to answer, except his eyes had blurred. Everything around him had an aura, and the auras had started to blend together into a giant ball of he couldn't see fucking shit.

"I can't." He cleared his throat. "Repeat, I can't see it."

His head throbbed as though someone had taken a chainsaw and wanted to separate his skull from the inside out. His headaches had never taken him out of a mission before. He'd always managed. What the fuck was going on?

"They're crossing the street." Steele sounded annoyed. "Confirm the four so Plat and I can grab them with the van."

Zach would love to comply and anger at his inability to do so made the whole thing so much fucking worse. "Not going to happen. My eyes have gone." The other Ghosts would have known what he had meant when Zach said that. It dawned on him perhaps Steele and Plat wouldn't. "Head injury from the explosion. Flare. I'm out. Repeat, I can't do it."

He stood. The best thing he could was move out of the way.

"Roger that," Plat responded. "I'm fairly certain, although I can't use my scope out here in the open in Manhattan. There are four. I think. Sarah, bring the van around the corner. Steele and I will take the four who are here."

"Got it. No further people leaving the building. I'd say we have four. Total of four."

And Zach was totally useless. He wanted to throw something, only what would he pick? His hands shook, and nausea formed in the pit of his stomach. Having gone through pain and recovery enough, he knew he was minutes away from puking.

Not enough time to hoof it back to the hotel room.

A screeching of tires in the distance caught his attention, and a blurry view of a van in the distance told him the mission was taking place, with absolutely no help from him. He hurried across the street. If he was going to puke, he'd do it in a garbage can.

"Zach? You okay?" Sarah's voice over the microphone. "We're still missing the man with the tattoo. The fellow who was outside the shop yesterday."

Horns honked, making his headache situation worse.

The taste of metal filled his mouth. God, it was going to be a bad migraine. Gritting his teeth, he crossed the street.

"Get out of here, Sarah. You managed to kidnap four guys off the street. Don't worry about the fifth." He clenched his hands in frustration. What was the point of being here if he couldn't help? His fucking head. His broken, worthless body. God damn son of a bitch.

"Steel and Plat have it covered. They're taking off. We'll meet them at the airport. I'm coming to you."

"No." He groaned, finally getting to the garbage can right in time. Everything he'd eaten for breakfast came back, and when he raised his head, it was to find both Sarah and a group of strangers staring at him, the later in disgust.

Sarah brushed his hair off his forehead. "Bad?"

"I can't believe I had to bail out." His vision had cleared a bit, it usually did if he puked, but not the pain. "And before you ask, I took the fucking pills."

She shook her head. "I wasn't going to question you, love."

"I don't need to be babied either." Bad enough he'd blown his role today. He got to live with looking at pity in the eyes of the woman he was sleeping with.

"Zach..."

He shook his head. Whatever she was going to say—

Zinc caught a glimpse of the guy—the man with the tattoo on his face—the same second the guy saw Sarah. Unlike them, the kidnapper seemingly had no worries about getting caught on the street. He raised a gun.

Things moved slow and fast at the same time. Zinc had only known another day in his whole life where the same strangeness of time took place, and that had been Operation Phoenix, when he'd died. He couldn't think, only react.

With an abrupt shove, he knocked Sarah onto the street

as he shouted into his microphone to Steele about the gun. He might have made sense, he might not have. The bullet missed its target. Sarah was safe.

It was a full thirty seconds before he realized it struck him instead.

"We're coming," Steele's voice screamed in his ear. He could hardly hear it. The gunman was still there. He had his weapon raised, and he was going to shoot again. Zinc couldn't reach his own gun, jammed in his pants, but he could reach Sarah's. She'd stuck the weapon in her back under her jacket. He pulled it out, and before the man could fire again, Zach laid a shot right between his eyes.

"Zach!" Sarah screamed from beneath him, finally getting out from under him. He dropped the gun, and she grabbed it. Women on the street were screaming, and it wouldn't be long until there were authorities involved.

Sarah was pale, her eyes huge. He wasn't in pain, and as he placed his hand over the bullet wound in his gut, he knew his lack of agony was a very bad sign.

"What did you do?" Her voice wobbled before she placed her hand over his bleeding insides.

"Sarah. Stop. Look at me." He didn't have long. "I told you. I wasn't going to die in an explosion."

She gasped, her mouth quivering. "You aren't going to die period."

He was losing a lot of blood, and she was getting covered in it. "You have to go."

"Are you out of your mind?"

He laughed. "Yes. And I've had the goodbye conversation once before with Steele. Terribly reminiscent. You're a CIA operative. You can't explain what happened here to the police." As if on cue, sirens sounded in the distance. "You can't be here, Sarah. It's okay. You need to go."

"No."

"If you care about me, you won't let the last things I think about be worrying about you getting hauled in by the NYPD. Please, baby. Go. I'm asking you. My job is to protect you. Getting you to go is the last thing I can do."

Her voice trembled. "Zach."

Damn it, she had to run the fuck out of there.

He took her hand off his stomach and replaced it with his own. It wouldn't do much good. Only what the hell? "You were seriously the best thing that's ever happened to me. Ever. I wish I had known when we were young and there was time. If I had to live the last three years to have had a blip of happiness with you, then I'm glad for the whole damn thing."

Tears slipped from her eyes. She'd not lost it during an abduction, a plane crash, or an attempted second abduction, but for him, she cried. Even with her hair shaved and her ill-fitting clothes, she was still the most beautiful sight he'd ever seen.

"Go. Hurry."

She nodded, tears streaming unchecked as she reached over and kissed him on the lips. "I think I've always been in love with you, Zach."

"Sweet lady, you saved my heart. Whatever good there is of me in the world fell for you. Try to remember me well."

She shuddered, and he pushed her off him with his free hand. "Damn it, Sarah. Go. If you love me, then save your-self. Run. Hide. Do what I know you can do. Call your brother. Be safe."

Sarah pulled back. "I love you."

Those achingly sweet words filled with a warmth he shouldn't be feeling. He leaned back on the ground, closing his eyes to the pain he knew would be coming. She'd gotten away. Sarah was amazing. The cops would never find her.

A wrenching burning started in his stomach, and he tried not to cry out. Some helpful bystander shouted something at him. He didn't answer.

If there was one thing Zach knew well, everyone died alone.

Screeching tires somewhere caught his attention. The sounds around him didn't matter, the world faded away. Once again.

SARAH COULDN'T STOP the tears from falling as she rocked back and forth on a park bench in Central Park. She had to look crazy, and she didn't care. Zach had taken a bullet in the gut for her. He had to be dead.

He was dead because of her.

Her hand shook as she stared at the burner phone her brother had given her before they'd left the hotel. It didn't take incoming calls, allowed the user to make outgoing. For an emergency, he'd told her.

In her fog of disbelief, she'd not phoned him yet. How much time had passed? It was almost evening.

Zach was dead.

I got the only man I've ever loved killed. A sob wracked her body.

She should have stayed. Fuck the police. She should have—

A large body plopped next to her, and she gasped in surprise for a second before she struggled in the next as the stranger pulled her against him into a hug.

"Relax. It's me, little sister."

"Adam." Her voice broke. "He's dead. He took a bullet for me. The man with the tattoo, he found us and—"

"He's not dead. Not yet, anyway."

"What?" She pulled back. "I saw his bullet wound. I know about these things. His was a fatal injury."

Adam snorted. "Zinc survived an explosion. Trust me, he should have died. You think something as small as a gut shot is going to kill him? I'm starting to wonder if he's the bionic man. The doctors have kept him alive, and as we speak, my people are stealing him from the hospital to bring him back home to Texas to recover. There could be complications. Moving him to the medical plane is risky. Fuck, I'd put odds on Zinc living through a bullet wound."

Was it possible? Her mind was slow, it wasn't taking information in the way she wanted it to. "He's still alive."

"He is."

She nodded. "How did you find me?"

He pointed to the phone. "Traced it."

"I thought it was a burner."

Her brother shrugged. "Yeah but it's my burner."

"Adam." She stood. "If he's still alive, you have to do something for me."

"What?"

"You have to go steal a motorcycle in California and bring it to Texas. Adam, please. I need to be with him, and you need to go steal his bike from that bitch, Ally." She couldn't be kind right then. Fuck that woman. No way would Sarah be marrying anyone in six months if Zach died, and she wasn't even engaged to him. "She's got it."

Her brother grinned. "Actually, that sounds fun."

9

Zach sat by the pond listening to the birds in the distance. He didn't know how long he'd been there, and he was getting a little tired of being alone. Where was Sarah? Where was Adam? Shouldn't they be here? They'd always been with him in the past.

Only, no. Life drifted by him, and he sat alone, all the time.

A sound caught his attention, a high-pitched beeping, and it seemed really out of place for his lake getaway, so he ignored it.

"Zinc, can you hear me?" He knew the voice, and he whirled around. "Enough is enough with the crap, man. We're not doing three months of you nearly dead again."

Titanium. He owed him something, didn't he? Something he needed to say to the man. Except, what?

The Ghost leader was nowhere to be seen, so Zach shrugged, and he went back to looking at the lake.

Something was wrong...

~

"THE LAST TIME, HE WOKE ALONE." Sarah turned as the man who had flown them from the plane wreck to Miami approached her. "I don't know how long he was conscious before anyone noticed. We'd all become convinced he was a goner, and then suddenly, he was back."

She'd spent four days sitting next to Zach's unconscious form waiting for him to wake. The doctors had pulled back his pain meds and seemed to feel he would soon start to regain consciousness. His blood pressure was good. They'd managed to repair most of the damage to him, although he would likely hate moving around for a while.

A miracle. One of the surgeons who had gone over his case with her when they'd arrived finally had used that word: miracle. No permanent damage.

Maybe Adam was right, maybe Zach was somehow superhuman. He survived where most men fell.

Her brother had gotten back with the bike the day before, and he and several other guys had spent the day stripping the identification numbers and the license plates so it could never be identified. Amazing what the guys here could do.

"He's not going to wake alone," she finally answered. "Thanks for coming by again."

"Let him know we're all thinking of him."

She nodded. "I will."

Sarah heard rather than saw Tungsten slip out. Everyone had been doing that. She didn't know what would happen to her once Zach woke. At some point, she'd have to let the CIA know she wasn't coming back. After everything, she knew she wanted to be a plain old lawyer and not responsible for life and death decisions with the possibility of being kidnapped off the street. Titanium wasn't done with the interrogation of the guys who had kidnapped her or her former handler. She made sure not to ask what would happen to them when he was.

She couldn't die, not even fakely. If her parents buried another child, it would kill them. Adam thought they could probably work something out. She was working overseas or something, would be the story.

She closed her eyes. She wasn't going to worry about it yet.

Zach groaned, and she sat straighter, squeezing his hand. "Zach? Can you hear me?"

His lids drifted half open, and he stared at her silently. Finally, she spoke again, "Sweetie, you were shot. You're going to be okay. I'm here. You're safe."

He nodded and then spoke slowly, "Sarah. You're. Hot. Bald."

It took her a moment to react. "All of that, and those are the first words you say?"

She laughed until she couldn't stand it anymore, and then for the second time in four days, Sarah Steele cried, holding Zach's hand.

"I'm Sarah Steele, you lunatic, I look hot no matter how I wear my hair."

"Damn straight," he answered before he closed his eyes again.

He was going to be fine, and eventually—when she could remove the image of him nearly dying on the street out of her head—so would she.

∽

Three months later...

"What do you propose to do with your new purchases?" Zach fingered the paddle she handed him before looking at her, his expression guarded.

Sarah sat next to him. "I propose to spank your behind. What did you imagine I wanted to do?"

She loved getting these reactions from him. He always objected when she pushed a limit, and then he always adored the final result. If he really objected, she backed off. He still hadn't done so. Some day, she might tell him he really preferred being submissive in bed. Not then. He'd lived through an explosion and getting shot, she didn't want to risk giving him a heart attack to boot.

"We talked about my ass being out of the question. A couple of times, if I recall."

She set the paddle down. "Something to think about."

Before she knew what was happening, he flipped her over onto her back. The soft mattress of their bed caught her, and she squealed. "I'll give you something to think about. Two things, actually."

"Oh yeah?" She wrapped her legs around his waist. "Such as what?"

"The first." His face fell serious in what she thought of as business Zach. It came close to when he actually assumed his Zinc persona. Although, Zinc had total focus and a real tendency to end up kicking someone's ass. Serious Zach was less likely to throw a punch. Neither version was ever an issue to her. He always treated her as if she was the best damn thing he'd ever seen.

She loved the fuck out of him.

"The four assholes who harmed you won't be bothering

anyone ever again. Money trail followed. Loose ends tied up."

Not the most romantic thing ever said, yet great news nonetheless. "Awesome. And the second thing? More shop talk while I have my legs wrapped around you?"

He reached into his back pocket and pulled out a small black box. "How about my latest buy?"

Slowly, he opened it until she saw a diamond ring. In her life, Sarah had never really imagined a proposal moment. Lots of girls wanted the whole romance deal, she had wanted poker nights. But with her man?

"Damn it, Zach, you're making me cry again."

He shook his head. "That's not an answer."

"I haven't heard a question." She ran her hand across his arm. A perfect guy—even though he snapped at her when his head hurt and could manage a funk akin to no other—had been made for her. Did he really think there was a chance she wouldn't say yes?

"Will you marry me, Sarah Steele?"

"I will, Zachery." She leaned forward to kiss him hard on the lips. "Thanks for asking."

"Well, you gave me back my bike. I give you a diamond ring. Seems a fair trade."

"Hey." She pinched him, and he grinned from ear to ear.

"I love you." He slipped the ring on her finger. It fit perfectly, as she'd known it would. She loved him too. And spent the rest of the night showing him so.

I am Sarah Steele. I am Zach's. Or he is mine. Both, really. Any threat will have to go through Elite Metal to find me. I'm good to go.

VOLUME THREE

VOLUME THREE

1

Russell "Francium" Burke stood in the center of the dressing room while the tailors and salespeople fussed over him. He was about to spend thousands of Titanium's dollars to appear exactly the way he needed in order to summer in the Hamptons. Some events would require a tuxedo, whereas others might need a suit—and never the same one twice. The trip also involved the acquisition of polo shirts, shorts, khaki pants, a seersucker jacket, and some shoes.

He loosened his jaw and breathed through his nose. Men, like the one he was about to become, didn't sweat the small things like the cost of their clothes. If Titanium did, then too damned bad. He could find someone else to spend the summer schmoozing with the assholes with too much time and too much money to be ethical.

No one pretended as well as Francium. He'd been doing it his whole life, and now he got to do it for the good guys. Well, the semi-good guys.

His phone dinged, and he looked down at it as the second seamstress started on the hem of his left leg.

Why am I getting pinged on my credit card that you have just spent thousands of dollars at Tom Ford?

Since operation Too Fucked Up In Russia had gone from bad to fucked, Francium's boss, code name Titanium, had lost his vision. He was totally blind. And yet somehow, he never missed a thing.

I'm being downright frugal. I've got to project the role. Being seen here isn't bad either. Could have been 10k if I'd let them design my own personal tuxedo.

It took a full minute before Titanium answered. He must have been fuming. Or talking to his wife-slash-assistant-slash-nurse-slash hot number woman in his life. Titanium and all of his various men worked on the same projects Francium did, but they took twice as long to get results. Maybe because they spent so much time falling in love and not enough time killing bad guys.

Of course, his own team had started doing that as well. Russell shoved thoughts of Wen and his woman out of his head and returned to the matter at hand, which happened to be Titanium and his purse strings.

Surely there was something you could have found that looked as good as the Tom Ford and didn't cost Tom Ford prices?

He rolled his eyes. *I don't remember you complaining about my price when I was pulling your ass and the rest of your team from death on the cold ground in Russia. If you want half-priced service, I'd be happy to take a long break, eat some dinner, watch some television, and get to Red Wolf sometime in the middle of August.*

He could feel Titanium's annoyance over the text messages. In person, the other man would probably have lowered his voice and made Francium stand there for a while without speaking.

We'll talk when you get back.

Francium had never been military, but his years with the CIA had taught him discipline and not to be insubordinate when the boss gave you an order. He'd cow-tow as necessary. Titanium would probably have him inventory the supply house to teach him a lesson on expenditures. He'd eat his shit if it meant getting the job done correctly.

The buzzing of an air conditioner and the chitchat of people making purchases tempered the loud bang of sensory overload from the always hopping Manhattan outside. The salesman who had helped him pick out the tuxedo brought Francium a scotch, meant to relax him, anesthetize him from the pain of the purchase, and loosen his purse strings so he bought more. If only they knew the man writing this particular check was in a compound in Texas.

Titanium could probably use the scotch.

The warm sting of the alcohol slid down the back of his throat. He smiled like he enjoyed the sensation. Francium only drank when he was on the job. Left to his own devices, water and tea were his drinks of choice.

His phone buzzed again, and he exhaled loudly, smiling at the seamstress. "I suppose I'm never really not at work."

She grinned at him, kneeling on the ground in front of him. He liked a woman on her knees but not for hemming his trousers. His best friend, Wen, had texted him.

You left without even saying goodbye?

Yeah...it had been a shitty move. Wen had been Russell's friend since forever. They'd been lovers once, but that had been more like a comfort fuck than anything else. These days, they were more like brothers. Francium had always preferred women, but he'd fuck anyone who moved if the day called for it. Sexuality was fluid, and so was he.

He'd never not told Wen where he was going or when he

expected to be back before. The thing was, Wen had gone and fallen in love. She was a great girl. Russell even liked her. But how the hell was he supposed to deal with Wen now?

Happiness had never been on either of their radars before. Running and hiding suited Russell. He wasn't above hightailing it when the need presented itself.

Didn't want to bother you. Seemed you were busy.

Wen, a defrocked priest, would see Russell's response for the pissed off passive-aggressive move it was.

For real on this?

Francium shut off the phone. Enough was enough. He didn't do emotions, and he wasn't going to come off like some jealous ex because his best friend was happy. Russell's job was going to take all summer, it would be enough time for him to get his shit together and be back in control when he returned.

The tuxedo was ready to be tailored for him. His job had officially begun.

STANDING on the porch of the deck overlooking the ocean, Russell watched his target from across the beach. Remington Reagan—every time Francium even thought the name, he snorted, he'd have to get his response under control—fucked his very good-looking wife up against the wall of their seven thousand square foot home. Unlike Francium, who had rented the house—thank you, Titanium—for the summer, the Reagans owned their beach house. They also owned their co-op in Manhattan and their ski home in Vale. Of course, they were getting later and later in their payments.

Remington was being fed information—or rather his underlings were—leading to bad investments and loss of income. Since the money he invested, well eighty percent of it, was Red Wolf's, the big boss was going to need answers soon. His pockets were getting mighty empty. They'd come to all this information thanks to Zinc, who had, in the process of rescuing his then girlfriend now wife, Sarah, had pulled a ton of information off an island where Red Wolf's now-dead lawyer lived. Sarah put a bullet between the man's eyes, and their intel had doubled.

Oh, the dramatic love stories of his colleagues and friends...That wouldn't be happening to Francium. Leave lovelorn nonsense to others.

As long as the Reagan's underling continued to make such bad calls, they'd all be fine. He'd soon be fired, and Francium would walk right in because he was going to be Reagan's best friend. Six months in place, then Reagan would have an accident. Oh, not one that would kill him—although he was such a scumbag, Francium wouldn't miss him—but it would put him out of work. Red Wolf would then turn to him. They'd have his finances by the throat.

Bye-bye money, bye-bye Red Wolf. Or at least, it would help. His team was taking care of the rest. It might even be possible to shorten the timeline, if Russell could get really friendly, fast.

In the meantime, Reagan had three mistresses and a hot wife he was not satisfying in bed. Russell strolled to the edge of the porch, sipping his tea and watching. Francium loved to watch. Truth was, he was a total voyeur and not at all ashamed at letting his freak flag fly when circumstances allowed.

Lara London-Reagan had the best legs he'd ever seen. Currently, they were wrapped around her husband's waist while he slammed her into the wall over and over in his Neanderthal-esque fucking, if it could even be called that, display. Francium wasn't sure he'd ever seen a woman so completely uninterested in sex before.

Was she frigid, or was Reagan's banging routine not what she was into? He didn't suppose it mattered. His intel told him Lara was a nice woman. She'd been an art dealer, once upon a time, before she'd been Mrs. Reagan.

She'd helped return art stolen from Jewish families during World War II by the Germans. Not every dealer would do that, not when there were millions on the line. He'd been impressed. Why did she marry such a scumbag? Francium sighed. He'd never understand romance. Fucking, yes. Loving, no.

He set down his teacup on the table next to him. This was deadly dull. He liked to watch, but usually at least both of the parties he spent time with were having a good time. It was their own fault if they didn't close their curtains. Francium sat in his chair like he had nothing better to do in the world than sit there and observe.

Reagan's underling sent information to Francium earlier in the day. Red Wolf's portfolio would be down another few points. Tap by tap, it looked like incompetence instead of an attack. Acting anonymously, Zinc demanded Danny Clyde, the underling, do this or they'd tell his wife and then the authorities about the other women—all twenty-four of them, and not all of age. When this was over, Francium would turn old Danny right in. He didn't like men who dated fifteen-year-old girls. Three more months, and those kids' parents would know.

He didn't like the way predators hid, whether they were the rich or the poor kind. At least prey should know they were under attack. Red Wolf had been the predator for too long. He wouldn't be around to harm anyone else.

Lara turned her head, looking out the window and caught his attention. Her eyes widened when they made eye contact. A distance away, it was hard to see him, but not impossible. Francium groaned. This was going to be a problem. He was going to go from nice new neighbor to creepy guy next door. Best thing to do was to quickly walk inside like he was embarrassed for having seen her.

Except she smiled at him. With his forehead pressed into her shoulder, her husband couldn't see what she did. Lara bit down on her bottom lip, her entire demeanor suddenly changing. As her husband continued his attempt, Lara suddenly became engaged in the act. Only...it wasn't Reagan's lovemaking exciting her. It was Russell. He'd been a voyeur long enough to know the difference.

Well, if she liked to be watched, he'd give it to her. Francium sat back in his seat, put his feet up on the nicely placed footstool, and watched.

Her cheeks got pinker, and her head arched back where it leaned against the wall. He couldn't hear her, but he'd bet she'd gotten louder, wetter. If she'd been one of his women, he'd have directed her ahead of time for certain acts to increase both her pleasure and his. Things she'd be doing to Reagan right now would get Francium off watching, and make her own excitement double. He couldn't instruct her, but he liked that she wanted him to watch.

Red-headed, five foot seven, thin, with long limbs and small but perfect breasts, Lara was the stuff of fantasy. He was a man who dealt very well in the idea of pretend. That was the thing about watching. Anyone could be anything. Debbie the lawyer and Jon the cook could be perfect, for one genuine moment, when they lost themselves to pleasure. He got off on seeing it. His cock hardened in his pants. She was going to come, very soon, and his body had taken note. God, she was beautiful.

Her mouth opened. She was close. Francium leaned even further forward. When was the last time he'd been so enraptured? His last trip to his favorite club had been downright dull. Lara was close, she was...

Reagan came, nearly collapsing on his wife, who he lost hold of. She slipped down the wall, and Francium groaned. The fucker hadn't held out until his wife was ready to come? Russell placed his palm over his eyes.

She appeared so disappointed, and Francium was, too. He needed to know what Lara London-Reagan looked like when she came. Reagan walked away, leaving Lara standing in the living room. She turned to the window, her eyebrows raised. Lara smirked at him before she turned on her heel and sauntered away.

He was stunned. Who was Lara London, and why did he suddenly, in the middle of a mission, need to know more about her?

LARA WALKED PEACEFULLY into her very large closet and sank down onto the floor. What the hell was wrong with her? Her hands shook, and she placed her head on top of her knees. First, she agreed to have sex with Remington, something she'd sworn after the last time she would never do again, and then she'd been turned on because she caught the neighbor watching them. Why had she liked that so much? She should have been so seriously mad he had dared to not just stand there and stare, but he'd sat down to watch.

The way she had stared back—she'd practically encouraged and certainly consented for it to continue. Hell, she had liked it so much.

Now her husband was going to think it had been his magic cock to make her all hot and bothered. He could blackmail her to stay in this marriage, could make her pretend she had feelings for him, but he couldn't get her turned on anymore. Those days were long gone. The day she'd found out about his illegal dealings.

She didn't even know why Remington came to her today, it had been months since he wanted her. Something with him was off...

And what was the deal with their new neighbor? She knew very little about him. The rumor mill in their East Quogue moved fast. The realtor who rented him the house had told one of her acquaintances he was a single man, worked in finance, and he'd be staying there all summer. No one had told her how incredibly handsome he was, or the way his gaze seemed to move through her like he could see all her secrets and wanted her anyway.

Lara groaned. This was so ridiculous, and she had things to do. Forcing herself up, she took a fast shower, scrubbing her body until she felt clean. Or the closest thing to it. She hadn't been clean in five years. When had thirty years become so old?

She slipped her Lili Pulitzer maxi dress over her head and let it fall to the floor around her feet. A quick spin in the mirror showed her she was all put together. Her arms looked fit, thanks to her trainer, and no one would criticize her choice of attire. Pairing it with Salvatore Ferragamo sandals, she officially looked the part she was stuck playing for the time being.

Lara steeled her shoulders. Someday, she'd be back in a little apartment in New York City, wearing jeans and a white tank top before she went out to a movie. She wouldn't be making small talk on a veranda with people she hated.

One last glance in the mirror before she pasted on a smile and let the driver take her to another summer party where she had nothing in common with anyone.

"This is what happens when you sell your soul, Lara." And yes, she'd gotten to the point where she spoke to herself in the mirror.

Time had a way of moving without her paying much attention to it. Hours could pass, and it felt like she blinked. Today was not one of those days. For once, she was intently focused on the conversation around her.

Desiree Garcia had been talking about her Mendoza for hours. Its place of honor, above one of their fifteen fireplaces, certainly drew attention to the new purchase. She stepped to the side to get a better look at the piece.

Someone moved to her right, standing too close for comfort. She turned her head, assuming it was one Remington's friends trying to sleep with her again, and stopped short. It was her neighbor. The one who had watched her having sex. Heat infused her cheeks, and her heart rate kicked up.

Tall, dark, with the most intense brown eyes she'd ever seen, and he smelled like a cool breeze. "She's certainly in love with her new purchase. Does she have a party every time she gets a new piece?"

She chewed on her bottom lip. "Yes, actually. First time here?"

"Met her on the beach yesterday, and she invited me. You seem unimpressed. Not a big fan of Mendoza?"

She laughed as softly as she could, not wanting to draw attention to herself or her neighbor, whose voice—low and in her ear—felt like a private conversation she didn't want others to hear. Did she dare tell him the truth?

"I love Mendoza. But that," she nodded toward the painting, which was badly hung and had way too much sunlight on it, "is not a Mendoza. That particular Mendoza is in a warehouse in Miami and will likely not see the light of day for the next forty years or so. That's a fake. A very expensive, very ridiculous fake that she is going to keep hung above her fireplace until she dies or gets divorced. Then it will be appraised and the truth will come out."

"My, my." He sucked in his breath. "How did you come to this conclusion? Been hanging out in nefarious warehouses in your five-hundred-dollar shoes?"

She laughed. He'd insulted her, or at least taken a bit of a jab, and she was still amused. Something was wrong with her. "Before I had the expensive shoes, I used to be a little shadier than I am now. Then again, I might still have a little bit of a bad girl in me. I did get all kinds of turned on letting you watch me earlier."

He sucked in his breath. "If we're going to talk about that, we should know each other's names. I know you're Lara London-Raegan. When I was invited here, our host squealed how I'd taken the house next to yours. My name is—"

"Russell Burke." Since he'd confessed to knowing her name, the least she could do was to offer him the same. "You work in finance."

"Finance is a big area. But, yes, I do." He smiled, but it didn't hit his eyes. Was he...faking it? Lara didn't know what gave her that thought. She doubted anyone else would notice. But she spent so much time having to pretend to be happy, she knew another faker when she saw one.

She took a sip of the champagne she remembered she

held in her left hand. "Is there a Mrs. Burke, or a fiancée to Mr. Burke, or someone who won't like it that you were watching me have sex with my husband?"

"There isn't a soul in my universe who would care. But I imagine your husband might."

Lara shrugged. She shouldn't be talking like this. Telling him she knew where the real Mendoza was had to be the stupidest she'd been lately. What was it about this man that made her behave so completely out of character?

"I think the less said to my husband on that subject, the better."

"All right." Russell touched her lower back, and heat travelled through her. "Before I leave you alone, because any second we're going to draw attention, and I think that's the last thing you want, I have to tell you something. That dress on you is utter perfection. Most of these women here, they have all the right clothes, but when they come in the room, they look wrong...like the fashion is wearing them. You are why they make clothes. You're perfect, Lara London. We will see each other again."

He backed up, winking at her once, before he turned and left the area. Desiree had just finished her speech about the dealer who had loved her, and that was why he told her all about the Mendoza that someone else wanted, but he would sell to her.

Lara raised her glass to Desiree. "Congratulations on the find, Desiree. I'm sure this a painting that will stay with you...forever."

Desiree grinned, her forehead not moving thanks to what Lara guessed was her most recent Botox injection, and practically twittered at the compliment. Lara nodded at Desiree. The people she socialized with over the summer loved to talk about her art background as though it was something they understood. The image they held of her... standing alone in a gallery, looking at artwork, waiting for Remington to find her and bring her to the better world they all lived in.

Most of her time had been in dusty warehouses, pulling paintings out of boxes and listening to artists yell. She sighed. It shouldn't have been fun, but wow, she missed it a ton.

Her husband's laugh caught her attention. He must have just arrived. She turned to see him in a circle, talking to several men she knew casually. They were mostly his business associates. And...Russell Burke. Well, now. That was interesting.

WITH THE LIGHTS OFF in her home, Lara could see the scene across the way at Russell's home. Her husband was there, and at least twenty other men, all of them loud, all of them drunk or high. Normally, she would be thrilled to have Remington out of the house. Better he spend the night with one of his women than come home to her. He'd likely leave Russell's late and go on to one of the cottages in Southold where he kept the long-term girls.

Her body felt itchy. She didn't want Remington over there with Russell. She wanted to be there. Why did Remington get everything when he was such a terrible person?

She shoved off her lightweight coat and threw it on the couch. Her type-A personality didn't usually allow her to leave her things where they didn't belong. There was a closet to hang her coat in. Instead, she stormed across the house to her walk-in closet. This had become her space, the one spot in the house that Remington never came, where he left her alone.

The only place in the house where she could hide anything.

Going into her black purse—the unnamed one that she'd come into the marriage with—she pulled out the cell-phone he knew nothing about. She quickly dialed her sister, who answered a moment later.

"Lara, you okay? I'll come get you right now."

Hearing her sister's voice always made her feel better. "I'm okay. Just wanted to hear from you tonight. How are things?"

Remington had taken everything away from Lara, and she'd gladly given it over. But the second she'd pushed back, he'd gone after her sister. Lara would do anything to keep Margot okay. The woman had been through enough. She'd find a way out of this for both of them.

2

Update? Wen wanted to know how Russell was doing.

Taking a deep breath, he answered Wen. *I've got a hard on for the target's wife. Never quite had this experience before. Not sure how I'm going to handle it. But I'll get the job done. Anyone heard from Arsenic?*

Their teammate had gone missing, and everyone was worried, especially her brother Kryptonite. It wasn't that Francium didn't trust Addison to take care of her business. No one was better qualified at managing her own shit, but it had been a while since she'd gone off holding hands with the dubious Uranium. It would have been nice to have some kind of heads up that she was alive and not rotting in a gutter somewhere.

He finished dressing and looked out the window. Since he'd woken an hour earlier, he'd been unable to stop himself from checking for Lara. He'd had to put up with her husband until one in the morning. Francium wanted to throw him off the balcony, and generally speaking, he was the most patient person in any room.

The bait had been placed. Francium had given Remington a couple of tips on moves to make the next day, which would result in a better day for his portfolio. The other man wouldn't have to sweat it out as much as he had other days. Manipulating the market was complicated, but not too complicated for Zinc, in small ways. He wasn't going to let anyone lose money in their 401ks or screw the little guy. Fake companies, fake stocks, fake funds. All of it looking perfectly legit.

Red Wolf was going to have a good day. Then Francium would be unavailable for a few days, and everything else in Remington's life would go to hell. He'd be back in time to help again. Then, he was in like Flynn.

No, Wen finally answered, *and it's starting to become an issue around here. Finish up and come back.*

Just as fast as I can, brother.

He looked out the window again, this time seeing who he looked for. What was more, she saw him too, and if he wasn't mistaken, had been looking for him. He smiled. She was in her bathrobe, a white, warm looking garment. Was she naked underneath? Would she be willing to drop it to the ground?

He grabbed his phone and held it in the air, hoping she'd grasp his meaning. He wanted her number. In the meantime, the binoculars that were always something he had, and he hoped she didn't question, would come in handy. He waited to see what she'd do. She'd either respond, or she wouldn't. He could get her number easy enough, but that would expose more than he wanted to at this point in the game. He was still playing nice guy.

She disappeared for a second and came back with a piece of paper with numbers scribbled on it. After lowering his lenses, he grabbed his phone and sent her a text.

Hey, gorgeous.

He watched as she looked down and then back up. His phone dinged. *Hi, yourself. Have fun last night?*

No. *Yes, of course. Always up for a good time. Drop the robe.*

Russell didn't expect her to obey. He didn't generally give orders. A few instructions before he and his partners went into the club, and then Francium sat back and let her do whatever turned her on. The more she got off, the more he did.

She stepped out onto her porch so they could face each other without the wall. Or maybe she was really pissed. It would be easier if she hated him. He could do his job without distraction. His dreams he couldn't force into compliance, but his days he could manage.

To his utter shock, she dropped the robe. Her hands went onto her hips as she threw her red hair over her shoulders. Her eyebrows raised in challenge. She knew he hadn't expected her to do it.

Good girl...

She'd been dressed when she fucked her husband against the wall. Now, she was on full display. Her breasts were small, but perky. They'd fit perfectly in his hand if he ever decided to touch her. Her hips were round, and her belly flat. She waxed her pussy, leaving it totally bare. His mouth watered. Usually, he didn't care if he actually got to touch, skin-to-skin, but now he wanted to. Although, he'd also love to watch her.

I'd love to watch you, honey. To take you somewhere where you could find pleasure, and I could watch you do so. It would be so hot.

She looked down at her phone. Watching as she read, his cock hardened to the point of pain. That was fast. Just staring at her naked shouldn't have made him so completely turned on. Not so fast, anyway. He had to adjust his pants. Shit, when was the last time this had happened? He couldn't even remember. Sex was so boring lately.

Her hand shook slightly when she texted back. *Why can't you?*

Well to begin with, you're a married woman. I'm not full of a lot of morals, but I do try to avoid getting in the middle of other people's unions. Second, I don't know if you'd like the club.

She walked closer to the balcony. They were as close as they were going to be without one of them actually leaving their home to go to the other. She typed back. *You spent last night with my husband. Do you think we have a real marriage? He plays. Why can't I?*

Well, that was a really good question. And if he were allowed to be Francium, he'd agree with her. He couldn't afford to express that opinion. *Leave him and I'll take you anywhere you like.* Eventually.

Like I could? I don't want anything from you but this. I've had enough of your kind.

She didn't know his kind, and she never would. Sleeping with the target's wife...well, that hadn't been on the agenda, and Titanium probably wouldn't like it. He wasn't exactly sure. Titanium seemed to be in favor of love and romance.

But Francium wasn't sure that was exactly what was going on here.

I'm not a kind any more than you are. Shit, I'm sick of this. Come to your front door.

He stormed away, berating himself the whole time. What the fuck was wrong with him? Why was he bothering with this woman at all?

Why couldn't he leave her alone?

It took him exactly five and a half minutes to reach her front door. Other than the place where their balconies faced each other, the houses weren't close to one another. She swung open the door, wearing a robe, which was smart considering this side of the house faced the street, but disappointing nonetheless.

"What?" she practically shouted. Her outburst forced him to reassess her. She didn't look as put together as she had the day before, and it wasn't because of the bathrobe. No, Lara had become a woman on edge.

Before he could overthink it, he placed his hands on her shoulders. "Are you okay?"

She swatted his hands off her shoulders. "No, I'm not. Why do you care? You don't deal with married women. Fine. I'm stuck in this marriage. I can't get out. I'll never get out. Don't worry, it's not your problem. Maybe I'll hire a prostitute and do something with him."

He forced himself to breathe. "Why do you think you can't get out? Surely there are thousands upon thousands of lawyers in the Tri-state area alone you can hire. I'll find you one."

Francium bordered on going too far, on losing the character. Would good old financial genius and millionaire Russell Burke want to help this woman? Probably not. But the reality was Francium had a hard time with women in distress. He always had. Maybe it had to do with the fact his father had killed his mother, but he couldn't stand to see a woman in trouble thinking she had no way out.

"It's more complicated than that." She looked down at the ground and pursed her lips. He understood her nonverbal quite well. No one read people better than Francium, and no one was better than he was at getting people to open up.

Did he want to use his abilities right now? Not particularly. What he really wanted to do was to hold her in his arms and tell her he'd make it all better, which was weird considering how little he liked to be touched outside of the bedroom.

"You don't know me, and I don't know you. But we saw each other. And I don't mean spotted, like I saw you on the street. I mean we saw each other." He was more than a little disturbed that as he spoke the words, he found he believed what he said. She might very well have seen right into him while she fucked her husband against the wall. "If you need help, I do know people who can provide it."

"There's no one you know who can help me with this. What I want is to feel good for a little while. Do you want to fuck me while my husband, thankfully, fucks one of his many whores?"

He shook his head. "No, I don't, and you don't want that either."

Francium let himself into her house without being invited. Getting inside would solve a twofold problem for him. First, he needed inside the Reagan's house to scope things out, and the second was to make sure Lara London-Reagan was not being held hostage inside by armed guards or something equally as worrisome.

He doubted this was the case. She couldn't have dropped her clothes the way she had if she was being observed. Or if she knew she was...

Russell did a quick look around. There were no obvious security cameras anywhere. That didn't mean there weren't any, and maybe Remington didn't want to be observed any more than he wanted to watch his wife. Still, it was a seven thousand square foot home. Someone had to clean it, and they might have wanted to be sure no one was stealing.

That was the world they lived in.

He put on his game face and swung around to face Lara. "Tell me why you're afraid."

"Will knowing make you want to fuck me more? You're a stranger. Why do you care?" She covered her eyes with her hand. "No one can help me. You'll run straight to my husband. He's rich and powerful. Everyone I know is one of his people. You spent last night with him. I'm sure you're no better."

Russell grabbed her and pulled her up against him, whispering in her ear when he did. If there was security system in this house, it was sophisticated; he had no intention of getting caught. "Lara, do you want to get out of here? Do you want to be out of your marriage fast?"

Lara smelled like baby powder and strawberries, both were probably from her morning routine. The day before, he'd scented a light wisp of lavender, a perfume or a body spray she'd put on. This was so early in the day, Lara hadn't even finished dressing yet. There was something intimate about this, something about seeing a woman who was never seen in public looking like anything but perfect, rumpled up a little bit.

She was sexier like this than in any of her couture pictures he'd seen or how she'd appeared at the Mendoza showing.

Lara nodded, slowly. "Why ask me if I can have the impossible?"

"Would you be willing to do whatever it takes?"

She stepped back, wiping at her eyes. Lara hadn't cried, but she must have felt like she was going to. "Anything. Why are you asking? Do you want a sex slave in return for some help? This is a ridiculous conversation."

He pointed at her and crooked his finger. She needed to

follow him outside. Titanium was going to need to be consulted.

LARA WASN'T DRUNK. She wasn't stoned. Hell, it had been a long time since she'd been either of those things. So why on God's green earth was she telling this man—this stranger, whose most profound statement to her had been to take off her robe—that she couldn't get out of her marriage?

Pacing in front of her house, not dressed to be seen, she decided she was out of her mind. This was going to be either a great turn of events or an utter disaster.

What was he doing? Russell's face was blank, hard to read. Every so often he seemed to say one word or another, eventually he disconnected the call. He walked over to her.

"Have you changed your mind?" Why did his voice have to be so sexy?

Calm down Lara. As if ordering herself to do so had ever worked. "Are you kidding? No."

"Here's the deal. I can help you. I know some powerful people who do this kind of thing. They do it well. They're willing to help, they're even happy to. But I have to gather some information before they'll give me the complete go ahead."

Her throat felt tight, and she found it hard to believe. As per usual, she ignored the sensation. "I suppose that is fair, but so help me, if this turns out to be some kind of joke, some kind of test you and my husband are playing on me, than I swear to God, I don't know how, but I will burn you. I will get you in your sleep. You'll never be able to rest because you'll always know I'm coming, some day."

He raised his dark eyebrows, his face blank. "I know

some people who would love you. Good thing you're never meeting them. Start talking."

"He said if I leave him, if I ever even think of leaving him, he'll tell the people who want to kill my sister where she is. He'll have her killed." Her voice broke, and she looked away. She would not cry, not in front of this stranger making her bare her story to him while he stood listening. "My sister and I used to do some things a lot of people— most people—would find illegal. It was to a cause we believed to be a greater good. We were both in the art world, and we decided we could help, um, families of Jews who lost their artwork in the Holocaust."

He rocked back on his feet. So far, she hadn't shocked him, and he wasn't running for the door. "Noble cause."

"Yes, well, there is a right way to do things and a wrong way. I tended to help the victims use the court system. Friends who were lawyers helped. There are tribunals. It's complicated. Margot, that's my sister, she stole the paintings and returned them. Pissed off a couple of families in Buenos Aires who are the sons and daughters or grandchildren of Nazis. They aren't happy to have their Picassos disappear. I betrayed my sister when I confessed to my husband two years ago the real reason my sister spent her time in hiding. He's going to...destroy her if I leave."

A muscle ticked in his jaw. "Why so much trouble? He cheats on you. You seem to know. Are you such a stupendous wife? No offense, but it seems to me Remington could get another wife, any number of arm candies."

"Ouch." She rubbed the space over her heart. She'd been called worse—whore and sellout were rougher—but arm candy wasn't her favorite. "Not sure why you dug at me like that. I hear what you're saying. Yes, he could have any wife he wanted. But I saw some things he didn't want me to see, about a business associate, and he's terrified I might talk. He also thinks they might kill me if I were to ever come out. So, in some sick way, I think he truly believes he's protecting me."

He put his hands on his hips. "Why continue to sleep with him?"

"Is that a question for your people who can help me or for yourself?"

Russell's mouth twitched. "My own edification, I suppose."

"I don't dare piss him off. What if he exposed Margot?"

He was silent for a moment. "Alright, so we'll take your case, so to speak. I suppose I should re-introduce myself. My name is Russell Burke. I'm not in finance. I'm here to destroy your husband's career so I can get close to Red Wolf—the name I presume you are aware of, and the one that has gotten you into trouble. I work for a group that has sworn to bring him down. Although Russell is certainly one of my names, many people call me Francium. For the purposes of this, I think you should stick to calling me Russell."

"You want to stop him? Red Wolf? The man funding my husband who is doing...bad things with the money my husband makes for him?"

He nodded. "That's right."

"And if I help you, you'll help me." She could hardly believe the words as she uttered them. Could this be happening? Could this be real?

The man who said people called him Francium nodded one more time. "Has Margot been moved? She's not still sitting where Remington could out her, right?"

"No, but it wouldn't be hard to find her once he gives over her picture. Photo recognition software. Her life would be over, and then she'd be killed. This is all my fault."

He shrugged. "Is it your fault that you told your scumbag husband the secrets of your sister? Maybe. I'm not really concerned with you putting your faith in the wrong person. What I see is that you are a smart, beautiful woman who is being abused—held emotionally captive by her husband, a very bad man. Let's get out of here. I don't want to be here when your husband gets home. He's not supposed to see me for a few days. You need a break, and since we have time to figure out how you can help me, I'm going to take you somewhere I think you'll like."

She looked down at herself. He wanted to take her out at some time between nine and ten in the morning—she didn't even know exactly—while she looked the way she did?

"I'm going to need some time to get ready."

He shook his head. "You have ten minutes. Yoga pants. Tunic. You don't need makeup, but if you insist, then fine."

She turned and ran back in the house. Even Remington didn't give her orders like Russell did. Where were they going? She hadn't even asked. But she wanted to do what he said, and not just because he was going to help her. Lara wanted to please Russell. She didn't dare examine the need too closely.

It had been two years since Lara experienced a shred of happiness. This very second she was, and she intended to go with it. If she could cause Remington and Red Wolf pain, then even better.

Eight minutes later, she appeared back outside. Russell must have gone and gotten his car, because a sleek S-Class black Mercedes waited for her, and she got inside. Whoever this group was who employed Russell and would help, they were certainly not without their finances. He sped down the driveway and out the front gate, his attention on the road.

"We're a few hours from getting where I'm taking you.

We'll be in Manhattan, but don't worry, no one will recognize you where we're ending up. It's private. Only a few individuals, carefully screened ladies and gentlemen, even know about its existence."

Her heart rate kicked up. "The club you talked about?"

"One of them. I'm a particular kind of man, and I'm not going to lie about it, since I've gotten into the truth telling business, all of a sudden. I'm deeply attracted to you. I wouldn't have told you to drop the robe otherwise. You're hot as hell." He gripped the steering wheel tightly. He wasn't, in any way, as calm as he pretended. She wondered if anyone else would ever notice.

"Thank you for the compliment."

He nodded. "I'm not a good person, per se. I've done tons of shit. A psychologist would probably have a field day with me. My father killed my mom. I don't remember it. I was then put in a place where they tried to drive all the Apache out of me. I snuck out, managed by the age of ten to cross the border into the United States. At one point, I ended up in the CIA. They were training me to be an assassin. A friend of mine stopped that."

Well, he'd told her a lot she had to digest. Her training on saying nothing when there was nothing to say helped right then. "I see."

"I doubt it, and that's fine. I'd rather you not see. The other part of me that you should understand is that I'm an equal opportunity lover. I've never been in a monogamous relationship. I don't do love. I'll have sex with whomever. Women. Men. Both at the same time. Whatever works. You may have already figured it out, but what I really want to do is watch two other people together."

The tick in the muscle in his cheek was back. Images flooded her head. Russell with other men, with women, with both. She wet her panties. Squirming, she tried to control her pulse. This was a new development. She'd never been so...excited by hearing what someone else did before.

"I'm sorry, I'm quiet. I'm a little..." She stroked her throat. "Overcome. Are you taking me to the club to be... with other people?"

He shook his head. "I'm not really sure what to do with you, to tell the truth. You make me feel...protective." For a second, he took his gaze off the road and looked out the side window. She'd almost have missed the tell, he did it so quickly. "I want to make sure you like it there. Then we'll start out slow."

"I'm not a wilting flower. I mean, I have been, but before that, I wasn't. I was the kind of woman who knew how to get things done."

She could almost see herself as she had been, as she'd been when she'd been introduced to Remington Reagan. He'd seemed so charming and interested in her in a way no one had ever been before. What she knew now was that Remington seemed that way to everyone. When anyone spent time with Remington, they felt like the most important person in the universe. He'd wanted a wife who could speak on many subjects: art, music, theater, fashion—all the topics he thought his wife should be able to speak about with the other wives.

They'd discussed children. She was pretty sure she didn't want them, and he was fine with that. They'd be on charity boards together and help fund hospitals.

All of it had sounded like heaven...she'd fallen, face first, into Remington and stayed that way up until she found the file he kept on Red Wolf. Was he planning on blackmailing the terrorist? She didn't know, but suddenly, it all felt like blood money, and she wanted nothing to do with it.

Hypocritical? To quote Russell, maybe. But she had changed, and if she wasn't stuck between a rock and a hard place, she'd already be gone.

"I'm looking forward to knowing who you are."

So was she.

3

Francium led Lara through the door of Erin Harden's private club in the East Village. He'd been to all the clubs in New York City catering to his particular tastes. Some of them were small, intimate, like this one, and some were a romping good time. A woman who could be a grandmother ran a dungeon out of her small apartment on the Upper East Side. That had been a strange, but memorable night.

This particular place was in the back of a tattoo parlor. Or maybe it was more appropriate to say that the tattoo parlor was at the front of the club. Either way, he was comfortable here, and despite an occasional moment where she rubbed the back of her neck, Lara seemed pretty comfortable too. Russell never drank alcohol when he came to play. Hell, he only drank when he was in character. Left to his own devices, he hated the stuff.

"Lara, do you want a drink?"

She shook her head, leaning on the couch next to him. "No, I'm okay. Are we going to be sitting here all night?"

"It's still day, so I should hope we're not going to be sitting here all night."

She rolled her eyes at him. "You know what I meant."

He did, but he was glad to see the spunk in her gaze. "I do. No, we'll not be sitting here all day. Come on."

They'd been waiting in what basically amounted to the lounge, but now they would move on. There were plenty of spots in the club to indulge in whatever kink the member liked. Dr. Kenneth Kent, ophthalmologist and Master extra-ordinaire, kept the place clean and running smoothly. Ken knew Francium as well as anyone did, which meant—with the exception of Wen—not very well.

Lara would be safe here. No one would recognize her, and if they did, no one would say a word about her presence.

He brought her into the viewing room. Like the rest of the club, Ken seemed to like to decorate his rooms in burgundy. Maybe it made people feel safer. He didn't know.

The viewing room was on the other side of a two-way mirror. Whoever sat in the room could see the other side, but the participants couldn't do the same.

"If you decided you wanted to participate in this, then we would play a little game. I would need your consent. And we'd come up with a safe word so you could tell me if you got uncomfortable. Then you would perform, and I would watch. Afterwards, maybe we'd have sex. Right here on this couch, or somewhere else."

Her breath hitched. She liked the idea. But which part? The bit where she did as he instructed her so he could watch, or the sex on the couch? Because he knew which he preferred. If she was going to pretend she got off being watched, this wasn't going to work. She had to mean it.

"What would you want me to do?"

He leaned against the glass. "Not much for now. You're married." Something he was going to change at his earliest chance. Plans were going to have to change and fast. Lara was more than a distraction. She could easily become an obsession.

She reached out and gently placed a finger on his chin. "If I wasn't married?"

He raised an eyebrow. God, this woman was so sexy. "More." He knocked on the window. "Let's start slowly. Shall we? You want to try this with me? You want to let me watch you?"

"I do." She looked down at the floor. "It's been a long time since I've been allowed to really want anything. It's hard for me to admit to it, to tell you what I want."

He stroked the side of her face. Her skin was ridiculously soft. How did she get it that way? How much product did it take? Or was she naturally the equivalent to silk?

"You're going to have to do better than that, honey. This only works when you tell me the truth. Pick a word. Tell me what it is. You say it, I know you don't want to go any further with the scene."

"I know what a safe word is. I'm not living entirely in a bubble." She smelled great too. He took a deep breath to take her deeper inside of him. What was that? Vanilla? "How about turtle? If I say turtle, I'm safe-wording."

"Turtle." People picked what they picked. "That works."

"Tell me something, Russell." The way she said his name —or at least, the closest thing he'd ever had to one—made heat travel to his groin. Oh yes, he was in so much trouble with this woman. "While you are getting to know me, while we are learning what I like, will I get to know you? Or are you hidden away?"

The room felt uncomfortably small. "I am not a man who shares myself easily."

"Then maybe this could be good for both of us. There's something about you, something that keeps me coming back. I can't imagine how this happened. I'm taking a huge risk, and yet with you, it doesn't feel that way."

His heart beat fast against his ribs, the rate kicked up way higher than it should have been. "I almost never tell the truth. Lying comes more easily to me than the truth ever could. You should never believe a word I say."

She lifted her eyebrows in what seemed like a challenge. Was she? "Duly noted."

"Remember your safe word. The door to the room is right there. We have two choices. I can instruct you over a microphone, or you can listen to me now and then go in there and perform. Let's start with the second way."

She pointed at the window. "Can anyone see me but you?"

"No." And so help him, no one would be seeing her except him for a long time to come. He could see himself becoming downright proprietorial over her.

"Unless someone comes in here while I'm in there."

Smart girl. But then again, she'd have to be. She'd been living with a man who abused her trust and threatened her family. "You're going to have to trust me to protect you. I would never let someone in here without your permission. That's a contract between you and me. The same way you won't tell anyone about my kinks and interests."

This seemed to satisfy something with her. Her spine unstiffened a smudge. "In there?" She pointed at the glass. "Will I always be alone? Or will you want to watch me with others?"

"Eventually. Unless you safe word it. Not today." He

tapped on the glass. "Head on in there. Orient yourself. I'll be here on the couch, watching you. You make me hard doing nothing at all. Drop your clothes, and I want to watch you get yourself off with your fingers."

She started to move, and then she stopped. "If I said no? If I said 'turtle' right now, what happens?"

"Is that what you want to say?" He had to give her the chance to get out of this, she couldn't walk this road with him unless it was entirely consensual. "Say it, and this stops here with no ramifications. We head back to your home. I'll still help you with your husband problem. You don't owe me this. You can say no."

She nodded once and continued into the room. Francium quickly locked the door and dimmed the lights a bit in her room. Trying to get comfortable, he sat down on the couch to watch what she would do. He wasn't expecting much. There was a difference between this and the game they'd played from their porches.

Alone in the room with just herself and his instructions, she might not get through this the first time, even if she continued to be interested.

It was one thing to get off on being watched in the privacy of her living room, and another in a private viewing room. But they wouldn't always be porch-to-porch, and the public voyeurism was part of what got him off.

His day couldn't have been any stranger. He didn't do this. Francium had never played with anyone who wasn't already a part of this life. And he had a job to take care of. And...

Lara pulled her shirt over her head, her gaze fixed on the glass where he knew she couldn't see him. Yet, her gaze seemed to find his, zooming in on him on the other side. She knew where he sat, and yet he couldn't help but dive into the feeling she could see through the glass right to his soul on the other side.

"Get a hold of yourself, man," he whispered to the room. She was a woman, just a woman. Exactly the same as any other girl in the world. Married, to boot. Women were fickle. They didn't stick around when the going got hard. They left their children...they left their...

She unhooked her bra, and the everlasting replay of his issues with women fled his mind. His mouth watered. For the first time in a long time, he wanted to touch, not only watch. He shifted in his seat, his cock straining. This was okay—they'd get to it. Once she didn't wear the bastard's ring, legally or otherwise.

Lara's hips swayed when she took her bra off. He hadn't told her to dance. That would be instruction for another time. But he didn't mind the movement. Lara had such a natural grace. Maybe she lived with music in her mind.

Her bra fell to the floor, exposing her breasts. She massaged her breasts, and he had to shift in his seat, his cock strained for release. Her hands travelled lower, and she pushed her pants down to the floor before she stepped out of them. Russell was once again struck with the image of a dancer, this time, ballet.

Normally, by now, he'd be stroking himself harder. But he didn't need any help with that, and he was fixated on Lara, he couldn't take his attention off her at all to do anything but watch. His body was on fire. When had he felt so alive?

Lara slipped her index finger under the hem of her panties, and they were soon on the floor also. She was totally naked. Her pussy was waxed smooth, and her toes were painted pink. Small details. Were her toes always pink, or did she change colors?

How did she decide?

He watched, practically transfixed, as her hands traveled upwards, finding her pussy. She still stood. It hadn't occurred to him to tell her to lay down. Would she think of it? Or would she make herself come and then have her knees buckle? Russell did not want her to hurt herself.

Her knees sunk slowly, and eventually, she lay flat on her back, spreading her knees so he could see her better. Good girl

He stood to press himself against the glass. Francium couldn't ever remember doing so before. Her finger found her clit, and she stroked it. One finger—two—he moaned. She was a woman who clearly knew her own pleasure. It didn't take Lara any time to find her own bundle of nerves. Two fingers seemed to do the trick. She made a circular motion and arched her back.

Francium wasn't certain how long it went on. She'd hit a certain spot, and her back would arch. He loved the sound of her breathy moans. Russell knew one thing as he watched her, aching to touch her in a way no viewing had done for him in years, she belonged to him.

Lara was his girl.

She finally came, and his cock jumped in his pants. He was so hard, he was about to come without her touching her at all. Boredom was nowhere to be found.

He walked slowly to the couch and sat down, trying to appear less strung out. Lara rose, slowly, and walked back into the room, completely naked.

She looked at him with a level gaze, her emotions shielded from him. "How was that?"

He crooked his finger, and she came toward him. With hands as steady as he could make them, he pulled her against him until she straddled his lap. There was no way she couldn't feel the hardness of his cock.

"We're getting that ring off your finger, sweetheart. As fast as possible. My plans have rapidly changed."

She was not going to be married to the asshole any longer.

LARA SIPPED her wine and wandered through the beautiful crowd at Jamie England's third cocktail party of the summer. Remington seemed happy today, he'd made some more money for his terrible clients, and now he was going on and on about needing to see Russell again. Exactly what her Francium wanted.

She took a deep breath. He wasn't her Francium. At least not yet. He seemed very preoccupied with her marriage fidelity. Remington didn't heed his marriage vows, she wasn't exactly sure why she had to. Except Russell was stubborn about it, and she couldn't get him to budge on the subject.

He'd been hard as a rock, and he'd kept his hands to himself.

Smiling at the waiter who gave her another glass of champagne, she wondered if she looked any different. Was there a glow around her? Could anyone tell she had dropped her clothes and masturbated for Russell's pleasure—and her own—via a two-way mirror?

Heat rose in her cheeks, and she rounded the corner, exchanging pleasantries with the women around her. She'd often wondered if she could do this song and dance in her sleep, it turned out she could since she was completely on auto-pilot.

Not only was she in the hottest sexual relationship of her life—and he still hadn't touched her—but she had the means, almost, to save her sister and be rid of Remington.

Thinking of her husband seemed to make him appear and next to him, the subject of her musings, Russell Burke, pretending to be something and someone he was not. Now that she knew him—and despite his proclamation about being a liar, she started to feel that she could, actually, see right through him—his faking-it persona ate at her. Francium didn't really smile like that. When he was really happy, he didn't show quite so much teeth.

His gaze caught hers, and for a second, time seemed to slow. He pulled their connection away, looking back at Remington and nodding before throwing his head back to laugh. Oh, he was good. She slowly approached.

Their drive back in the car had been quiet but not strained. She'd watched him quietly as he drove. A muscle in his jaw kept ticking. He was stressed, and she didn't think it had to do with Remington.

Like the good wife she was supposed to be, she put her hand on Remington's arm. "You two solving the world's financial problems over here?"

Francium's eyes flashed to her hand. It was a split second of time, but she saw it. He didn't like her hand on Remington. She didn't much care for it, either. But until the ruse was over, they'd both have to deal.

Her husband winked at her. "Russell and I are going to do some business together."

"How lovely." She smiled. That was her standard answer, although she found none of it to actually be so.

"So, if you would excuse us..."

She nodded, her smile in place. That's all she was anymore. A nod. A smile. A gaze. Except when she'd done what Francium told her. Then she'd been...present. Why? She didn't want to know, really. Why question what finally felt good?

Turning her back on the conversation between the pair, she decided to enjoy the view. She'd always loved the water, and when they bought the beach house, she'd assumed she'd spend happy days there. Of course, once it had become her jail, she'd hated it. As she had the New York City apartment and the home in the mountains. Viewing the sea tonight started a countdown in her head, she wouldn't be forced to look at the waves anymore. Unless she wanted to.

"Honey." Remington kissed her cheek, catching her attention. "Russell and I are going to go somewhere to where we can talk privately. You're fine getting home, aren't you?"

Smiling as sweetly as she could manage, despite the bitter taste in her mouth, she answered, "Sure. Of course."

"See? That's what you want from a wife, Russell. She never says no."

Francium raised his eyebrows. "Oh, I bet she does. I bet she knows how to open her mouth and say no."

"Not if she wants to keep having pretty things." Remington laughed like he'd made a great joke before he headed for the door.

Russell leaned over as though to say goodbye. "Fuck him."

She almost dropped her drink.

❦

IT WOULD BE hours until anyone came home. She walked through the house. In all the years since she first discovered her husband's terrible business dealings—and he'd threatened her sister—she hadn't made any moves into his office. He kept it locked. Of course, she knew where the keys were. The time he'd stumbled home stinking of whiskey and practically pissing himself, he'd been so sloppy, he'd shown her where they were.

She walked slowly to his dresser drawer, finding the removable portion, and she yanked the key out. All the way home, she'd fixated on the idea of helping. Lara could do more than shadow Francium around and basically be useless. He needed information. She could get it for him.

Save them all some time...

Grabbing her secret cell phone, she texted her sister. *I might be nuts. But I think we might all be okay. Stay tuned for more news.*

With a goal in mind, she let herself into her husband's office. The door opened wide, and no monster jumped out at her, which for some reason, shocked her more than it should have. The office looked exactly the same as it had the last time she'd been inside of it.

An expensive desk, a computer with a screen saver that flashed various beach locations worldwide, a black chair adjusted to fit him perfectly, and a Persian Rug—her wedding gift to him when they'd gotten married. He'd paid for it, but she'd picked it out. The lines were perfect, and she bent over to stroke the softness.

The girl I'd been...

It was possible he'd changed the password on his computer. A smart guy would have altered everything after their fight when he'd threatened her sister. But he'd locked the door, and he probably thought that was enough. He'd frightened her enough to keep away.

Only tonight, she wasn't afraid.

Fury fueled her hands and surprisingly, kept them steady.

After she entered the date Remington earned his first million, the computer let her in. He was such a jackass, and she was the bigger fool for having loved him at all.

A few swipes of the mouse, and she was into the folder where he kept his tax returns and his client lists. Remington was nothing if not organized. He had to be to keep control of all the lies he told.

Although it would be hours until her husband returned home, she moved as quickly as she could through the files, emailing them all to herself. She didn't have Francium's email, or she'd have sent it directly to him. When next she saw him, she'd give him what she found.

Shutting everything down was quicker than getting into it. Minutes later, she'd left the room and relocked it. No one would ever know she had been there.

With her back straight, she walked to her bedroom. Today, for the first time in forever, she could remember who she was.

Once upon a time, she'd been the kind of woman who knew the difference between right and wrong. She'd stood up for something when it mattered to her. Maybe she really could be that person again.

Lara went through her bedtime routine, taking the makeup off her face and hanging up her clothes—some of them going to dry cleaning, some of them not. She put on her pajamas and shut the door to her bedroom. Remington wanted to fuck her, he didn't want to sleep with her, and that suited her just fine.

If he stumbled home, he'd pass out in his own room as he'd been doing for the last year. Otherwise, she wouldn't see him at all. The sounds of the ocean were soothing for a change, and she didn't take her sleeping pill to conk out. She had insomnia, and the doctors couldn't figure out why. If she ever felt like telling the truth, they would have paled at the reason. But she wouldn't place the doctors in danger. Keeping her mouth shut was the name of the game.

Things were going to change now. She closed her eyes, and after a few minutes, she slept.

A noise woke her suddenly. With her heart in her throat, she sat up. What had woken her? She tried to identify the sound. There was nothing she could pick out exactly, but there had been something. She could sleep through Remington's staggering, and unless he'd fallen face down and made some weird noise, that wasn't what disturbed her.

Lara would never know what made her move. She darted to the left, just the second the first bullet fired. She hit the floor, hard, spots flying before her eyes. A second bullet exploded right above her head.

She screamed, unable to stop herself, and crawled for the bedroom. What the hell was going on? Terror became a living, breathing entity in the room for her. Someone was trying to kill her. She couldn't breathe, and she wasn't an idiot. She knew she wasn't crawling out of there alive.

Life had caught up with her. There could be any number of reasons someone tried to kill her. She would die without know what exactly that was—

A loud bang sounded, followed by a clunk.

She raised her head. If she wasn't dead, she could look. The figure in the doorway took her breath away. Francium stood like an avenging angel, gun pointed, head cocked to the side.

"Russell?" Her voice shook.

He put the gun in a holster on his side, still not having

spoken to her, he picked up his phone. "Titanium, I need a cleanup and Wen."

His gaze turned to her, the hallway light making it easy to see him. He was with her in two strides. Russell bent down and embraced her. "Baby, you okay?"

"What is happening?"

"Your husband is trying to have you killed. Why did you go into his office? Hell, I don't care. He called Red Wolf, and they sent an assassin. Just that fast."

Russell smelled safe. He was warm. And he'd killed someone for her. "I...Oh my God, I can't believe this. Russell, I..."

"Sshh. All will be well."

He picked her up like she was a Hollywood damsel whose hero had shown up to save her. She didn't believe in heroes, and Francium had told her he was a liar. Maybe the world didn't really have any. She was fine with that. He'd shown up, he saved her. Maybe he was the most flawed, difficult guy on the planet.

Francium never needed to tell her a true thing for the rest of her life. He was her hero. End of story.

4

F rancium sipped his ice water and stared at the ocean. It was well past midnight—maybe three AM —and he couldn't really see the water. But he could hear the waves. Tonight, they weren't soothing. He had almost been too late.

If he hadn't heard Remington on the phone, Lara would be dead instead of asleep on a sedative he wished he could take as well. Titanium had thought to send Platinum with some drugs. The sniper had two years of med school under his belt. For the moment, that was good enough. His girl was asleep and alive.

Wen had waited in silence until Francium wanted to talk. That was what was nice about the other man—he never insisted on making conversation.

"Do you remember when you ripped me out of the CIA?" He turned to his oldest friend.

Wen's expression remained passive. "I remember many things about that time."

Russell bet he did. After Wen saved his life, they'd fucked like bunnies. "I'm not thinking about the after-party at the moment. More like when you walked in, took me by the arm, and told me I wasn't an assassin."

"You weren't. Not now. Not then. You're not regretting this shit tonight, right? That scumbag was one of Red Wolf's exterminators. He's killed more women than we can count."

He shook his head. "Just the opposite. I'm not at all bothered. I was terrified for Lara. But, no, I raised the gun. Pop. No issue there. I don't feel a thing about it. Maybe I should have been the assassin."

Wen snorted. "I stand by that decision."

Zinc walked outside, joining them on the deck. "Debrief me, would you?"

"Well, years ago, I saved your life." Francium didn't know why he chose that moment to share that piece of information, but what the hell, it was a night for truth-telling—which made a nice change.

Zinc rocked back on his heels, his brown hair falling into his eyes before he shoved it away. Zachery needed a haircut, but who had the time anymore?

"Well, thanks for that. Wow. It was you. Okay. You got it wrong. I wasn't supposed to be saved. But I'll say thank you because if you hadn't, well, I wouldn't know some things I know now, and I wouldn't have Sarah Steele as my wife. So, thanks." He held out his hand, and Francium shook it. Just days earlier, he'd have wanted to roll his eyes when Zinc brought up his wife. Now, he found he was equally obsessive about the woman sleeping inside.

He scratched his head. "You're welcome, I guess. Glad I screwed up that day."

Wen shook his head. "You'd think you'd be used to the sensation by now."

He glared at his best friend. "Don't help."

"Debrief, if you will. Catch me up. I can't get word one

out of Platinum." Zinc shook his head while he spoke. "All he said was Francium's lady almost got killed."

He leaned back on the railing. "She's not my girl. Not yet. Here's the deal. I came here to work on Remington Reagan. You know that much. I ended up getting mixed up with Lara, his wife. I didn't see it coming."

Zinc looked at Wen. "We never do. Go on."

"I got permission to read her in on the mission. She must have taken initiative. I was out at a party with him when she set off a silent alarm, having gone into his office. He realized what she'd done and excused himself outside, not realizing I was tailing him. He's rather oblivious to be this high up in the organization." But then again, Red Wolf wanted people who obeyed, not who thought for themselves. If Francium was going to run a terrorist organization, he'd want the same damn thing. "I heard him set the hit. I guess losing his stability with Red Wolf didn't count as much as saving his own ass."

Platinum came outside and leaned against the door, watching them. He didn't speak much.

"And you did what?" Zinc prompted him, while he rubbed his head.

"I ran. I fucking ran. I got here just in time. He must have people locally. It was fast, man. It was fast."

Platinum took an audible breath. "Are you outed? Did he make you?"

"No." The fact that Remington hadn't gotten home yet was interesting. If Francium was going to guess, he'd suspect the ass would arrive in the morning, feign shock, a scandal would follow, and he'd have a new wife by the end of the summer. Or at least, that's what Remington wanted since he expected his wife to be dead.

Francium's blood hit boiling level.

"What do you want to do?" Zach walked to lean against the railing next to Wen. "What's the next step?"

That was a good question. "I know Titanium wants the mission salvaged, but what do I want? I want to take that asshole into my hands. I want to squeeze his brain. I want to harm him. I want him to feel more pain than he can handle while he signs divorce papers giving her everything. Then I want to make him so afraid—real fear, you know the kind? Not the, oh shit, this is bad afraid, but the kind of fear where you aren't sure you can draw another breath. I want to stand over him doing that while he hands me Red Wolf's financials for the next six months. Then I want him to drown in his own spit."

Zinc snorted. "Very vivid. I like it. I'm never much on staying on Titanium's guide book."

That was an understatement. Titanium and Zinc were never on the best of terms. They co-existed okay and wanted the same things as far as Francium could tell. They'd started to thaw.

"What Titanium wants," Platinum spoke from the doorway, "is Red Wolf. I don't know that he's all that married to the idea of continuing the con, if we can get it done faster. He gives you a long leash, Francium. Use it."

They all fell silent. He'd never heard Platinum use so many words together before. "Disposing of bodies make you chatty?"

The sniper didn't answer, and finally, Wen stepped forward. "Then let's go squeeze the fucker's balls—literally or figuratively."

Sounded like a plan.

∼

FORTY MINUTES LATER, they sat in an SUV a short distance from Remington's third mistress's house. Zinc and Platinum set up the back of the truck for the next passenger who would be unwillingly joining them soon.

Wen stayed silent in the front seat while Francium waited for the all clear to go get Remington.

His friend cleared his throat. "Penny for your thoughts."

Russell pointed at the house. "He has Lara at home every night. Up until two years ago, she loved him enough to tell him her deepest secrets. And he was never loyal." Or at least, as far as Francium's digging could turn up. Maybe there was a week when they first dated. "She would make the world spin for some lucky asshole. Besides the obvious, what is the matter with him?"

Wen scratched his head. "I'm going to help you pick out the best church."

"What?" He didn't follow.

"When you get married. Don't get married anywhere until I check it out."

He rolled his eyes. "She's only starting to understand what I need. I'm not sure she'll want it in the long run."

"You have pretty good instincts. Don't invent problems if there aren't any yet."

"Hey you two," Zach called out. "We're ready. Go get him."

He jumped from the car, knowing the others would follow. But this was going to be his show for a little while. This man had tried to kill Lara. Legally wed or not, somewhere in the last two days, Russell had decided she belonged to him.

He was going to cause Remington so much pain, he wouldn't be able to piss straight for months.

The door to the small beach cabin was unlocked. The

whole thing couldn't be more than two thousand square feet, which meant it was probably worth two million dollars at least, thanks to its beach location. Remington had three of these things set up for his women. He had spent money over the years like it grew on his trees.

On silent feet, thanks to his training in more nefarious organizations than he could count, he made his way inside the house without being heard. The sounds of grunts and moans caught his attention, and he rolled his eyes. First off, he could tell Remington struggled to hold off coming. Years in the clubs had taught him the telltale sounds. The guy wanted to get off. His partner faked her moans. She wasn't feeling it all. So far, in the watching Remington have sex department, Remington had been zero-for-two. Lara had only gotten off because Russell watched her, and this woman—whose name was Geraldine, and who in her spare time when she wasn't fucking Remington, worked as a barista—was clearly not having a great time.

He banged open the door with enough force, Remington was off his mistress in two seconds flat, his hands moving to cover his penis as though it were the most important part of his body.

Remington blinked rapidly. "Russell, what the hell?"

He didn't give the man the chance to say anything else. He punched the man square in the throat just to hear him gasp for air before finishing the job with a fast pound on his face. Red Wolf's CFO hit the ground, hard.

Flipping Remington over his shoulder, Francium turned around to face Wen, who waited behind him.

"You got this?"

He nodded. "Deal with the woman. She needs to never breathe a word of this."

Wen nodded. The nice thing about knowing him for so

long was he could completely count on Wen getting the job done. "And thanks," he thought to add.

His friend snorted.

They really didn't have a thank you relationship.

FRANCIUM STORMED into Lara's house like he owned the place while Zinc hauled Remington out of the trunk. It had been too long since he put eyes on Lara. He'd left her here asleep. On the drive back, he'd suddenly worried Reagan had hired a second hitman. What if he'd missed something?

She slept deeply on the bed in the guestroom, one leg scooting out from beneath the covers to reveal her long leg, the bathroom light illuminating her pink toenails. She'd been in complete darkness when the hitman had come. He'd told Plat to leave her a little light.

Lara had been very brave during the cleanup process. She hadn't cried after her initial shock, and she hadn't asked too many questions. Somehow, she trusted him.

He knelt down next to her. She breathed lightly, her mouth slightly open. Beneath her eyelids, her eyes moved. He smoothed the bangs off her forehead. She'd even taken the sedative without arguing about it and crawled into bed, believing he'd handle things.

Why was she so damned lovely?

"Hey man." Zinc's voice was low but filled the room. "You might want to come now. We're all geared up and waiting on you. I can take over this show. But he's yours to get rid of, if you want him."

Lara didn't stir, and he was just as glad. Let her sleep for twelve more hours, at least. Sleep had a way of loosening the bad thoughts and memories that clogged the brain. Or at least, he thought it did. He hadn't slept well in years.

He kissed her lightly on the forehead and followed Zinc out of the room. The Ghost waited for him in the hall and nodded. "Tough to leave them."

"I've only known her forty-eight hours."

Zinc shrugged. "Guys like us, we live with our instincts right up front. We react, or we die. We trust out guts. We know things because somehow, we hear, feel, see, or taste things others don't. When we know things, we know them."

Interesting idea. He took the stairs two at a time to get back downstairs in time to see Wen dragging Remington out the back door toward the beach.

"He's going for a swim."

Francium stopped moving. It had been a long time since either one of them had made anyone go for a swim. They used to do it all the time. But Wen didn't necessarily do this level of crap anymore, and he wasn't sure he wanted to be responsible for sending him into the darkness or facing the wrath of Wen's lady if he did.

She was sweet, but he didn't want to turn on her temper.

"Hey," he yelled after him. "Don't do anything. I'll do it."

"No, this man threatened a woman, tried to have her killed, and works for Red Wolf. He's going swimming, and you're not as good at this as I am."

That happened to be true. Although when it came to this kind of thing, expertise only accounted for so much.

"I...I..." Remington stuttered. "There has to be a deal to be made. There's always a deal to be made. I didn't even know you liked my wife. Want to fuck her? I'll let you fuck her."

Russell sucked in his breath. "She isn't chattel for you to

barter with. Despite the fact, she would be dead if you'd had your way. But we will deal. Just not about your wife."

"Do you know who I work for? Do you have any idea..." Russell didn't know exactly what Remington would have said next, because Wen shoved his head straight into the ocean.

Running up next to him, Francium grabbed him and hauled him out of the water. "Do you like air?"

He waited long enough for the man to breathe in a gasp of air before he shoved him back in.

"It's more in the wrist," Wen called out. "You're using too much back. Wrists."

Russell pulled him back out. "Because I can make it so you never breathe air again."

Remington gasped. "What do you want? What can I give you?"

Platinum and Zinc arrived at the scene. Zinc spoke first. "Ten minutes 'til sunrise. I don't want to be spotted out there."

"I've got the papers," Platinum added. "He signs this, she gets three quarters of his net worth, the house, all property, and he stays away from her."

"What?" Remington squealed, and Francium shoved him under the water again.

"Seriously, Plat. How did you get those papers so fast?" He'd never seen divorce papers suddenly appear before.

Plat shrugged. "Chrome takes care of things. I don't ask, he doesn't tell. I told him what we needed. He sent it right over. He's good like that."

Francium was going to drown Remington if he wasn't careful. He pulled him out, and the man gasped for the air. "You could drown. Or you could freeze to death."

The water was cold, even during the summer, and especially in the morning. "I don't want to die."

"We all die eventually." Wen took a deep breath. "You're going to sign the divorce papers. Then we'll talk about all the rest of it. You have four new best friends. Maybe five. I keep thinking I want to bring in Platinum's friend Copper. She really has a good time with abusers."

Francium smiled. It was good to have friends.

LARA WOKE SLOWLY. Her mouth was dry, and her body ached. Reality didn't descend all at once, but slowly, one slow second at a time. Her husband had hired a hitman to kill her. She gulped. Russell had killed him instead. Then people had shown up, fast. They'd said something about jets. She hadn't really been able to focus on any of it.

A blond-haired man they'd called Platinum had dosed her with a sedative, and she'd been out like a light. Now, if the sunshine through the window was any indication, it was afternoon. She sat up, rubbing at her eyes. The sedative had been helpful, but she still had to deal with what happened, and she now had a medicine hangover.

Noise in the corner caught her attention. Russell was asleep in the chair near her bed. He wasn't, if the way his head moved left and right abruptly, having good dreams. Had he spent the whole night in the chair next to her bed?

She made her legs work, which was easier decided than actually done, thanks to the leftover medicine in her system, but she did eventually manage to get over to him. She placed a gentle hand on his cheek, and he jolted a wink.

Russell blinked rapidly before he seemed to finally see her. "Hey, gorgeous."

"Can't be looking too gorgeous right now. Thank you for saving my life."

He nodded. "Thanks for not dying."

"Think that's more on you than me." He looked exhausted, circles under his eyes indicating he'd slept very little before she woke him.

He took her hands. "I need to take you downstairs. But, before we do that, I need you to know I have nearly nothing to offer you. I've got money stashed away various places. But I'm the kid that literally no one wanted. Ever. I'm all kinds of fucked up, and I have done seriously bad things. Not even necessarily for a good cause every time. You should take the out you're about to get and never look back."

She kissed him lightly on the lips, loving his gasp when she did. "Thanks for the warning. You might find you want to be rid of me. It's been a long time since I did anything but get dressed and look pretty. I have to figure out who I am, too."

"I know who I am, and it isn't...pretty, to say the least." He stood. "Thanks for the wake up, by the way. Bad dreams, which is weird. I don't usually dream at all."

Francium took her hand and led her from the room. She didn't know where he was taking her, but she'd follow him to Mars if he wanted her to go. Instead, she ended up in the kitchen. Remington sat shaking at the table, a man she recognized only because he'd given her the sedative sat next to him. He was blond with blue eyes. With barely a nod, he acknowledged the two of them.

Her husband's eyes were huge, his skin very pale, and his bottom lip quivered. She'd never seen him look so frightened before.

The blond man pushed a piece of paper toward her.

Finally, Francium spoke. "If you sign at the bottom, you'll be divorced."

She gasped, all air temporarily leaving her body. "How did you make that happen?"

"I'm a man who gets things done. Or, at least, I have friends and colleagues who do." He handed her a pen.

Remington cried out, "Please sign it and don't let them kill me. Please, Lara."

"He pissed himself earlier." Blond man looked bored.

Russell snorted. "Hard to be a terrorist all on your own, isn't it? Hard to be the one making people afraid when you're locked in a kitchen with us?"

"Sign it, Lara. Please. I'm sorry for everything. I'm so sorry."

Francium sat next to him, and Remington jolted. "You're only sorry you got caught."

She took the pen in steady hands. This was what she wanted. "Does someone want to summarize the terms?"

"You get three quarters of his net worth and all of the property. He'll stay away from you, too. Or he'll live to regret it." Russell placed a hand on her arm.

Remington's voice shook. "I'll stay away. I'll stay away."

What had they done while she'd been out of it? She signed fast, and the blond man took it from her hand.

She nodded. "Thanks."

Francium looked between them. "This is Platinum. He doesn't say much, but you can trust him. Well, as much as anyone can be trusted for anything."

"Cynical, man." Platinum grinned, taking Remington by the arm. "Don't worry about this guy. He won't bother you again. He's coming with us to get started on the rest of his penance."

Remington was dragged from the room like a rag doll. Francium didn't move. What was she supposed to do now?

"You can pack and leave." It was like Francium heard her unasked question. "Go anywhere you want. I'll set it up."

He seemed so anxious to be rid of her. Only as he lifted his eyes, his gaze met hers. It was the same as he'd seemed when they'd been at the club, and he hadn't been sure she'd go inside the room by herself. She doubted he even knew how he seemed. Francium was wounded.

And unsure.

He needed a hug, but she'd sell her kidney in a bet he wouldn't take one.

She extended her hand. "Come up with me?"

Russell rose, linking their fingers. "Need help packing?"

"No, if I'm still rich, I'll pay someone to do it soon. I'll have to get him off the bank accounts." This was all too much for her to really process it. She had to do one right thing, and then another. Just the night before—or was it? How much time had passed?—her now ex-husband had tried to kill her.

Now she was divorced with beefy, armed men hauling Remington around.

Her brain stuttered. Her sister was safe. Her. Sister. Was. Safe. Tears pooled in her eyes, and halfway up the stairs, Francium tugged her against him.

"What's the matter?"

"Something is finally right. You did that for me. Thank you."

His mouth tensed. "I've never made anything right for anyone."

"That must be why this one is so huge. You were saving it up for one giant explosion of help."

She brought him with her to her bedroom. In the few minutes she'd been out of the room, someone had removed all of her ex's stuff. He hadn't slept in there with her in forever, but he'd had a presence in the room—a globe, a picture she hated on the wall. How had they known what to get rid of?

Lara didn't care.

After closing the door, she stepped away from Russell. This was going to take guts on her part—she didn't initiate things easily—but she wanted the connection taking a risk would bring. On a day when she'd opened her eyes, and the world righted finally, could this happen, too?

"What do you want me to do right now?"

He rubbed his eyes. "About what?"

"About anything. I'll take off my clothes. Do a little dance." God, she really hoped it wasn't that one he wanted. She didn't dance particularly well. "Do jumping jacks."

She counted at least five different emotions crossing his face before he finally spoke with his eyes heated. "You want to play?"

"Can we? I mean, we're not at the club. People are here. We don't have a window between us. Is it still possible?"

Francium groaned loudly. "Beautiful lady, you can have whatever you want from me. You could bring me to my knees if that is what you wish. I don't know why, but the second I saw you, and you were in the arms of another man, I knew you were mine. Last night was probably the most harrowing night of my life. You want to play? Here in the bedroom? You've got it."

"I have one thing to do. I want to let my sister know she's safe."

He nodded once. "That works. I'll take a quick shower. I'm a sweaty mess. Then I'm going to make you one."

She blushed at his words, even though she loved the images pushing through her mind they created.

~

FRANCIUM FELT the water pound on him and hoped it would wipe away some of the fear he couldn't seem to get rid of. He hadn't been afraid since he was a child. When he'd run from the so-called foster home, which had really been an organization devoted to getting rid of anything native left inside of him, he'd been sure they'd chase him down with dogs who would eat his insides.

The idea was, of course, ridiculous. He wasn't worth that much to them. Another kid to write off as lost and never to be heard from again.

That night he'd known terror. But then he'd figured out the sun always rose the next day. A new start, a new way to figure out how to get what he wanted by any means necessary. Wen had given him a chance, years later, to see himself as useful. He could make a scene and become whomever he needed to be. He could watch himself from the outside and not have to live in reality if he didn't want to.

Last night, he'd known fear again and not for himself. Caring about someone else, even in the early stages, was a damned terrifying experience. What if she died? How would he manage to live through that pain? What was—

The door to the shower swung open. Lara, wearing a white robe and nothing else, stared at him. His heart skipped a beat. She looked fresh, alive, and not at all like she endured hell because he wrongly yanked her into his world. So far, she hadn't blamed him, and she had every right to do so.

"When we designed this bathroom, we made sure the shower was big enough for two."

He blinked. She wasn't wrong. It was a large washroom, for sure. Plenty of space. Why didn't she come in if she wanted to? He was hardly going to say no.

It dawned on him all at once. She wanted him to tell her to, she was giving him permission to watch.

5

"Drop the robe." He stepped back so he couldn't reach her. He didn't want to touch, not yet. They needed to see if this worked. Hell, for Lara, he'd probably give the whole thing up. She owned him. Did she know?

The crazy thing was she kept asking for it. He wasn't begging, he hadn't yet dropped to his knees and sworn whatever she wanted to hear. She pursued him. It was the hottest thing he'd ever seen.

She did as he asked. Her lean body in front of him made him hard. As he was also naked, she had to be able to see how turned on he'd become. This was a big change for him. The mirror usually gave him a chance to get himself under control, if he wanted to, before he had to face the person on the other side.

But they were both completely exposed, and he loved that—which should have freaked him out.

She lowered her eyes. "Now what?"

"Don't rush me when I'm enjoying looking at your naked body."

Color heated her cheeks. "Thank you."

He wanted her eye contact. "Raise your eyes. You should never be embarrassed by how gorgeous you are."

She lifted her gaze. "You're pretty damned beautiful yourself."

He laughed, the levity making him grin. This wasn't supposed to be amusing. Or maybe it was. What did he know, anymore? The rules were different with Lara.

"I am covered in scars. Trust me, not beautiful." He lifted his hand when she would have spoken. The question about whether or not he was good looking was neither here nor there at that moment. "You're not married anymore. I guess it has to be filed with the court. I can guarantee it will be. That means the rules have changed."

She nodded. "You can touch me now, actually make love to me."

"I don't know if I've ever made love to anyone. But I can try."

Her eyes flared. "Then don't you think it's beyond time you did?"

"One of the things I have come to admire about you in the brief time we have known each other is how you are really not afraid of anything when it comes to yourself. Someone you care about, sure. You feel fear, but not for your own well-being. Not one person in a thousand would speak to me the way you do. I love how you never back down. Come under the water with me."

She nodded and stepped into the shower spray. The water covered her fast, droplets traveling down her body, over her breasts, past her stomach, and touching her pussy before they hit her legs and eventually, the ground. He was transfixed, like a teenager seeing his first naked woman, instead of a guy who had fucked every manner of person over his lifetime and felt very little about any of it.

Lara made him feel brand new.

"Touch your breasts."

She nodded, her hands coming down her neck to where he'd instructed her to stroke. His hands ached to touch her, but he wanted this more. For now.

His cock jumped at watching her take her nipples in her hand and squeeze them. Lara threw her neck back, leaning a little bit on the shower. "My nipples are not usually sensitive. But when you tell me to touch myself, my whole body seems to come alive. Jolts of pleasure when I touch them right now."

Well, that was seriously awesome. He kept his grin to himself. Russell didn't want her to think he was laughing at her or not taking her seriously.

His own body was on fire. Her nipples peaked and hardened. She rubbed them, a circular motion, and a small moan escaped her mouth. Would she want her clit stroked the same way?

He changed how he stood. They'd only gotten started, and already, he wanted to be in her—pounding her into pleasurable completion.

"Remember your safe word?" His voice broke when he spoke.

A small smile passed over her mouth. "I do. But I don't want to use it."

"Just checking." He backed up a bit and sat down on the bench on the other side of the shower. "Make yourself come."

She nodded once, her hands traveling down her body. There were things they could do, things they would do, when he had the tools with him. Dildos, handcuffs. His mind could go a million different ways. For now, he was so happy to have each other and the shower.

Her hand had almost reached her pussy, when he stopped her. "The showerhead. Make yourself come with the showerhead."

Her eyes widened, and he waited. She had her safe word, and although they were new at this together, he trusted her to use it if she wanted it.

Lara turned a half degree and unhooked the showerhead. She ran her hand over it. When she turned to face him again, it was with a steady gaze. Lara chewed on her lower lip. "I've never done this before, not like this. It's going to take a second or two for me to figure this out. Bear with me?"

He pointed at the settings. "Push the button that says massage settings."

"Ah, good call. Nice, you've had some experience with this." She did as he told, and the water changed. With the showerhead otherwise occupied, the water no longer beat down on him. He hardly noticed. Between the heat Lara generated and the steam in the room, he wasn't going to feel cold anytime soon.

Still standing, she bent her knees, positioning the spray right over her vagina. It must have felt good because she let out a moan, deep in her throat, and closed her eyes. Lara bent her knees to take the showerhead farther inside of her. Francium wasn't sure he could take any more. Right about then was when he should have started to be turned on, not already so far gone, he was going to come from watching her alone.

He moved until he had her in his arms. "I don't usually want this. And don't get me wrong, there are going to be times when all I want to do is order you around and watch you find pleasure—maybe even in that club. But I want you now. Can I have you?" He wasn't above saying please if she wanted him to.

Lara flipped her hair over her shoulder. "Are you kidding? Take me. You always could."

Not until she could have been his. He didn't know why it was a hang up, and naked in the shower was not the time to explore his hidden feelings about the sanctity of marriage. He shut off the water.

Francium scooped her up. The bathroom counter was safer than the shower. He didn't want either of them to fall. They'd had enough bad luck lately.

He placed her on her rear end on the counter with her back on the mirror. Russell would have preferred the opposite, being able to watch her while he made love to her rather than the current situation, but he wasn't going to take her from behind the first time.

Unless she asked for it.

"Fuck." A thought dawned on him, and he wished reality could slip away, but it couldn't. "We don't have a condom. It didn't even occur to me. I've been busy. I—"

She placed her hand over his mouth. Her fingers were soft, and he kissed her palm. If he had to shut up, at least she told him so with the softest skin ever. "Second drawer over there. Condoms."

This woman was a queen. He opened the drawer, grabbed the aforementioned condoms, and sheathed himself with shaking hands.

Lara stroked her hand down his cheek. "I'd love to get you in my hands, but I want you in me. You seem close."

"You make me weak."

She kissed him lightly on the lips. "Not possible. Maybe you know you can trust me."

"Maybe you're the hottest woman I've ever seen."

She grinned, a look of pure female satisfaction crossing her face. "Thanks for that."

He inched her slightly off the counter so that her pussy positioned close to his cock. In one swift move, he pressed upwards, pushing inside of her balls deep. The world tilted on its axis. He'd never had a home anywhere in the world. But inside this woman, he suddenly felt like maybe there might be one for him—right in between her thighs.

They moved together. Lara had to position herself slightly on the corner of the counter, but she didn't seem to mind. When he pressed upwards, she moved down his cock. His balls throbbed, and the colors passed before his eyes. He didn't care. He'd hold out until she came.

Lara whispered in his ear, "I don't think I'm going to be able to come until you tell me to."

Was she fucking serious? He fell hard, head over heels for Lara right that second. If he'd had any doubt about his feelings, they fled. He was hands down in love with her. "Fucking come, Lara. Come now."

She exploded around him, her juices soaking him. The sounds of their lovemaking filled the room as she cried out his name. He was done. Russell didn't have another second in him. He came, hard, every bit of him emptying inside of her.

They breathed hard together, his face pressed into her shoulder. This was too much. The poor woman had just gotten out of one abusive relationship. She really, really didn't need his crap. The best thing he could do was to leave her alone.

She ran her hand up and down his back. "What are you thinking?"

"I should stay the fuck away from you. You need time,

safety, and a guy who can be on the up and up. I'm a con artist. Just because I'm currently on the right side of things, doesn't mean you should be mixed up."

Lara pressed her forehead to his. "Don't be scared and run away, Russell."

How did she read him so well? "I don't even know if that's my name. It's the first one I can remember, but I think I had one before it. They might have given that to me in my first foster home. Or maybe it was the second. No one has ever wanted me."

"I do."

He closed his eyes so she wouldn't see the tears in them.

～

LARA HATED PAPERWORK, but there was nothing like tracing something through documents to make finding things easier. Maybe she should have been a lawyer. Back in the day, before she'd become basically useless, she'd done this to trace ownership on stolen works of art. Now, she was reading her ex-husband's financials and dreading each paper more than the last. She had three quarters of his money which wasn't—when the debt was taken care of— going to amount to very much. That was okay. She'd sell the houses and be glad to be rid of them.

She'd left Russell asleep on the bed upstairs. The man was seriously sexy, even down to the vulnerability he clearly tried to deny. The smart move would be to leave—he'd even told her as much. But she wasn't going anywhere. Whether it was random coincidence or the universe had brought them together, she was keeping him.

He called himself a con man? Maybe he was still trying to figure out who he was supposed to be. She certainly was.

As she went through the books, she kept stumbling on one figure that didn't make any sense. What did DG stand for? Why did they keep getting paid? She'd already figured out who the mistresses were—

A knock sounded on the office door, and she turned to see the blond guy—Platinum—come in. He was followed by a man with brown hair she didn't recognize, but then again, she really had no idea how many people Russell had running around the house at the moment.

"We're looking for Francium." Platinum's face stayed serene. She wondered if he ever showed emotion. He wore a ring on his left finger, which meant either he was married or he wanted people to think he was.

The other man extended his hand. "Zinc. Pleased to meet you. Ma'am."

He also wore a wedding ring.

"Pleasure." Lara nodded. "He's asleep upstairs."

She hated the thought they'd wake him up. He hadn't expected to sleep. That much she realized. He'd been two seconds into telling her a story about a horse he'd once seen run at the Kentucky Derby, when he'd conked right out. That kind of exhaustion meant he should be left alone. Then again, everyone except her was here to do a job. Sleeping on the job was probably frowned upon. Maybe she shouldn't have told them.

Platinum and Zinc made eye contact. She cleared her throat and smoothed her skirt as she stood. Fortunately, she'd had the presence of mind to properly dress herself in a sundress and sandals before she left the room.

"Something wrong?"

"We have Remington, and we're having a little trouble getting a final piece of information out of him. He'll need to touch base with Red Wolf tonight." Zach walked to the window. "Francium tends to be good at this kind of thing. Wen, our other colleague, is too, but he went back this morning. I can make him talk, but I've got to do something about my head first."

Platinum shrugged. "This is not my forte. I'd rather shoot him in the head."

They needed Remington to speak, and they wanted to wake Francium to do it. "Maybe I could get him to talk. If you could help me."

Zinc looked at Platinum. "I don't know. My girl could do this easily, but she's trained to."

"Rose really wouldn't want anything to do with this. But Lara just said she did. If she said she can, she can."

Zinc crossed his arms over his chest. "Shit. Can we bring her in there without discussing it with Francium?"

"Yes, you most certainly can." She'd been in a relationship where she got told what to do. That wasn't going to happen again. "Where is he?"

When Lara had designed the pool house, she'd never imagined it would ever serve as a means to keep Remington prisoner, tied to a chair, and covered in his own piss. She stood by the door to watch him for a second. He stared at the ground. His face didn't look swollen. In fact, she couldn't see any noticeable injuries on him anywhere. Whatever they'd been doing to him to get information, it wasn't physical.

He raised his head to stare at her, and she wondered if she'd ever known him at all. Zinc had talked strategy with her before he'd gone off to sleep off his headache. She didn't know what had happened to him, but at some point, that man had been hurt.

She inched into the pool house. It could have doubled as a guesthouse if they'd ever had enough people to fill up the main house and the actual guesthouse. Now, it was where these people who had stormed into her miserable existence and let in the light were somehow forcing her ex to speak.

Except they weren't. They wanted Russell to. Maybe—just maybe—he'd had enough of that for a lifetime.

"Lara, you have to get me out of here. These people are crazy. And someone is going to come looking, and then we're all dead."

She knelt down in front of him. "What have you done to us?"

Once he had loved her, or at least, he had liked her as much as he did anyone on the planet. She'd been good enough to marry, when the other women he'd kept purely to fuck. If she could reach him, in that place, maybe she could get somewhere. He was tied to a chair, an expensive chair, as the case turned out to be. She'd way overspent on the lawn furniture, but it had been one of her first married expenditures, and she liked being able to charge and not worry about it.

Of course, if he'd ever told her about the dire states of their bank accounts, she wouldn't have done it so frequently.

"Why did you do this to us?"

"Me?" He spit on the ground. "You're sleeping with one of them."

She tried to ignore the revolt being close to him brought out in her. "You really want to compare notes? Which one of us slept around?"

"Okay, fair enough." He took an audible breath. "You have to help me."

"Who is DG? Another mistress? I can't help you, if you don't help me. I can cut a deal with these guys. They like me. But I won't if you don't come clean. Why are you paying DG a monthly stipend, and who is your business partner? They know about Red Wolf. But they think you've got a third person on the hook. Is that true? Let me help you."

This wasn't what Zinc had told her to do. He'd told her to go in and ask. If he didn't tell her, he wanted her to get out. Platinum stood outside with a gun. She wasn't at risk, but this kind of situation was so fraught with stress, and she had no training.

"DG is my business partner. Don't go near her. She and Red Wolf, they go way back. If she doesn't see me today, she'll report it. Then we're all dead. She's his redundancy. I pay her to give me a little bit of leeway. She doesn't report my indiscretions to him. He wouldn't like it. Too much attention with the mistresses. I am sorry, Lara. We're all going to die. These guys seem like they're good? They're going to be why you die."

She wouldn't pretend her heart didn't race or that her mouth hadn't gone dry in terror. What was the point? This was scary as hell. But that didn't mean she would give up. This wouldn't get better unless she got him to talk.

Lara made herself swallow. Outside, she could hear the ocean and even closer, the sound of the pool filter turning on to clean the pool. Someone must have put on the washer. She could hear that, too. This moment was nothing. It was small. She would crush it.

"Tell me who DG is. I can't help us if I don't know. I'm not dying today. And neither are you." She didn't care if she lied. He wasn't getting out of telling her. "Unless you don't fill in this information gap. DG—the same problem in the ledger—is your partner, who also works for Red Wolf. Who is she?"

He spit on the floor again. She'd never known him to do

that and wasn't entirely certain why he did then. "You know her. Desiree Garcia."

The woman with the fake painting. Lara stood before putting her hands on her hips. She had been forced to go to that woman's house over and over for the last three summers. They were high up in Hampton society. She was haughty and stupid.

Lara wanted to throw something. All that time, he'd been paying her because she was some kind of terrorist?

"Lara." She turned around at Francium's voice. He leaned against the doorway, actually appearing bored. Well, that was what he wanted to portray. Her guy wasn't at all at ease. If anything, he gave off so much tension, he could have filled the room with adrenaline.

Turning once more to Remington, she took what she knew would be her last look at her ex-husband. Whatever else happened, from this moment on, she'd never see him again. She wasn't even sorry.

She walked slowly to Francium, keeping her steps even. When she passed him, he closed the door behind her before pushing her up against the outside of the pool house, blocking any escape she might want to make with his body. Only she didn't want a way out. She imagined she'd always want to be close to him.

"Are you okay?" His gaze scanned her face. Perhaps his intensity would frighten others. It would never intimidate her.

"He's tied to a chair. Of course I'm fine, sweetheart."

She let him keep her pinned where she was. He was a man who liked to be in control. Where she was, he'd put his body between her and danger. No one would get through.

Platinum stood to the left of the door. He cleared his

throat, and Francium held up a finger to indicate he wasn't ready to speak.

"You don't want to talk right now, Plat. I'm fuming. You guys let her go in there while I took a nap."

She touched his chest. "I told them I wanted to. What they did was listen. Big difference. No one lets me do anything. It's all about choice. All of it."

He closed his eyes like they pained him, and a muscle ticked in his jaw. "I have to be able to protect you."

She nodded. "Yes, you also have to be able to trust me. I'm not interested in getting killed."

"You went into his office. That's why you almost got killed. If I had been late..."

She hadn't known that. A shudder rushed through her. There she'd been thinking she was helping, and she'd nearly made everything much, much worse. "That was dumb."

This was seriously hard to listen to. "It was untrained. Big difference. Okay. This moment is over. Desiree Garcia. The idiot with the fake painting is the other half of this problem. Good work."

At least she had finally done something right.

6

Z inc, now up from his headache recovery, stood in front of Francium as they studied the specs of Desiree Garcia's house Plat called up on the computer. Between the three of them, they should be able to plan a home invasion. Only the woman seemed to have designed the house for the purpose of stopping anyone from doing what they wanted to do.

He should have noted that the last time he was in the house. That time, however, he'd been totally unfocused, thinking about Lara, and how he wanted her husband dead. He had Lara now, and the second they deemed Remington totally useless, he'd get rid of him too.

They couldn't get in through the windows without setting off alarms. The doors were rigged. "Who was this architect?"

"You'd think she was a terrorist and paranoid, or something." Zinc laughed. "Can you get back in? She invited you once."

Russell nodded. "I can always put back on my finance

persona and make up a reason to get through the door. Then we'll have to work out how I'm going to disarm the room and get you two in without getting caught. I can do it. I've done it many times."

Even if he'd decided he was seriously over this lifestyle. When Red Wolf went down, he was going to figure out if there was anything in the universe he could do other than this.

Lara cleared her throat from the doorway, and they all turned to regard her. She was so lovely. He thought it every time she came near him. He held out his hand. "You okay?"

"I wasn't eavesdropping. I really came to see if I could get us all some food? I'm trying to be useful."

Zinc rubbed his forehead. "You totally were. That spreadsheet and finding the DG. Took lots of time off our task. Then you were great with Remington. You don't have to order food."

"Thing is...I can get Russell and I in to Desiree, no trouble. I just have to want to look at the painting. I can distract her. She wants my approval on that thing. We can talk art for hours. Then you could get in, get what you need, get out. Take her out. Whatever you want."

Francium shook his head. He had to make himself very clear. "You aren't trained to be a spy. I spent years learning how to be fake. I never open my mouth without knowing exactly what I'll say if I'm engaged in a conversation. You're not prepared for this."

He expected her to argue. Her self-confidence was shot. But he wouldn't place her in danger to make that better. She'd have to forgive him. In some ways, he wouldn't compromise.

"I'm not going to fake it. I'm simply not going to tell her

everything. I'm good at it. I do it nearly every moment I'm awake and speaking every day. I'm not lying. I'm being me. I can do this. I won't place anyone in any danger. I swear it."

He wanted to argue or better yet, to send her off to Titanium's compound where he could wrap her in bubble wrap and keep her safe for the rest of her life. But that would make him no better than Remington. The other man threatened her, locked her away. He wouldn't be guilty of doing any of that.

"I would really prefer you not do that. I'd rather you wait here. I won't tell you what to do. Ever."

She raised her eyebrows. "Thank you. I'm going to do it. I'm going to help."

"Alright. Then let's plan it. Down to the smallest details."

Plat lifted his hand. "I'd like to point out I can take her out. I'll grab my sniper rifle, and we can be done with this crap in no time flat."

"Titanium's going to want to question her. That's why Remington's not dead." Zinc sat back in his chair. "But if worse comes to it, you shoot her in the head."

Platinum nodded. "That works."

RUSSELL WAITED while Lara changed in her closet. He'd been dressed for half an hour. He'd used Remington's phone to text Desiree to get Lara invited to look at the painting. When she showed up with her neighbor, who happened to be nearby, he'd hit on Desiree. Let the woman think he'd come to fuck her. She was just the kind of asshat to believe that.

He pressed a hand on the window. Things went wrong

all the time. People died. They were slaughtered. They were blown up. Mothers left their children to wander the streets.

But damn it, nothing would happen to Lara London anymore.

She stepped out of the closet, a vision in light blue. She usually wore long skirts, which showed off the sheer length of her legs, but today she'd gone short. The dress was chiffon, and the best description he could give it in his head was that it was a party dress. Spaghetti straps on top and layers of chiffon on the bottom, which stopped right on top of her knee. Peteled flowers layered the bottom half of the dress. To finish the outfit, she had heeled sandals in silver.

"Wow."

She looked down at herself. "This is an old one. I always wanted to wear it again. One thing I will miss about this life was the need to own clothes like this. If I end up going back to the art world, it'll be few and far between. Suits and more professional clothing, I imagine."

Once a year, he would find a reason for her to get dressed up. His lovely, lovely Lara. Maybe twice a year...

He extended his hand. "Zinc will be watching you the whole time and listening from the mic. If something goes horribly wrong, Plat takes her out. Boom. Don't hesitate to scream for help."

She stroked the side of his face. "I've got it. I'm going to have ten minutes of conversation about the painting and get out of there. No problem. You be careful. You're breaking into rooms made not meant to be broken into."

"My specialty."

Lara kissed him. "I'm forcing myself to think about the future. We've never slept next to one another."

She was right. The night before, he'd stayed up going

over schematics and fallen asleep in his chair. Lara had gone to bed alone.

"I'll be honest, I've never slept with anyone except the little nap I took yesterday. I think it comes from my years in the foster home. Twelve of us in one section of the room." She had made him feel comfortable. Of course, then he'd woken in a panic because she hadn't been there.

She put his arms around her. Why hadn't he thought to hug her tight? Why did she have to tell him? Why was he so defunct?

Lara didn't seem to mind, she cuddled closer. "Then you're overdue. Like the making love thing, which you did really well."

He snorted. "Thanks. My male ego appreciates the stroke."

"I'm serious. Tonight. When it's over, you'll sleep next to me."

It was like she was constantly giving water to a man dying of thirst. "I'll see you here."

DESIREE GARCIA LOOKED every bit the part she played. Francium grinned at her, doing his best to put sex in his gaze. The role was harder today than it had been the last time he'd been at her home. For the first time in his life, he wanted to be himself, but he had to get through this obligation, and then he could do what he wanted. He wouldn't object to kicking Red Wolf in the balls either.

"Russell! What are you doing here?" she practically purred. "I thought I was having a girl's afternoon with my darling Lara."

Her darling Lara was probably throwing up her in

mouth, even as she smiled and wore her dull, pleasant expression.

"Well, when I heard it was a chance to see you again, Des, I was absolutely compelled to come and see you. Once was not enough."

Her cheeks pinked. She could either make herself blush or she wanted him. He leaned forward to whisper in her ear. "You look smashing in pink."

"Thank you." She touched his arm.

Lara raised her eyebrows. "Shall I leave you two alone?"

"Oh, no." Desiree looked down at the floor. "If Jose thought that, I'd be in very big trouble."

"Well, darling, what Jose doesn't know won't kill him, so to speak." He winked at her, and her color deepened again. "Why don't I step out back and make some phone calls, and then when you girls are done, we can get to know each other better, Desiree? You have a view, don't you, of the ocean from here? I was so preoccupied with looking at you last time, I hardly noticed."

Without waiting for her by your leave, he walked to the other side of the house as though he headed for the back porch. He rounded the corner in time to hear Lara's fake laugh. He wasn't the only one who knew how to do what was needed.

Instead of going to the porch, he walked toward the office. Zinc spoke in his ear. "You made me want to throw up."

"Made myself sick. What are you doing out there?" Zinc and Platinum were positioned where Plat could see in the house and fire if necessary. "Got any good take out?"

"Nah, Plat's gone all organic on me. His wife has gotten him into the green juice phase."

Desiree's office was locked, but that had never stopped

Francium, and unlike Lara, he wouldn't bust through the door only to get caught. "I'm at the office."

"Roger that," Zinc replied. "Bringing down cameras now. Temporary loop installed. You have three minutes."

"Copy. I'll have the lock open in thirty seconds."

He'd had to break locks to eat when he'd lived on the streets. These days, he managed much more expensive devices. But they all came down to the same basic principal —to keep him out of where he wanted to be. He'd never been very good at being told no.

"Interesting note." Zinc's voice came over the line again. "Jose doesn't exist. Not so far as anyone connected to Desiree. She's invented a husband."

He shook his head as the lock gave way, and he walked into the office, closing the door behind him. "Good to know."

At least they wouldn't have to deal with Jose. Desiree was enough all by herself. He walked to the computer, pulling his external drive out of his pocket. "Ready?"

"Roger that," Zinc answered. "Preparing for password lock on your go."

He inserted the device that would hook Desiree's computer to Zinc's. After they cracked the password, they'd download the contents of the hard drive. Zinc had never seen a hard drive he couldn't get into. Firewalls were jokes to him.

All of that was great, as long as he came through when it counted, which was right then. He figured Lara could talk about the fake painting without letting Desiree look for him for ten minutes. After that, it might get tricky. Desiree didn't know her newest purchase was fraudulent. A woman with her ego and ties to Red Wolf wouldn't allow herself to be taken in like that.

He wasn't going to risk Lara on this going on too long.

Francium moved toward the door and listened. Female laughter greeted him. They couldn't take down Desiree without Titanium's say-so, not unless it was life or death. The boss man wasn't going to give them the go for it based on a ledger and the word of a man who funded Red Wolf. They needed what was on this computer.

For his part, Francium would be happy to let someone else take over the second they were done here, and he'd never felt that way before. Giving up wasn't in his nature. Only this didn't feel like that, this felt like moving on.

Francium knew what he had been doing when he took his name. Outside of the laboratory, the element was almost never seen. It had to be created to exist, and so had he. If he hadn't made himself to be whoever he needed to be, he'd have died on the streets before his tenth birthday.

He was proud of how strong he could be.

But maybe it was time to see if he was adaptable, if he could be there, full time, for the bravest woman he'd ever met...

"We've got it. Disconnect. Get the girl. Get out. I'm calling Titanium. There is serious shit on this computer. I imagine extraction will come, but not now. Oorah. Good job."

Francium grinned. He'd never been a Marine, but he knew what it meant when they said that. "Thanks, man. See you soon."

He walked toward the hallway, pulling himself back into character. Only it wasn't female laughter he heard. No, it was screams, and it was Lara.

Oh, hell no.

～

LARA BACKED UP, forcing herself to stop screaming. Nothing had ever gone well or gotten better by yelling about it, and being faced with a gun wasn't going to be any different. Men who knew how to handle these things surrounded her. Somehow, she had to give Russell more time.

"Answer me. Where is your husband? Cut the bullshit, because I can spot a lie a mile away. You think I don't know you're here with one of them? We know every move they make."

She didn't know if that was true or not. Lara did, however, pay close attention to details. Desiree hadn't used anyone's name. She suspected Francium, fine. She thought there were others around, all right, well, she wasn't wrong. But she didn't really know anything, and if her shrieking tone illuminated any truths, then she was really on edge.

When Lara couldn't come up with a lie, she decided the truth would have to do. At least, it would give them more time to make conversation. "I'm not sure where he is at the present time. The last time I saw him, he was tied up in the pool house. Since then, he's been moved, but no one has told me where. Can you put down the gun? We can talk this out. I really shouldn't be in the middle of this. Let's have tea instead. I wouldn't want you to accidently hit your new painting."

Okay, she was rambling, but it turned out she really didn't do well with guns, not in any capacity. Too many guns lately.

Desiree swung the gun around like it was a part of her pointer finger. "When he picked you out, I told him you were going to be nothing but trouble, but he was so taken with you. I couldn't talk him out of it. And here you are, bringing nothing but destruction with you."

"Honey." Francium's voice caught her attention. He leaned against the doorframe, staring at the scene like it wasn't a gun wielding disaster waiting to happen. Russell caught her eye for one second. She saw the anger in his gaze before he covered it. He wasn't unmoved. She steeled her back. He'd get them out of this. "You want to put down that gun. It doesn't go with your shoes."

Desiree flushed. She was clearly not blasé about Francium, despite knowing who he was. "We're both professionals, whoever you really are. We know how these things work. We have people who we work with, who give us orders. She interfered in things that don't concern her."

"Oh, do we?" Francium took a step toward Desiree, then another. They were easy movements, as though he were unworried, not concerned with what happened around him. "You take your orders from Red Wolf, yes? That must be a hell of a relationship. Is he fun at the Christmas party?"

"And how fun is your Titanium? Must be loads of laughs with his being blind and—"

Francium lifted his hand. "Don't go there. Not if you want to keep living."

"I'm not going to fool around. You're going to give me Remington and disappear. I'll let you live. That'll be the deal."

He laughed. "What do you think, Lara? Should I give her Remington?"

"No." She shook her head.

Every few seconds during their entire discussion, Francium had inched forward. She knew he was armed—she'd seen the gun before they left her house, and yet he hadn't pulled it out yet.

The device hidden in her ear, which had stayed silent

since she came in the house, turned on. Zinc's voice spoke quietly to her. "Hi, Lara. Don't answer me. All is well. I know that's a lot to say with a gun pointed at you, but Francium has gotten her to move just enough that Plat can shoot her."

Hence the inching. She took a deep breath. "I don't want you to be scared. But I do want you to hit the floor, now."

As though she'd been following instructions like that one her whole life, she threw her body on the ground. Anything that happened after that was lost in the sounds over her head. A shout, a whoosh, a bang. She really had no idea what was happening. The only thing she could focus on was the painting. The bullet that Desiree had wanted to shoot at her had slammed straight into the painting.

Desiree lay dead on the ground, and Francium squatted in front of Lara. "You okay?"

"Peachy keen." She rose to her feet, still staring at the fake painting, which had been destroyed in the escapade. Papers came flying out to the ground, like feathers moving in the air conditioning.

He pulled her against him. "You're okay. I thought I was going to swallow my tongue in terror."

It wasn't that she didn't want his affection, but the floating papers held her attention. She gave his cheek a quick peck and stepped away before kneeling down to look at the mess. "Desiree must have known it was a fake. She was using the damn thing to store information. This is a cypher." She handed it to Russell. "Smugglers use it to transport art with unverified backgrounds. I can probably decipher it for you, but I'm wondering," she spun in a circle, "if every paper in the house is really a hidden depository of information."

Russell put his hands on his hips. "Is any of it real?"

"The paintings? Fifty-fifty. I thought she had a bad eye

for it." She handed him another piece of paper. "Don't get me wrong, I'm sure I'm going to have a freak out, but right this second, all I can see is all this hidden code and something we can do about it."

The door to the room banged open, Plat and Zinc running in. "Good job taking direction."

Francium held up the papers. "Looks like Desiree stored her secret information other places than her computer. Lara says she might be able to decipher them."

Plat grinned. "Then let's get to it." He bent over to grab the now dead Desiree by her shoulders. "After I deal with her. She was an unsanctioned kill, but I don't think Titanium will mind."

"Particularly if you dispose of it properly," Zinc added.

Lara barely heard any of them. She looked down at the papers in her hand. Years earlier, when she'd decided to do something about the stolen artwork she encountered, she'd had to learn to figure out the shipping methods of the people who moved the art around. It had taken her weeks, but eventually, she'd worked it out.

"I can try, but I'd imagine you guys have really smart people who could do this faster than me."

Francium shook his head. "We most definitely do. Come on. Let's break into the paintings and see what you can do. We all have our strengths. If this is one of yours, we aren't looking a gift horse in the mouth."

She grinned. It was sick to do so, considering the dead body on the ground and the events of the day, but she might prove to be useful after all.

RUSSELL HAD WANTED to spend the night sleeping with Lara

but that didn't seem to be happening. One night had turned into two, and now she was still working on the cyphers. She made enough progress, Titanium had left them to it. Francium wouldn't have minded if someone had gone and taken away the job from her.

And yet...Lara seemed alive. She sat straighter in her chair, she smiled with her eyes. They were small changes, but he could see how doing this made her feel like she contributed. So, he kept quiet, and he fielded questions from the team.

They were eliciting results. Most of the disguised code seemed to be pickup and delivery spots Red Wolf used to move cargo. Some of it might even be weapons. There were others looking through it. "You're staring at me." She didn't look up from where she worked at the dining room table. "I can feel you doing it."

He grinned. "Only because I want you to."

She finally lifted her head. "If you didn't want me to know you were there, I wouldn't?"

"Correct. How are you doing?"

She held up one that had been printed in red ink. "This one is scary. It's written straight out. Same basic code, although slightly harder. I've gotten so I can almost just read it, almost." She shook her head. "This is how you were all going to die."

He took it from her hand. "Let me see that one."

Sure enough, as he read the words as she'd translated them, there was no question about the wording. Red Wolf had planned all their deaths. One particularly scary killer for hire was going to take out Titanium and then the rest of them. He folded the note and put it in his pocket.

"I've been thinking about things." He sat down next to her. "I have some things I have to take care of, things you can't be a part of. That doesn't mean I don't want to be together. I do. More than you can imagine. I think the best thing I could do would be to finish this and then find you."

There, he'd spoken the words. They hurt to even utter, because she could easily move on in the time they weren't together. She sat back in her seat. "When I finish this, I'm going to sell the houses, and then I'm going to find out what I'm going to do with the rest of my life. We should probably let each other do these things."

"Right." He nodded and wanted to throw up. "Then let's agree to meet back up, and then we can—"

She placed her hand on his arm. "I don't want to be smart. I don't want to be right. I want you. If you have to go, then fine, we're still together. I'm not giving you up. You're not getting lost from me. End of story."

He let out the breath he held, and his shoulders sagged. "I probably have to help get rid of pretty much the worst person on earth. You get that's my life, right?"

She held his gaze. "I get it." Lara pointed at the paper. "Go take care of that card I just gave you. But tell me where to go to meet up with you."

He kissed her cheek. "Okay. You can change your mind."

"Don't assume that everyone leaves. Some of us stay, even when we shouldn't. You're something I want to do. Forever."

It hurt his head, his heart, his stomach, but he decided to believe her. Forever might be possible.

～

One month later...

He stared at Lara, asleep on his bed. They'd said they were going to spend the night together, and it looked like they might finally get that chance. He'd been away for a month. Henchmen had to be killed. Cut off all of his resources, and eventually, Red Wolf would die. Or at least, that was the idea. He would be dead, soon, of that, Francium was sure.

Russell had felt safe enough to come home. To Lara. She opened her eyes, staring at him in the darkness. "Did you mean for me to hear you?"

"Actually, no." He walked toward her and lay on top of her on the bed. "That's impressive."

She sat up, hugging him around the neck. "You're safe."

"I'll always be safe. I'm like a cockroach. It's hard to kill me."

She pinched his arm. "Talk about yourself as a cockroach again, and I'll beat you."

He grinned. "Okay. Fair enough."

She pressed her ear to his chest. "Can you tell me what happened?"

"I can tell you that a lot of people who shouldn't be breathing, aren't anymore. And those still alive will find that's a temporary state of being for them. They won't live to bother anyone again. They didn't stand a chance, and that was because you went ahead and saved us all. Thank you so much."

"Don't you dare thank me." She kissed him on the lips. "Are you done?"

"Almost. I might have to leave for a while again. But that will bring the whole thing to an end. I'm sorry it has to be."

She nodded. "That's okay. I had this idea for something we could do together when you're finished. I think...I was wondering if you might like to help me track down art thieves?"

Lara kept talking, but all he could do was smile. Yes, he would help her. That sounded like a great idea. But first, he was going to tell her to take off her shirt, because he wanted to and she was his girl. Lara made him believe that fairy tales could have truth to them. Even for a guy like him.

ABOUT THE AUTHOR

As a teenager, I would hide in my room to read my favorite romance novels when I was supposed to be doing my homework.

I am the mother of three adorable boys and I am fortunate to be married to my best friend. I live in Austin Texas where I am determined to eat all the barbecue in town.

I am in love with science fiction, fantasy, and the paranormal and try to use all of these elements in my writing. I've been told I'm a little bloodthirsty so I hope that when you read my work you'll enjoy the action packed ride that always ends in romance. I love to write series because I love to see characters develop over time and it always makes me happy to see my favorite characters make guest appearances in other books.

In my world anything is possible, anything can happen, and you should suspect that it will.

I'd love to hear from you! Please visit my website at www.rebeccaroyce.com to sign up for my newsletter and learn about my books!

Here's where you can find me online:

Rebecca's Randomness Reading Group https://www.facebook.com/groups/RebeccasRandomness/

https://www.rebeccaroyce.com

https://www.facebook.com/authorrebeccaroyce/

www.twitter.com/rebeccaroyce

Instagram: rebeccaroyce79
MeWe: RebeccaRoyce
Cheers!!
Rebecca

OTHER BOOKS BY REBECCA ROYCE...

Wings of Artemis

Kidnapped By Her Husbands https://amzn.to/2BQdUxy

Rescued by Their Wife https://amzn.to/2Rr9as4

Crashing Into Destiny https://amzn.to/2VkyXRL

Meeting Them https://amzn.to/2BLPaXm

Reclaiming Their Love https://amzn.to/2GKAw8E

Loving Them https://amzn.to/2BKDmEK

Ship Called Malice https://amzn.to/2BNputj

Saving Them https://amzn.to/2SsrBtH

Dark Demise https://amzn.to/2VidXv3

Light Unfolding https://amzn.to/2GO6Yqr

Still Waters https://amzn.to/2CFePT8

Rising Tides https://amzn.to/2MCdTlM

Lost Star (coming soon)

Pointed Arrow (coming soon)

Last Hope (completed series)

Tradition Be Damned

Past Be Damned

Destiny Be Damned

Compassion Be Damned

Future Be Damned

Dragon Wars (completed series)

Driven

Subversive

Redemption

Justice

Warrior World (spin off of The Warrior, completed series)

Deacon

Micah

Jason

The Westervelt Wolves (completed series)

Her Wolf

Summer's Wolf

Wolf Reborn

Wolf's Valentine

Wolf's Magic

Alpha Wolf

Angel's Wolf

Darkest Wolf

Lone Wolf

Fallen Alpha

Alpha Rising

Alpha's Strength

Alpha's Sacrifice

Alpha's Truth

Alpha Enticing

Hidden Alpha (coming soon)

The Capes (completed series)

Seductive Powers

Adrenaline Rush

Last Ascension

Illicit Minds

Illicit Senses

Illicit Connections

Illicit Alliance (coming soon)

The Outsiders

Love Beyond Time

Love Beyond Sanity

Love Beyond Loyalty

Love Beyond Sight

Love Beyond Expectations

Love Beyond Oceans

Love Beyond Flames

Love Beyond Lies

Love Beyond Death (coming soon)

Cascade (completed series)

Haunted Redemption

Phoenix Everlasting

Fragility Unearthed

Persuasion Enraptured

Reverse Harem Story (completed series)

Unconventional

Unexpected

Undeniable

Kiss Her Goodbye (completed series)

Hard Truths

Dark Truths

Deadly Truths

Shifter World

Planet Bear

Planet Wolf (coming soon)

The Swamp

Hidden

Pursued

Caught (coming soon)

Stand Alone Titles

Under The Lights

No Quitting Allowed

Mr. Wrong

Bite Marks

Bitten Surrender

The Vampire and The Virgin

Demon Within

Crimson Lust

Call Me Crazy

The Storm (writing with Ripley Proserpina) completed series.

Lightning Strikes

Thunder Rolling

The Deluge

Heart of the Nebula (writing with Heather Long)

Queenmaker

Deal Breaker

Throne Taker (coming soon)

Stupid Boys (writing with C.R. Jane)

Stupid Boys

Dumb Girl

Crazy Love (coming soon)

Through the Gates (writing with Skye MacKinnon)

Purgatory City

Infernal Land (coming soon)

The Coveted (writing with Ripley Proserpina)

Eyes in the Darkness

Voices in the Darkness (coming soon)